The Devil finds work…

… for Idle hands

Acknowledgments

Many thanks to Jim, Richard, and all the staff and customers of the Idle Draper for their help, knowingly or otherwise, in the creation of this novel. Without their input, interest and encouragement it would not have been completed.

Special thanks to my good friend Linton Greenwood for suggesting the character name 'Mrs Semtex'.

The cover image was kindly provided by Jim Emmett.

This is a work of fiction. Although many of the places referenced in the book are real, some characteristics have been changed to fit the story. The characters and events in this book are products of the author's imagination or are used fictitiously. Any resemblance to actual persons, living or dead, is entirely coincidental.

Finally, many thanks to my army of proof-readers. If there are any errors in the published text, it's their fault.

CHAPTER 1

They walked slowly and apparently aimlessly across the large shoppers' car park. It was almost deserted; the only cars belonged to local residents who had nowhere else to leave them overnight. Easy pickings. The area was poorly lit, and though ostensibly protected by video surveillance, in truth the solitary camera was directed at the same spot every night - at the delivery trunkers parked at the far end at the rear of the supermarket, their drivers already asleep in the cabs.

They completed one circuit and split up to work the area once more. It was Darren, Daz to his mates, who spotted their target for the night. Keeping to the shadows as he skirted the car park, he emerged close to a dark coloured hatchback and peered casually through the driver's window. No visible alarm. Just an old-fashioned lock of the type which supposedly secured the handbrake and gear lever. No problem. The engine would probably be immobilised, but the switch would be simple to locate. He'd nicked these before. In less than a minute, they could be in and speeding away. He couldn't wait to tell Andy. He felt a high, a buzz. He always did. He cleared his throat, fetching up a thick wad of phlegm which he spat with unerring accuracy at a nearby bollard, watching with satisfaction as it clung and then gradually slid down towards the base.

Andy joined him beneath the trees which lined the exit slip-road. They discussed the options available. Andy wanted to go for the old Beemer, a 316, but Daz, as always, got his way. The Focus was to be the target. No questions, no arguments. Daz made the decisions and Andy fell in line with his older, more streetwise, brother. The night was perfect for it. Dark, moonless and quiet. The earlier showers had ceased some time ago and the January wind was light. But most importantly, it was after midnight, and midweek. Nobody around. All tucked up in their nice warm beds. Getting a good night's sleep before driving to work in the morning. Well, one of you, Daz thought, won't be going anywhere tomorrow. He grinned. He always did when he was about to nick someone's car. Someone's pride and joy. He looked around at the buildings which bordered the car park. Many were totally obscured from view by the trees. Others were offices, and shops, only occupied during the day. And from the rest, including the retirement housing flats, no lights were burning. Ideal! The town planners couldn't have made it any easier for them if they'd designed the scheme specifically with car thieves in mind.

****

The old fox emerged cautiously from beneath the bushes at the far end of the car park, close to the rear of the supermarket. He stood stock-still and sniffed the air before edging his way warily towards the rubbish bins behind the burger takeaway. This had been his regular route for some time. A round trip of eight or nine miles, it was no problem and provided an easy source of food. As the nights grew colder and longer, he'd begun to forage further afield, and had no fear of this unnatural environment. As long as he remained wary and alert, he could come and go as he pleased. And always leave with a full belly. He stopped again, nose in the air. He'd picked up a scent. Human. And more. A different, animal smell. His instincts told him it was canine. He skulked back into the undergrowth, ensuring he remained downwind of the approaching threat. He had time. He would wait patiently.

****

Daz stiffened as he thought he heard something. He couldn't be sure, but instinctively he grabbed Andy's arm and pulled him back deeper into the dark shade of the trees. They stood quietly together in the darkness as an old man shuffled slowly into view trailing an equally old shuffling dog on a leash. They passed within ten yards of the teenage pair, but old Walter's sight and hearing wasn't too good these days, and the same applied to Bonnie, his Labrador-cross companion. Daz's grin instantly returned, and he and his brother lit up a cigarette each and casually waited until the old man had shuffled out of sight towards the far end with its patches of grass and shrubbery which Bonnie regularly used as her toilet.

Minutes later the youths emerged from the shadows. Their routine was well rehearsed and practised, and verbal prompting was unnecessary. They walked briskly towards the car, Andy making for the passenger side while Daz approached the driver's. In position, both stopped and gave the area a quick final once-over. All clear. They exchanged nods. Daz unzipped his jacket, and extracted a heavy metal bar, a foot in length. The rear offside window shattered. Daz shoved his hand through the hole, reaching inside and forward until he was able to open the driver's door. Then he was prising away the dashboard trim until he located the immobiliser exactly where he'd expected it to be. He easily disabled it and jumped in to the driver's seat, reaching across to open the passenger door for his impatient brother. Andy immediately got to work releasing the so-called anti-theft lock securing the gear lever and handbrake while Daz pushed the iron bar through the steering wheel. The steering lock offered no resistance to the pressure as he pulled hard down on the end of the bar. Inserting a screwdriver behind the wheel, Daz prised the cover off to expose the ignition wiring. Expertly he made the connection and the engine fired. He revved hard, slammed the car into gear and raced toward the exit road.

Old Walter was returning home with Bonnie after completing his circuit of the area. Bonnie had been acting a little strangely, he thought. As if she'd picked up a scent of something vaguely familiar but scarcely remembered. Even at her age, her sense of smell was quite acute and she'd criss-crossed the area for a minute or two before deciding that whatever it was she'd smelt wasn't worth the effort of pursuing at her time of life. She squatted in a dark corner before returning with a languid wag of the tail to her master and stood patiently while his arthritic fingers struggled to clip her lead to the loop on her collar.

The Focus whizzed past within ten feet of him, and even with his poor eyesight he could see the two young occupants - the passenger with his bright red baseball cap worn back to front. Neither of them noticed him as the car sped down the road towards the dual carriageway.

"Bloody stupid kids", he muttered to Bonnie. "They'll knock someone over driving like that."

He shook his head slowly and shuffled home.

****

The gamekeeper's cottage stood fifty yards off the main road, set slightly back from the unmade and bumpy track which led to the fields. The cottage came with the job, rent-free, so Bill, the present incumbent, couldn't complain about its poor state of repair. It was cold and damp. When he first took the job, almost three years ago, the landlord had promised a number of repairs and improvements which, however, never materialised. He never mentioned it any longer; the last time he raised the subject, his landlord made vague threats about the security of his job. Nothing specific, but he got the message very clearly. Put up and shut up. Tonight, he didn't care. The previous weekend had been a good shoot, and the party up from London were well pleased with the bag. One of them had given him a bottle of whisky as a thank you. Grouse, it was, which was rather inappropriate as they'd been shooting pheasant. Probably didn't know the difference. What the hell. He'd accepted it graciously and opened it earlier that evening. Just a drop to keep out the chill. By the time he fell asleep slumped in the armchair, he'd consumed almost half the bottle.

He didn't hear the car bounce at speed down the track.

Fifty yards past the cottage a faded sign nailed to a tree proclaimed 'Private land. Keep out. Trespassers will be prosecuted.' Daz crashed the gearbox down into second and spun the car through the narrow opening on to the concrete single-track road that skirted the flat fields. Running the length of the road was a wide ditch to one side. Beyond that were the tall thick hedgerows which conveniently shielded them from view. And on the other side were nothing but flat fields, featureless except for a single weathered oak which stood dark and tall a mile or so away. The headlights showed the track ran straight for some distance. Daz knew that anyway. They'd been here several times before. He put his foot down hard and changed up through the gearbox, soon reaching the end of the straight and flinging the car round the corners. He was in total control, and though he'd never taken a test, he considered himself an 'ace' driver. The car was used to being driven in more sedate fashion but responded well as he slammed through the gears, eventually leaving the road and ploughing through the damp yielding black earth of the fields. He practised his favourite manoeuvres; handbrake turns through one hundred and eighty degrees, slewing the car's rear through the mud as the suspension creaked and bounced. He raced toward the oak, concentrating, judging the car's speed and handling as the distance between the stolen car and the unyielding oak rapidly diminished. He glanced at Andy, watching the colour drain from his face. He grinned. This was the part he enjoyed most. He judged it perfectly, braking and spinning the wheel at the very last moment so that the rear end slewed sideways and clipped the oak's trunk, ripping off the rear bumper. The colour returned to Andy's face and he laughed out loud and gave a little whoop of pleasure.

"Nice, Daz. Nice. Fuckin' ace."
"Want a go?"
"Yeah."

Daz hit the brakes hard and brought the Focus to a sliding halt in the middle of the field. Both got out and walked round to exchange seats. They stopped at the rear to inspect the damage. The bumper had gone, torn straight from its mountings, and the quarter panel was badly dented.

"Just a scratch, Andy. See if you can do better."
"No problem. Just fuckin' watch this."

He kicked the rear light cluster, shattering the panel, then kicked again to ensure all the bulbs were broken. They got back in, wiping the mud off their trainers on to the dashboard. Clearing his throat, Daz spat a gob of phlegm at the rear-view mirror. It caught the corner. He tried again and this time scored a direct hit on the centre of the mirror so that the rear view was totally obscured.

Andy liked driving. He liked the speed, and regardless of the fact that he kept missing the gears, he thought he was every bit as competent and in control as his brother. His handbrake turns were improving and he was confident of his ability. Soon, the field had become deeply rutted, and fearful of getting bogged down, Andy drove back on to the concrete track to content himself with pure speed. He raced along until the muddied headlights picked out a metal gate barring their progress. He hit the brakes, but not quickly enough, nor hard enough. The gate buckled but didn't give. The car felt the impact as the headlights exploded and the front panel caved in, buckling the bonnet and front wings. The offside wheel arch had crumpled, its jagged metal edge resting on the tyre. The occupants were pitched forward but had braced themselves and escaped injury.

"Bastard!" hissed Andy, slamming the car into reverse and putting his foot down hard on the gas.

The car careered at speed along the track until Andy lost control at a bend as a tyre exploded, the engine note changing abruptly as the remaining tyres lost traction. The car left the track and came down hard in the bottom of the ditch, bouncing along for some distance as the hedgerows clawed at the bodywork, ripping off the wing mirror. Steam rose from under the crumpled bonnet as Andy crunched once again into first. The car moved forward slightly as he lifted the clutch and revved. But the front tyre had shredded totally and the others were unable to gain any purchase from the muddy ditch. He increased the revs and rode the clutch until he could smell it burning. And finally, he stalled the engine.

"Fuck it!"

Darren tried first to get out, but his door was jammed tight against the hedgerows. He kicked hard at it, but it only opened a matter of inches before the springy hawthorn branches pushed it back inwards. Andy had better luck and was able to force the driver's door open by kicking and pushing it against the yielding mud bank of the ditch. He squeezed out and scrambled up the bank, followed by his brother. They stood there and surveyed the damage as best they could in the darkness. The car was covered in mud. One tyre had blown out and was almost totally free of the rim, exposing the suspension arm which had collapsed, leaking fluid. The bonnet was crumpled, and the front end badly damaged. The front and rear wings, visible from where they stood, had suffered considerable impact damage. And the doors had taken a good kicking. All in all, a good night's work. They looked at each other and grinned. And without saying a word, they performed their final ritual. Their trademark, like the string of phlegm hanging from the mirror. Together they unzipped their jeans. And together they urinated through the open door and shattered window. Spraying wildly. And giggling.

They zipped up and walked back along the track. Back to the entrance with its faded sign. They walked in silence, taking a right by the gamekeeper's cottage, along an old overgrown path which eventually joined a wider footpath. Soon they reached the footbridge which crossed the dual carriageway. They paused before crossing. Checking for traffic. Checking for police cars. But all was quiet. They walked quickly across, down the path at the other side and through the back alleys of the housing estate. They met no-one. And twenty minutes later they were back at the rented ex-council house where they lived with their mother.

She was asleep in an old armchair in front of the TV. Her last client had left some hours ago, and since then she'd consumed four cans of Special Brew and a dozen cigarettes. She never stirred when her sons entered. At least not until Darren tenderly lifted her arm from her lap and slapped her hard in the mouth with it.

"Come on. Wake up, you old twat!"
"Oh, fuck off! Leave me alone."
"Come on. Make us some supper."
"Get your own fucking supper."

Darren's reaction was predictable. She should have expected it. Yet it still came as a shock as she felt his fist explode against her cheek. He was a grown man now. And he could punch just as hard as his father used to. But whereas she was never afraid to strike back at his father - once even with a bread-knife - she daren't raise her hand against Darren. He'd kill her: she was sure of that. And it wouldn't be long before Andy summoned up the courage to hit her as well. He'd watched Darren often enough, with evident pleasure. And she knew it was just a matter of time. Once he'd done it for the first time there'd be no stopping him. He'd be worse than Darren. Andy was evil. Whereas Darren only had his dad as a role model, Andy had both his dad and Darren. And that was twice as bad. Without a word, she staggered into the kitchen, prized two burgers from the freezer, and put them in the greasy frying pan. Ignoring the spitting fat, she spread two rolls with margarine and wiped a plate with the dirty tea towel. She placed the plate close to the cooker and tried to hang the tea towel on the hook by the sink. Twice she missed. Closing one eye, and squinting, she managed to hook the towel where it belonged at the third attempt. She lit up a cigarette and balanced it on the edge of the worktop as she realised the burgers were burning. She flipped them over with the dirty green plastic spatula, which had deep grooves burnt into the handle as a result of previous drunken attempts at cooking. She took a pull at her cigarette as she slid the burgers onto the rolls, using her fingers to ensure they reached their intended destination. And this time, for a change, she remembered to turn off the gas. She'd learnt. Darren had hit her once before for forgetting. She staggered into the living room where the boys were sprawled on the settee.

"So, where you two been tonight?"
"Been here with you all night. Watchin' tele. Haven't we Andy?"

"'S right."
"'Course you have, boys. Here's your supper."
"Where's the fuckin' sauce?"
"Sorry, Andy. I'll get it darlin'."

CHAPTER 2

The alarm clock sounded at 4.45am, as it did every weekday when Terry was on the early shift. And as usual, he ignored it, allowing it to ring until it woke Linda. Sleepily, she nudged him and shook his shoulder gently.

"Turn it off, Terry. Time to get up."

He silenced the alarm, swung his legs lazily out of bed and switched on the bedside light. He looked at the clock, scarcely able to believe it was that time already. He put his fingers to the corners of his eyes to dislodge the crust of sleep which threatened to glue them permanently shut and trudged wearily into the bathroom, closing the bedroom door behind him as his wife snuggled beneath the duvet. He turned on the bath taps, slipped a robe over his shoulders and walked barefoot through to the kitchen. He switched on the electric kettle, sat on the sofa and lit a cigarette. As the kettle reached the boil, he docked the cigarette in the ashtray, and made himself a mug of strong coffee. He took it through to the bathroom, set it down and turned off the taps. Perfect timing as usual. A smooth, well-practised routine which never varied. He didn't know it yet but this morning would be different.

Emerging from his bath, he towelled himself dry and pulled on his working clothes, which as usual were piled tidily on the wicker chair in the bathroom. As ever, they had been laid out the previous night in the sequence in which he dressed. He finished his coffee, combed his short sandy hair and walked quietly back through to the kitchen. He made a second mug and relit the cigarette he'd started earlier. He put two slices of bread in the toaster and by the time they were browned he'd finished the cigarette. He spread the toast sparingly with margarine and ate it quickly. Leaving the plate by the sink, he selected an unread section of his Sunday paper and took it into the toilet along with his coffee.

At exactly five thirty-five, he laced up his boots, picked up the carrier bag containing his sandwich box, grabbed his keys and opened the door into the long corridor. He closed the door behind him carefully and quietly, so as not to disturb Linda, and walked along the corridor towards the rear staircase which led to the car park. He opened the back door, ensuring it clicked shut and locked securely behind him and stepped out into the cold dark morning air. The path to the car park from the back door was only a few yards long. He walked towards the spot where his car was always parked, fumbling with his keys, turning them between his fingers until he had the car key gripped between his thumb and index finger. And suddenly he stopped in his tracks. Where the hell was the car? It should be here. Where it always was. He tried to recall if Linda had used the car the previous evening. But no. She went out on Thursday evenings. And this was Wednesday morning. Besides, when she took the car, she always parked it exactly where he did. It was their space. Everybody knew that. So, where the hell was it? He walked past the vacant space, looking around as he went, trying desperately to remember where he'd parked it, and thinking he was now going to be late for work. He walked on for a further fifty yards before the penny finally dropped. His car had been stolen. Shit! He walked quickly back to his parking space as if to convince himself he wasn't dreaming. And then he saw at last. The tell-tale evidence. Twinkling on the frosty ground as they caught what little light there was from the few functioning lamps. Tiny squares of glass. Beneath where his car's rear door should have been. Broken glass from a broken car window.

Linda woke suddenly. She looked at the illuminated display on her alarm. Five-fifty. The alarm was set for six. Something else must have woken her. And then she heard the sound again. The one which had awoken her. The sound of someone in her flat. Beneath the bedroom door she could see the thin sliver of light from the hall. Oh my God! A burglar! She slipped silently out of bed, her heart pounding. She lifted her housecoat, a thick fleecy pink passion-killer as Terry called it, pulled it over her naked body and zipped it up to the throat. She stepped into her slippers. And finally, taking a deep breath and steeling herself against the prospect of disturbing a desperate intruder, she pushed open the bedroom door.

Terry was standing in the hall, his back to the bedroom, his ear to the telephone. Hearing the noise behind him, he turned to see Linda's puzzled face.

"Terry? What's going on? What's happened? Why aren't you at work?"
"Hang on a minute, love. Yes. Morning. I'd like to report a theft, please. My car.... Erm. OK... Hello? Yes, my car's been stolen....

Well, overnight.... Erm, just a second.... around six last night, and it was gone by five thirty-eight this morning...Stanton... Terry Stanton....A Ford Focus....Burgundy red..... FG10 ECP... It was parked in the corner of the car park at the Hutton Centre, near the flats.... Mellington House... 44.... 286442. Yes, that's right. OK, just wait a second, please, while I find a pen.... Right...C4872. Yes. OK. Thank you. Sorry? Oh, right, thanks. 'Bye."

"Terry, what's happened, love?"

"Car's been nicked."

"You're joking."

"'Fraid not."

"But it was locked. Wasn't it? It's always locked. You didn't leave it unlocked, did you?"

"Whoa! Hold it a minute. They've smashed the window, love. I don't know why they've done it. I don't know. The immobiliser was on. I'm certain it was. I always put it on. And the Krooklok was on. It always is. But it's been nicked."

"But why? Why would someone want to steal our car?"

"I don't know. All I know is it's gone. It's been stolen. I've informed the police, who were extremely reassuring in telling me that stolen cars normally turn up within twenty-four hours. If they turn up at all."

"Oh shit! Bastards!"

"My sentiments exactly."

"So, what do we do now?"

"Wait. For the police to ring to say they've found it. Apart from that, there's not a lot I can do. I'll have to phone the insurance company when they open. Get a claim form sent."

"What about work?"

"I'm not going. Not now. I'm going to have another cuppa and have a walk round for an hour or so. See if it's maybe been abandoned on one of the estates. You never know."

"And what about work? Shouldn't you phone them?"

"Can't. Not till the office opens at half eight. Till there's someone on the switchboard."

****

Alan, the production supervisor, walked into the factory at six-twenty and was surprised to find the place in relative darkness. Only the emergency lights were lit. The production lines were silent and the familiar deep rumble of the giant washer barrels was absent. He pulled on his white overall, and made his way round the factory, switching on lights, pressing buttons, turning handles, bringing the lines to life in time for production to start at six-thirty. Some of the workers were already making their weary way towards their positions. Alan barked a few terse instructions to his line leaders, then returned to his office, passing the unlit QC office on his way. He picked up the receiver and punched in the four-digit extension number, allowing the phone to ring repeatedly until a breathless voice answered.

"Hello?"
"Ronnie, it's Alan."
"Morning, Alan."
"Morning. Erm, what's happened to the QC this morning?"
"Terry? Hasn't he turned up?"
"No."
"Well. I don't know."
"Well, we can't hang about. We'll be running in a few minutes. QC or no QC."
"So, the checks haven't been done then?"
"No."
"Great! I'll try and pop down as soon as I can. I'll see if I can find Terry's number. See if he's slept in. I can't run both factories at once. I don't know how you expect me to be in two places at once..."
"Take it easy, Ronnie. I'm only letting you know what the situation is. It makes no odds to me whether everything's QC'd. I'm just responsible for production, that's all. So, don't take it out on me."
"All right, Alan. Thanks for letting me know. I'll see you later."

Alan returned to his duties with a smile on his face. He liked to throw a spanner into the works where Ronnie was concerned. She was a hard-faced cow! And he was quite happy to carry on without the interference of Quality Controllers. He had nothing against Terry personally. In fact, he quite liked him. But it was the breed as a whole he had little time for. He thought QC's were a necessary evil. They were there only because the customers demanded a visible commitment to quality control. But he found them a nuisance. Forever stopping the production lines. Forever querying. Rejecting anything. For whatever reason. Temperature too low. Or too high. Labels not printed correctly. Scales not weighing accurately. Hygiene rules not being adhered to. Well, this morning at least there were no such constraints. He could crank up the production lines and earn himself and his team some extra bonus.

Veronica Nicholls, Ronnie to her workmates, sat at her desk and cursed. She rummaged through the various piles of paper on her desk, looking for Terry's home phone number or his mobile. She couldn't find either. She could do without this sort of hassle at this time of morning. She was already due a bollocking from her boss, as one of their largest customers, a major supermarket, had just rejected a consignment of carrots. It wasn't her fault, but as supervisor, she carried the can. Well, never mind. She'd make sure the QC's took their share of the blame. She'd give them all a real roasting. She always did. And just wait till Terry turned up!

Veronica wore that look of a person permanently under pressure. Even when things were going well, she looked harassed, constantly on the move, checking this and that. She hadn't risen to the position of QC supervisor without displaying single-minded determination. The job was her life. Every night, she would return to her empty flat and think about the events of the day and plan her routine for the next. Generally disliked, even despised, by those who reported to her, she was nevertheless held in high regard by those who mattered. The bosses. She got the job done. By God, she did. And wasn't slow to vent her fury on anyone who didn't come up to scratch. She was surprised at Terry. He'd been fine until now. Worked diligently. Carried out her orders to the letter. She'd been surprised he'd taken the job in the first place. He seemed over-qualified. He was used to handling computers, not vegetables. But he'd knuckled down to it, and she'd been generally pleased with his progress. Until now. Now he'd let her down. And he'd pay for it.

****

Terry was already out on the streets, combing the neighbouring estates in the hope that someone had borrowed his car just for a ride. It had been raining. Perhaps someone had come out of the pub and didn't fancy the idea of walking home. He was hoping and praying that, just round the next bend, he'd find it, relatively undamaged. He'd just get in, start it up - it always started first time - and drive down to the garage to get the window fixed. Probably wouldn't even be worth making an insurance claim. But as the morning wore on he was becoming more depressed. He still clung vainly to the hope that he'd get the car back. It wasn't the sort of car anyone would steal to order, or to use as a getaway car, or anything like that. It was just a bog-standard family hatchback.

Nothing special. One in many millions. But it was special to him. It was the first decent car he'd ever owned. He'd had a good job then and saved until the day he'd walked in to the showroom and paid for it in cash. Only eighteen months old with hardly any mileage on the clock. He was so proud. But it was just the first step. He was going to keep it for a couple of years and then trade it in for a brand spanking new one. Then just before that time came, the bombshell dropped. He was made redundant. So, they kept the car, even though they had to give up their large house with its expensive mortgage and move into a small cottage. They economised wherever possible, doing without their usual annual holiday abroad, while he tried desperately to find another suitable position. But at forty, he knew he'd had it. The good times were over. He remembered the day he'd come home to Linda with the news that he'd taken a job, the way her face had lit up, and then dropped when he'd told her it was as a factory labourer. But they'd stayed together. Their marriage was strong. And she'd supported him and loved him even more for the fact that he was prepared to resort to hard manual labour to make a living. And he'd stuck it for three years, hating every minute. Feeling the calluses on his hands forming and hardening day by day. Scrubbing his fingers each night to cleanse his nails and skin of the dirt and smell of chemicals which lingered nonetheless. And in the end, he was both relieved and gutted when they made him redundant. Six more weeks on the dole, and then he saw the ad, and decided to go for it. His one last chance to make a decent living. A new computer site. Looking for someone to get it up and running and drive it into the future. He'd impressed at the interview. His experience and ideas, and very real enthusiasm to make a go of it had convinced them he was the man for the job. But it all happened very quickly. They'd driven down the following weekend, found a flat at the right price and put in an acceptable offer. Six weeks later they were in, and he'd started work, relishing the challenge. Linda found a job after a few weeks. But he'd never doubted that. She was the type who would get work anywhere. Smart, pretty, and intelligent, with good all-round office and secretarial experience, she was never out of work for long. And after a while, their cottage was sold, though for substantially less than the asking price. At least they had one less mortgage to pay, and with two incomes coming in, things were beginning to look rosier than they had for a long time. But still he kept the Focus, resisting the temptation to trade up. It was a good car. Never gave him any trouble at all. Always started first time, whatever the weather. As reliable as Bank Holiday rain, he used to call it. And he saw no point in trading in a perfectly good car for the unknown quantity of another used car. If you find something good, stick with it. That was how he looked at it. And for six months or so, things were fine. He worked hard - and so did Linda - and they took a two-week holiday abroad. Just like the old days. They soaked up the Mediterranean sun, drank too much, ate too well, and had a wonderful relaxing holiday. And returning to work refreshed, he was called to see the MD on his first morning back. To receive the news that the company was in trouble. Orders had slowed down, probably a seasonal thing, but the banks were becoming nervous and were reining in the overdraft and seeking to reduce the loan. Drastic measures were required, and the MD had no alternative but to dispense, reluctantly, with his services. He got a generous settlement, under the circumstances, and an empty promise of future employment when things picked up. And he knew that was it. Three times made redundant!

But Linda kept him going. She took on some freelance work as a proof-reader to keep things ticking over until he found 'something suitable'. But he knew that was it. His chance had gone. And though he attended interviews for highly paid jobs, he failed to impress. He'd lost that spark. That something special that once made him stand out from the rest of the candidates. Where once he'd had that arrogance, that positive attitude, that evident desire to succeed, now he came over as almost apologetic, crestfallen. He was beaten. And he knew it.

And when he was offered the job as a quality controller in a vegetable packing factory, he accepted immediately. He didn't want the job, but couldn't refuse it, or he could lose his only income, his Jobseeker's Allowance. So, he took the job, and worked as diligently as he could, but without much real enthusiasm. Every morning he'd get in the car and drive the eight miles to work. And at the end of the shift, he'd drive the eight miles home. And those sixteen miles of travelling were the most pleasurable part of the day. He was in his car. His beloved Focus. All that he had left to remind him of better days.

"And now some bastard's nicked it."

He stopped and looked round. He hadn't realised he'd been thinking out loud. But he couldn't care anyway. Never in his life could he remember feeling so angry. He abandoned his search and made his way home.

Linda was just about to leave as he arrived. She'd checked her hair and make-up and was making a desperate last-minute attempt to remove some scuff marks from the heels of her shoes. She smiled as Terry walked in. But it wasn't her usual smile, the one which could light up a room. This smile was little more than a flicker really. Anxious, a little sad, but reassuring to Terry, he acknowledged it with a small smile of his own.

"Sorry, love. No luck."
"It'll turn up, Terry. It's only been reported stolen a couple of hours. You can't expect miracles."
"I know. It's just I feel powerless to do anything. I feel as if I should be out looking for it. But I need to be here in case the police ring."
"Be patient, love. It'll turn up. I'm sorry, I'll have to go or I'll miss my bus. I'll see you tonight."
"See you."

Linda kissed him on the cheek, turned and left. Eight-thirty almost. Terry checked his watch against the time displayed digitally on the radio clock. He opened a drawer of the antique pine welsh dresser and pulled an A4 envelope from beneath an assortment of stationery. He tipped the contents on to the dining table and sifted through them until he found his car insurance documents in a smaller envelope. From the hall table drawer, he extracted a ball-point pen. He scribbled on the notepad, inscribing circles in the paper until the ink began to flow. Satisfied, he dialled his motor insurance company.

By nine o'clock, he was at a loose end. He'd registered his claim, which had been dealt with efficiently and sympathetically by a girl at the insurance company's call centre, who asked him to ring them as soon as the car was found. He'd rung work immediately afterwards, where he got a less than sympathetic response. He'd asked to speak to the QA manager, Mrs Gardner, but since she was in a meeting, he'd been put through to Ronnie. He groaned quietly on hearing her shrill, almost hysterical voice.

"Christ, Terry. Do you realise the problems you've caused this morning?"
"I'm sorry. But...."
"I've been running around like a blue-arsed fly. Trying to run two

factories at once. One of the washers in the bottom building has been running without chlorine because there was nobody there to check it first thing. The top dogs have gone ape-shit."

"Look. I'm sorry...."

"I've had to ring Davie and ask him to come in early to cover for you. But he hasn't arrived yet. I don't need this hassle. I don't need all this. My job's hard enough when I've got a full staff."

"My car's been stolen."

"So what time are you coming in?"

"I'm not. My car's been stolen."

"Well, get a bus. Or, better still, a taxi."

"I have to wait for the police to ring."

"What time are they ringing?"

"I don't know. When they find the car."

"And you're going to sit by the phone all day? Jesus Christ, Terry! This is a busy time for us. And you're going to sit at home waiting for the phone to ring. Well, thanks a lot!"

"I don't have a choice."

"So, will you be in tomorrow?"

"I don't know. It depends."

"It could be days! You can't stay off forever. You've dropped us right in the shit. You know that?"

"It's not my fault. I'll ring this afternoon if there's any progress."

"Give me your number."

"Why?"

"Because I want to know what's going on. I need to organise cover if you're not going to be back tomorrow. I'll be ringing you if I haven't heard anything by five o'clock."

"286442."

"Right. And your mobile number?"

"My wife's taken the mobile to work. You can't ring her."

"You've only one mobile between you?"

"Yeah."

"Great!"

She'd put the phone down, the cow! No tea and sympathy there. He felt sorry for Dave, and anyone else who'd come into contact with Ronnie today. She was in a foul mood, and somebody would suffer the brunt of it. He made a mug of coffee and lit another cigarette. Hearing the click as the central heating switched itself off, he walked over to the control panel and hit the manual override. It was going to be a long day. He was glad he'd lied to Ronnie about his mobile, which was by his side.

****

Bill finished his lunch of pork pie and sandwiches. During the morning he'd been working in the top fields, repairing some fencing. The manual work had helped him shake off his hangover, and he added a small dash of whisky to his tea to keep out the cold during his afternoon patrol of the lower fields. This was one of the benefits of the job; no-one clocked him in or out. If he wanted a long lunch, he took it. Nobody checked up on him. And this afternoon, all he had to do was check the lower fields and the bottom gate. Then he was free to collect firewood to dry out for use over the winter months. He pulled on his thick coat, reluctant to leave the relative warmth of the cottage. He stood by the door for some seconds, staring at the whisky bottle on the table, before finally deciding it could wait till the evening. He'd do a few hours work; then get drunk tonight.

At two-thirty, he came across the car. Taking a stub of pencil from his pocket, he scribbled the registration, or at least the first half of it which was legible from the broken plate and noted the model and colour in the little dog-eared notebook he always carried with him. Flipping back through the pages, he found several similar notes from previous occasions. He'd phone the police when he'd finished work. First, he had to check the gate, and collect his firewood.

****

Terry was dozing in an armchair when the phone rang. Quickly to his feet, he ran through to the hall and picked it up on the fourth ring.

"Hello?"
"Terry, love, it's me."
"Hello, Linda."
"Any news?"
"No, love. Not yet. When the phone rang, I thought it might have been the police."
"I'm sorry. Are you OK?"
"Yeah. Just pissed off."
"OK. I'll see you later. Don't worry. It'll turn up."
"I'm beginning to wonder."

****

Bill had to forget about the firewood for the day. He'd found the damage to the bottom gate and knew he'd better report it to the Estate Manager immediately. He checked it was still secure and hurried back to the cottage.

****

At three-thirty, Terry received the awaited call from the police. A member of the public had phoned them. Would he please arrange to have the vehicle removed as it was on private land? He wrote down the directions, put on his shoes and coat, picked up his car keys and left the house.

As he walked along the damp grass verge which bordered the dual carriageway, his thoughts were concentrated on the job in hand. The police hadn't told him the condition of the car; in fact, they hadn't known. They'd simply relayed the message to him. They hadn't mentioned anything about fingerprints, and as far as they were concerned, the case was closed. Just another crime statistic. He arrived at the roundabout built above the main link road to the airport. There was no pavement, nor grass verge, and so he walked round it in an anti-clockwise direction, balancing on the narrow kerb which separated the road from the crash barrier, and the thirty-foot drop to the carriageway beneath. He found the dirt track - he'd driven past it often enough - and turned down it, noting the gamekeeper's cottage with the wisps of smoke escaping from its crumbling chimney stack. Further along, he saw the faded sign and turned right on to the concrete track, following it slightly downhill. He noticed how the road became muddy with the parallel lines of tyre tracks, how they veered off into the field and returned at irregular intervals on their meandering course. And rounding a bend, he saw its roof glinting dully in the weak late afternoon sun. Approaching slowly, and full of foreboding, he tried to ascertain the extent of the damage. At least it was upright, and sunk deep in mud, which might, just possibly, have cushioned the impact. Then his heart sank as he drew closer. Now he could see the rear bumper was missing, and the rear wing caved in. The car listed toward the front offside, where the wheel was splayed out at a crazy angle, remnants of a tyre hanging loosely from the rim. One rear window was shattered. Both front doors were open, the driver's door buried deep into the mud banking. He walked quickly now to the front, dismayed to see the crumpled bonnet off its catch, the lights smashed, and the front panel and wings badly dented. He could see the trail of debris as branches of the hedgerow had snapped off as the car had lurched along the ditch bottom. Turning his attention to the interior, he saw the glove compartment gaping wide open. One of Linda's driving shoes was still tucked in the passenger door storage pocket, its partner missing. The electric wiring for the ignition lay exposed, the cover nowhere in sight. And mud everywhere! On the seats, on the dashboard, on the grey-weave cloth of the door panels. And then he noticed the smell, and the wet patches on the seats, and the zig-zag lines of damp everywhere, as if some demented graffiti artist had sprayed indiscriminately. But this wasn't paint!

"Bastards!", he breathed. "Fucking bastards!"

For a moment, he thought about closing the doors to prevent any rain from causing further damage, and then checked himself, realising what a futile gesture it would be. He knew it was a write-off. He didn't need an insurance company expert to tell him. That was it.

Terry had seen enough. He was boiling with rage, finding it difficult to understand why anyone would treat someone else's property in such a way. Didn't they realise he needed the car to get to work? Christ! He'd forgotten all about work. He'd better get home and ring Ronnie. No. Get the priorities right. Ring the insurance company first! Get the claims procedure in motion.

He was turning to leave when he noticed it. It had escaped his earlier inspection, but now he could see it clearly. A yellow, green, brown stain on the driver's rear-view mirror. Dried, almost crystallised. And it took a few seconds before his brain registered what it was. Dried phlegm! His rage welled up again.

"Bastards! I wish I could get my hands on the bastards!"

He walked home, seething in silence.

It was five-thirty when he arrived home. As he mounted the stairs to the flat he could hear the phone ringing. He unlocked the door, took off his muddy shoes on the mat outside and entered, carrying them. He allowed the phone to continue its persistent ringing as he took a newspaper from the rack, opened it out on the hall carpet, and placed his shoes carefully upon it. Finally, he lifted the phone.

"Hello?"

"Terry! Where the hell have you been? I've been trying to get hold of you for the last half hour. Are you coming in to work in the morning?"

"Hello, Ronnie. How nice of you to call enquiring about my welfare."

Christ, he thought, better go easy on the sarcasm. This bitch could make things even more difficult if he upset her.

"What's that supposed to mean? Look! We've had one hell of a day here."

"I'm sorry, Ronnie. But so have I. And no, I'm sorry, but I won't be in tomorrow. They've just found the car, and I've got to make arrangements to get it towed to a garage tomorrow."

"Well, it's just as well I've got Dave to come in at six in the morning to cover for you. It's not fair, you know. Just think how you're inconveniencing us all."

"It's not my fault. I'll try to be back on Friday. I'll ring about the buses. I'll do what I can."

"Right! Ring me tomorrow. Early afternoon. Make sure you do."

"I will."

"Right. 'Bye."

He heard the phone click dead before he had the chance to reply, but was content to say "Go wank yourself, you old whore" down the silent line.

He rang the insurance company, who promised to get a local garage in touch with him within the hour. He put the phone down and rested his elbows on the hall table, sinking to his knees. He put his hands over his closed eyes and immediately the image of the mud-spattered wreck appeared. He ran his hands upwards, pushing back his hair. Again and again, each time more gently, soothing his scalp. Calming down. He stood up and took off his coat, hanging it tidily in the hall closet, and walked wearily through to the kitchen. He checked the kettle. Half full. He switched it on and heaped coffee and sugar into the mug he'd used earlier in the day, watching as the dark brown and bright white granules merged into a muddy consistency in the bottom of the wet mug. Like the ditch. Where they'd pissed in his car. Bastards!

The phone was ringing again. He trudged through to the hall, hoping to God it wasn't Ronnie again. He took a deep breath and picked up the receiver.

"Hello?"
"Mr Stanton?"
"Yes."
"Hello, Mr Stanton. It's Salim Khan from Northgate Motor Services."
"Hello, Salim."

He knew Salim. He'd taken the Focus to Northgate for a service and had it MOT'd there only a month earlier.

"Mr Stanton, your insurance company has been in touch with us. Your car, I believe, has been stolen. And now it's been found?"
"Yes, that's right."
"OK, Mr Stanton. Is the car driveable?"
"I doubt it. It's in the bottom of a ditch. It needs towing out. And I'm fairly sure from what I've seen that one of the wheels is coming off. And the front suspension looks knackered."
"OK, Mr Stanton. It's getting a little late now, but I'll try to get a recovery vehicle out tonight. The procedure is, they will bring the car to us, and a representative from your insurance company will inspect the vehicle with us and assess the damage and agree a course of action from there."
"How long will it take?"
"You will have a decision tomorrow, Mr Stanton. Now, will you be at home for the next hour or so?"
"Yes. I'm unlikely to go for a drive. I'm sorry. I don't mean to take it out on you."
"That's OK, Mr Stanton. I understand how you feel. Don't worry. We'll sort things out for you as quickly as we can. What I'll do now is, I'll try to get someone to recover your car this evening. If I can't, I'll ring you about eight o'clock. If I can get someone to recover the car, they will ring you, so that you can give them directions. Is that OK, Mr Stanton?"
"Yes. That's fine. Thank you very much for your help."
"You are welcome, Mr Stanton. 'Bye now."
"'Bye."

Ah, well, he thought, at least something is happening. He put the receiver back down in its cradle and realised that his hand was shaking. It was rage. Pure rage. And he couldn't calm down. He tipped the remains of his coffee down the sink, opened the bottom right-hand cupboard of the welsh dresser and extracted a bottle of malt. His favourite. The one he only touched at Xmas, New Year and on his birthday. It was half full. He pulled the cork, selected a tumbler and poured himself a generous measure. He slumped in the armchair, glass in one hand, cigarette in the other and an ashtray on the arm. And brooded. He was tired. More tired than when he'd done a day's work with Ronnie on his back, complaining, criticising. Moaning, as if she was the only one who had problems. He wished to God he had the guts to tell her to Eff off and walk out. But he needed the job, needed the money. And needed it even more now, because of the excess on his insurance. Plus the fact that his premium would go up next time, because of this claim. And all because some bastard took his car and wrecked it for a bit of fun! He still found it hard to understand why anyone would want to behave like that. It was mindless! What did anyone gain? Except, maybe, pleasure. He wished to Christ he could get even. Find whoever it was who'd done this to him and give them - he was inclined to believe there were two of them from the state of the car's interior - a good pasting. But he knew the chances of their being caught were slim, and he guessed if he came face to face with them, he wouldn't have the guts to do anything about it. He drained the glass and refilled it.

Linda was annoyed at first when she arrived home to find him sitting, drinking. Normally, when he worked the early shift he'd have a meal ready by the time she came home. But she immediately sensed his mood and sat on the chair arm by him and put her arm round him. She kissed his cheek gently as he told her what had happened. She was careful to disguise her anger.

"It'll be OK, love. Don't worry. It's only a car."
"It's not only a car! It's our car! The only decent car we've ever had."
"We'll get another. The insurance company will pay out."
"Yes, but they pay book price. And that car's worth a lot more."
"Well, we'll get something to tide us over, and save up for something better."
"What's the point? If we get a decent car, some bastard will nick it."
"Come on, Terry. We've just been unlucky, that's all."
"But why us?"
"Just bad luck, that's all. I'm sure it's nothing personal. I mean we've hardly been here long enough to make any friends, let alone

enemies. Anyway, if it's a write-off..."

"It is a write-off."

"OK. Assuming it's a write-off, how much are we likely to get for it?"

"Fifteen hundred. Maybe sixteen. I don't know. But it's not much considering we've just spent over two hundred on it."

"We can still get something reasonable for that amount, surely."

"Not that easy, love. At that price range, we either buy privately or we try the small traders. Either way, there's no guarantee. We won't get anything from a reputable dealer at that price."

"What about a loan?"

"What's the point? What's the point of going into debt and buying a nice car and waking up one morning and finding it's been nicked. Or trashed."

She decided not to pursue that line of conversation. She'd wait another day till Terry was in a different frame of mind. Then they'd sit down together and talk about it. The way they discussed everything. Calmly, rationally. And they'd come to a joint decision.

The phone was ringing again. Terry leapt to answer it, and returned two minutes later, a look of resignation etched into his face.

"That was the recovery company. They can't come till the morning."

"Will the car be safe out there overnight?"

"I don't think anybody's going to nick it. Do you?"

His tone was unnecessarily sarcastic, and she wished immediately she hadn't asked such a stupid question.

"Give us a hand, please, love. Peel the spuds and I'll get the chops on and do the veg. Then we'll settle down with a bottle of wine, or something, and maybe have an early night. OK?"

"Yeah. Fine."

Terry's mood had lightened a little by the time they went to bed. They made love with urgency but little passion, fulfilling a need rather than a desire. And went to sleep immediately afterwards.

They both rose early the next morning, and at eight-thirty Terry was waiting at the roundabout over the dual carriageway when the recovery vehicle pulled up. He climbed into the cab and murmured 'Morning' to the driver.

"Morning. Mr Stanton, isn't it?"

"That's right."

"OK, Mr Stanton. Which way do we go from here?"

"Far side of this roundabout. There's an unmade road. About fifty yards down, there's a track on the right-hand side. It takes you down..."

"To Oakland."

"You know it?"

"Know it well. But I didn't recognise it from your directions. Sorry. Seems I've got you out of bed for nothing."

"That's OK. It's not a problem."

"Christ. I must have been down here about six or seven times over the last year for a recovery. It's my betting it's the same people every time. They race about the fields till they crash, or till they get bored. Then they just vandalise the cars for fun. Set fire to one once."

"Mine's just been crashed into the ditch. The one at the side of the track."

"They'll have lost control. Handbrake turns, in reverse, and all that. Bastards!"

"Agreed. Oakland, did you say? That's an odd name, isn't it? As far as I can see, there's only one old oak tree, standing on its own in the middle of all these fields."

"Aye. But it used to be all forest round here. And the name just stuck. There's one or two of us old lads still call it Oakland, but most people just call it the Estate nowadays. And that last oak won't be there for long either, not with them crashing cars against it all the time. You can see the marks on its trunk. Deep gouges. They've given it some right hammer, this last year or so."

"So, when did you first come here to pick up a wreck?"

"Last summer. Joy-riding's fairly recent round here. Well, no, that's not strictly true. But it's only fairly recently that people have been taking cars deliberately to write them off. Before, they just used to, like, borrow them for a lift home. Yeah, now and again they'd cause a bit of damage, but usually because they'd been driving too fast, or been drinking. But this last year or so, it looks like someone's doing it just for the pure hell of it. And I suppose it's ironic really but business for me has never been as good. I used to just get accidents and breakdowns. But this, for me anyway, is a welcome addition to trade. Sorry if that sounds selfish, like. But it's true. And it doesn't come out of your pocket, well, at least not directly. Your insurance company foots the bill. Though I suppose you pay for it with higher premiums."

"That's true... So, if this has only been happening round here for less than a year, it sounds like it could be young kids, who are only just old enough to drive."

"Possible. Or it could be someone who's moved here in the last year."

"Mmm, yeah. Suppose so."

"I think you're right though. It's most likely kids. And I'm pretty sure it's the same ones. I bet all your lights have been smashed, and the rear wings are damaged. And I bet as well that they've pissed in it."

"That's right. How'd you know?"

"'Cos it's the same every time I come here. Ah, there it is. Let's go have a look and work out how to shift it."

Sandy, the driver, shifted into neutral and applied the handbrake. He jumped down from the cab and walked quickly to catch Terry who was already on his way towards the ditch. They both stopped on the bank, looking down on the wreck.

"Well, Mr Stanton. It's definitely a write-off. I can tell you that from here."

He slid down the muddy bank to the car and worked his way round while Terry watched helplessly from the concrete track. He weighed up the options before climbing out of the mud and walking back to the truck, which he manoeuvred expertly into the optimum position to dislodge the wreck. He passed a length of steel cable through the car's towing eye, looping it through its own eyed end and securing the other eye to the hook on the hydraulic winch. He pressed buttons and pulled levers and the winch came to life, sucking the Focus from the cloying mud and dragging it up the banking. He switched off the winch, released the cable, and moved the truck into a more favourable position before letting down the ramps at the rear. He re-attached the cable and started up the winch once more, dragging the car on its three wheels up the ramp and on to the flat bed, where he secured it with chocks and cables. Even though the car was caked in mud to the top of its wheel arches, Terry could see the extent of the damage, and he struggled again to keep his anger under control. Seeing this, Sandy dropped him off close to home before depositing the wreck at Northgate Motors. Terry turned to watch his Focus being carried away. He knew it was the last time he'd see it.

****

Salim phoned at lunchtime to inform him that the loss adjuster had already inspected the car and deemed it an insurance write-off. It was what he'd expected. Now he could only wait for the insurance company's offer, which, Salim said, was likely to be 'top book'. Terry thanked Salim, who'd evidently spent some time with the loss adjuster explaining that the vehicle was in immaculate condition prior to its theft. And, sure enough, when the loss adjuster phoned later that afternoon, he made him an offer of seventeen hundred and seventy-five pounds. Terry accepted immediately, rather than delaying matters by quibbling. His cheque should arrive within ten to fourteen days. Until then, he'd have to use bus and taxi. He checked the internet to find the bus times of services to the outlying area where the factory was situated. He then had the unpleasant task of informing Ronnie he would be returning to work on the Friday morning, but that the earliest time he could get there would be eight-fifteen. It didn't surprise him in the least that she would be unhappy at such an arrangement.

"You're supposed to be on earlies this week. Six o'clock start. That's your contracted time."
"Cut me some slack, Ronnie. I've already told you I have to get two buses. Quarter past eight is the best I can do."
"What about taxis?"
"I can't afford taxis every day. It's a tenner a time. Can't you ask Dave if he'll cover the early shift for a while? Till I get sorted."
"I've already asked him. He'll cover tomorrow, and the next two weeks. But you'll have to do Saturday. Dave's away for the weekend."
"That's fine. Thanks."
"Don't thank me. If it was up to me, I'd leave the rota as it was. It's your responsibility to do the hours you're contracted to work."
"Give me a break. You know it's not my fault."
"I'm giving you a break. You've got two weeks on lates, apart from Saturday, to get sorted. 'Bye."

The phoned clicked dead in his ear. But the message had come through loud and clear. He'd upset the smooth running of Ronnie's little empire, and for that he'd have to pay.

CHAPTER 3

Thank God, it's lunchtime, thought Brian Peters. This Monday morning had seemed never-ending. He'd been in this open-plan office where Bradford CID was based on several occasions in the past, but always as a visitor, and he'd always felt welcomed. Today, though, it was as if he was disturbing his colleagues, his new colleagues, who evidently had more important things to do than help him settle into his new working environment. He'd been introduced to everybody, but the welcome was curt and cold. He could sense a little resentment from some of the current staff; a clique, it seemed, which preferred to do things their way, the way things had always been done. He'd been warned, at his interview, but was adamant he could handle it, and his old boss, Don McArthur, had written a glowing reference which swung it for him. His new colleagues would just have to work with him. At least he knew a few of the support staff with whom he'd liaised over the years when he'd been a member of the Counter-terrorism Unit, and he could rely on their friendship, help and support. But for Brian, there had always been days when he wished he'd never joined the force. This was one of them. He'd become used to having a pile of outstanding work. And now, suddenly, he had nothing to do.

He locked access to his PC, pulled on his jacket and walked up a flight of stairs to the canteen. He'd almost reached the door when he was stopped by a young DC whose name he'd already forgotten.

"Excuse me, DS Peters."
"Call me Brian when we're in the office, please."
"Yes, sorry, Brian. Muesli wants to see you in his office."
"OK, thanks."

He'd already heard about Muesli; DCI Moseley, who earned his soubriquet through his apparent addiction to a healthy diet, and who often lectured his staff about the dangers of their preferred breakfast of high-fat bacon and sausage sandwiches. He carried on climbing a further flight of stairs leading to a large room evidently used for meetings, with offices along one wall. He stopped outside the one with the nameplate DCI Moseley, took a deep breath and knocked.

"Come in."

He entered.

"You wanted to see me, sir?"

"Ah, yes, Brian. Please take a seat."

"Thank you, sir."

"How's it been so far, Brian?"

"A bit daunting so far, sir, to tell you the truth. They're a close-knit group."

"They certainly are. They need to be. As you know, once you're out in the field, as it were, you spend many long hours in the company of the same small group, and when it comes to the crunch, you have to be able to trust each other implicitly."

"Yes, sir. I'm well aware of that. It's no different to life in the CTU. They'll take time until they learn to trust me."

"Well, let's hope it won't take too long. In the meantime, you'll be working with another new recruit to our ranks. Someone I believe you already know."

"Who's that, sir?"

"DC Lynn Whitehead. Her transfer's been approved. She starts next Monday. It seems there's some major reorganisation taking place in the CTU."

"Well, I'll look forward to working with her, sir."

"In the meantime, I'd like you to have a look through this."

He passed a folder across the desk. Brian noticed its status, clearly marked, was 'Open'.

"Since you've got nothing on your plate as yet, I'd like you to have a good look through this, Brian. We've made no progress in recent weeks and I feel it needs a fresh pair of eyes. I want this case closed. Let me know what you think on Friday. See me at 3pm. Thank you."

"Thank you, sir."

After a quick lunch at an otherwise empty table, he spent the rest of the day looking through the file and making notes. The victim was Amanda Braithwaite, a 28-year-old single female, found dead in her flat on New Year's Day. Her body was discovered in the early afternoon by her flatmate who had spent the previous night at a party in Leeds. The Post Mortem examination estimated the time of death as the early hours of New Year's Day and established she had died from a cardiac arrest following ingestion of cocaine. Her flatmate, Victoria (Vicky) Armstrong, was adamant she was not a 'user', and had never known her take illegal drugs of any kind. The Scene of Crime report noted that no drugs nor any drug-taking paraphernalia were discovered in the flat. Neighbours were interviewed but nobody saw or heard anything unusual. Nobody was seen entering or leaving the flat. Her flatmate stated when interviewed that the entrance door of the flat was locked when she arrived. There were two locks, a Yale and a Mortice lock, and she stated to the best of her knowledge there were only two keys for each. Both sets were accounted for, Vicky had hers when she unlocked the flat, and Amanda's were on the coffee table in the flat. Nevertheless, the coroner felt obliged to conclude that death was due to an overdose of cocaine and should be considered as a suspicious death. The verdict was 'misadventure'.

He looked at the photographs enclosed within the folder. The first was a close up of an attractive, smiling young woman, well-dressed and clear-skinned. In stark contrast were the others - the crime scene photos of the dead girl with vomit on her chin and down her dress. Dishevelled, her previously glossy hair now lank; her sunken, lifeless eyes once sparkling and full of fun, but now dull and empty.

He noted the addresses he needed to visit in the morning and made appointments over the phone.

"Don't stay here all night. People will think you're a promotion chaser."

The voice startled him: he'd been engrossed in the file. He looked up to see the smiling face of one of his new colleagues.

"Gary Ryan. DC."

He held out his hand. Brian shook it and introduced himself.

"Pleased to meet you, Gary. Brian Peters."
"You're the guy from CTU. One of the team involved in the Bradford bombing."
"That's right."
"You'll be fine here, Brian. Everyone will soon get used to you. But they'll probably play some tricks on you. They do with all new staff.

Just try to take it and keep your cool. It's just like an initiation ceremony. Nothing malicious."

"Thanks. I'll bear that in mind."

"Some of the lads have gone down to the pub. You're welcome to join us."

"Some other time, maybe. It's been a long day."

"OK. See you tomorrow. And if you ever need any help with anything, just ask. I'll do my best to assist. Goodnight."

"Goodnight, Gary. And thanks."

"You're welcome."

Ten minutes later, Brian signed out at the front desk and left. Soon he was driving back to his wife and child at their home on the outskirts of Wakefield. The house was up for sale and had attracted some attention but as yet, no offers. Brian had resigned himself to spending yet another weekend looking at properties in Bradford, so that he could be nearer his work, and he knew that by the time he got home, his wife, Sarah, would have details of yet another half-dozen potential new homes for him to look through. Still, it would take his mind off the case he'd been assigned to investigate, and he would be able to start afresh in the morning. There were items in the report which had nagged at him. Something was not quite right. Apart from the body, there was no other evidence that a crime had been committed. It was all too *clean* to look like a crime scene. But a visit to the flat was on his list of things to do the next day. It could wait till then. In the meantime, moving the family to a bigger house was becoming a higher priority as every day went by, the birth of their second child being due in April.

Once home, he put work to the back of his mind. Sarah never asked him how his day went, preferring to let him raise the subject if it was weighing on his mind. Otherwise, home remained a sanctuary from the problems the nature of his work inevitably caused. Here, he played the dutiful husband, washing up, playing with Daniel and helping put him to bed, and only then, when the house was still and he relaxed with a drink in hand, would he open up about his day. Since his final case with the CTU, he'd adopted single malt whisky as his favourite drink, in honour of a friend, John Braden, who'd lost his life during Operation Coyote. He made sure he always kept a bottle of Glenlivet in the house. He'd never been a heavy drinker, unlike some of his colleagues, but enjoyed a glass of malt. It helped him relax. It helped him think. At least that's what he told his wife. In fact, it helped him cope with the horror of seeing his working partner being blown to unidentifiable small pieces by a terrorist bomb prior to his departure from CTU. As he relaxed, he looked at the latest batch of suitable houses for sale on his laptop, discussing the pros and cons of each with his wife, before deciding which, if any, were worth short-listing for viewing. By the end of the evening, they had listed two for further consideration. Sarah agreed to arrange viewing over the weekend. Brian was not overly enthusiastic but was pragmatic enough to realise it had to be done, and soon.

Sarah went to bed leaving Brian to have another 'small glass', as he frequently did these days. Just before midnight, he finished his drink and went up to bed.

CHAPTER 4

He was at his desk by 8 am. He needed quiet time to review the information contained in all the interview notes. In doing so, he made notes of his own, and questions he needed to ask when he spoke in person to those people who were interviewed at the time. Cross-referencing all the information before him, he noted the sequence of events recorded, looking for anomalies. He also planned to talk to the investigating officer on the original case whose name was printed and signed on each sheet of paper – Danny Hardcastle. He would leave that until last.

By now, most of the officers were at their desks, talking in small groups before setting about their allotted tasks. Brian's phone rang. He picked it up immediately.

"DS Peters."
"Good morning. I'd like to report an incident of indecent exposure."

He could hear laughter in the background. He turned to find four members of the CID team stood behind him, flies open, cocks out.

"Very funny. But you should know that CID don't deal with issues as small as those."
"Just a joke, Peters. You'll get used to it."
"Yeah. No problem."

Seemingly satisfied, they returned to their desks, passing the grinning Hardcastle on their way. His phone rang again. This time it was Muesli.

"Morning, sir."
"Morning, Brian. I'd like you to look into a call we've just received. You'll get the details from Mrs Shackleton. Take DC Ryan with you."
"Yes, sir."

He replaced the receiver, put on his jacket and crossed the room to Gary Ryan's desk.

"You're with me this morning, Gary. Muesli's orders."
"OK. What are we on?"

"Don't know. I've to collect the info from Mrs Shackleton, whoever she is."

"She's upstairs. She's a civilian, the senior admin officer, researcher and call scheduler. You'll love her. Everyone calls her Mrs Semtex. You'll soon see why."

"I can't wait."

She had an office to herself, quite a large space, but packed with files, folders and machinery. She had two desktop computers, a printer/copier/fax machine and a laptop, a landline phone and a mobile on her desk and didn't look up from her work although it was clear she had heard them approach. Brian broke the silence.

"Good morning, Mrs Shackleton. I'm sorry to disturb you, but DCI Moseley sent us to collect some information from you regarding a call. I'm Brian Peters."

"Good morning. I'm Teresa. Pleased to meet you."

"Pleased to meet you, Teresa. What have you got for us?"

"A body found in his flat. The pathologist should be there now, and SOCO are already on site. Here's the address."

"Thank you."

"You're welcome."

Out in the corridor, Gary shook his head in amazement.

"I've never known that before."

"What do you mean?"

"Mrs Semtex being so calm and friendly."

"I take it she's not normally like that?"

"Not at all. They call her Mrs Semtex because she's volatile. She's got a short fuse and is likely to explode at the slightest provocation. She must like you."

"Perhaps she just likes to be treated like a human being."

"Perhaps."

Gary drove while Brian tried to make the necessary calls to re-schedule his appointments for the morning. He was keen to get back to the case he already had outstanding and hoped this new one wouldn't take up too much time. He then reminded himself that *any* case, however trivial it may appear, demanded his full attention and concentration. He would remain focused on the job in front of him.

They soon reached their destination – a retirement housing complex close to Idle village – and parked next to the SOCO van. A constable had been posted outside the flat and he allowed them to enter after checking their IDs. The head of the SOCO team, Allen Greaves, was on the point of leaving but stopped to brief the newly-arrived officers.

"What have we got, Allen?"
"We have the body of an eighty-year-old male, Arthur Williamson, who lived alone here. I believe death probably occurred on Saturday, late evening, and was caused by blunt force trauma as a result of a fall when he smashed his head against the corner of the table. He'd been drinking heavily and was alone. The warden found him this morning. The door was locked, and there were only two keys – the resident's, and the warden's master key. He did not get a morning welfare call, having refused the service, but his neighbour became concerned she hadn't seen him for a couple of days, which was unusual. So, she alerted the warden. I don't believe there are any suspicious circumstances. In my opinion, it's an accidental death, pure and simple. You've just missed the forensic pathologist, but we're both of the same opinion on this one."
"Thanks, Allen. We'll just have a word with the warden, and then we'll talk to the neighbour, and that should be the end of the matter from our point of view unless the Post Mortem raises any issues."

They had a quick look at the scene, verifying everything Allen had told them, then went along to the office where a middle-aged pleasant woman was behind the desk, staring at her computer screen and typing. Brian knocked and entered.

"Excuse me, are you the warden?"
"No. Actually, I'm the Court Manager. We last had a warden here in 2004. Now, how can I help you?"
"I'm sorry. No offence intended. We'd just like you to repeat what you told Mr Greaves, for our records."
"Mrs Carr, who lives at number 46 came to my office this morning at about 9.30. She told me she hadn't seen Arthur, Arthur Williamson, since Saturday afternoon, which was unusual. She tends to notice everything that happens on the Court, if you know what I mean."
"Yes. Go on."

"Well, she seemed concerned, so I told her I'd call on him. Now, he doesn't have a daily welfare check. That was his decision and I have to abide by that, and I'm not allowed to enter a resident's flat alone without express permission. So, when I knocked on his door and couldn't get an answer, I asked Maureen, my cleaner, to go in with me. And we found him, lying on his side on the floor in his living room if you can call it that. He was obviously dead. So, I dialled 999 and they sent the policeman and a paramedic. They took over and called the other chaps. That's it, really."

"You didn't touch anything in the flat?"

"No. Nothing. I couldn't get out of there fast enough, to be honest."

"Could I take your name, please, and your cleaner's name? Just for our records."

"I'm Norma Cunliffe. My cleaner's Maureen Barratt."

"And when did you last see Mr Williamson alive?"

"Friday tea-time, when I logged off for the weekend. He usually goes down to the village for a pint on an afternoon."

"How did he seem?"

"Just normal. He's not very steady on his feet after a few drinks. But he usually waited till he was home before getting the whisky out. Mainly because of the cost."

"Was he a heavy drinker?"

"About a bottle of whisky a week in the flat. It's the first item on his weekly shopping list."

"Thank you. Could we just have a quick word with Maureen before we go?"

"Yes. She's in the lounge. Just knock and she'll let you in."

"One more thing. Does Mr Williamson have any family?"

"His wife died before he moved here, but he has a daughter, though she hardly ever visits. He's lived here more than four years and I've only ever seen her twice. I'll have to contact her. The trouble is, as far as I know, she'll be spending the winter in the Canaries like she always does. She's his next-of-kin, so she'll be responsible for clearing the flat. Otherwise she'll have to continue paying the rent and service charge till it's done. Whether that will cause her to interrupt her holiday, we'll have to wait and see."

"Thank you for your time, Mrs Cunliffe."

"You're welcome."

They walked over to the residents' lounge where they could hear the unmistakable sound of a vacuum cleaner being pushed back and forth. Brian had to go around the side and knock on a window to attract the cleaner's attention. She gave them the same story they'd just heard from the manager. Satisfied, they left her and called on Mr Williamson's neighbour, Mrs Carr, who confirmed what they'd heard from the Court Manager. Walking back to the car, Gary remarked,

"Did you notice how blasé everybody seemed about the whole affair? It was like they come across this sort of thing on a daily basis."

"Maybe they do. Just bury the bodies in the garden and rent the flat out again."

"God's Waiting Room for the coffin dodgers."

"Mmm."

"Your parents still alive, Brian?"

"Yes. Both still working and well, thank God. They've both got a couple of years before they retire. How about yours?"

"Both fine. Both still well short of retirement. Dad still plays a bit of cricket."

"Do you see much of them?"

"Every day. I still live with them."

"You're still single, then?"

"Still looking for the right man."

"Sorry. I didn't realise."

"No need to apologise."

"Is it common knowledge at work?"

"Yes. They accept it. Well, most of them do. Hardcastle often makes snide remarks. But I can live with that."

"Have you reported him?"

"No."

"Don't you think you should?"

"He'll get his comeuppance one day."

"Well, it's your call."

"I can handle it."

"Good for you. As far as I'm concerned, all I want to know is, are you a good copper?"

"I think so. I don't make rash judgments. I'm methodical and thorough. I may be gay, but I can handle myself."

"That sounds like a joke."

"I mean if things get violent, I don't stand back holding the coats."

"That's good to know."

"You used to carry a weapon, didn't you?"

"Yes. I'm still registered, but obviously, I'm not allowed to carry one on a daily basis any longer. I'm no Dirty Harry."

"Sometimes I think Dirty Harry's just what we need round here."

"Let's get back to the station. I've more interviews scheduled for this afternoon."

Back at the station, Brian discovered he had, in fact, only one interview lined up for the afternoon. A neighbour of the dead young girl had agreed to see him. As he drove to the address, he reflected on Mr Williamson's death, and his relationship with his daughter. He wondered whether she'd think her father's death was sufficient reason for curtailing her holiday, and whether the fact that it would cost her financially by not clearing the flat would be the deciding factor. He hoped his young child, and the other one on the way would treat him better in his old age. He made a promise to himself there and then that he would give more consideration to the needs of his own parents in future. He wondered how many of the residents of the complex he'd visited that morning received regular visits from family, and how many spent their lives just waiting for someone, anyone, to engage in conversation with them. These days, when so many millions of people are online and connected practically every second of the day, there are still those lonely people left behind and forgotten.

He parked the car in the street outside the small block of flats, a recently converted industrial building. He walked around the perimeter, noting the security fence and the CCTV cameras. Reaching the front door, he was dismayed at the absence of any cameras there. There was only the door panel, and a speech module which visitors would use to announce their presence and request entry, which would be controlled, he imagined, from inside each flat. He pressed twenty-four and waited until he heard a click and then a voice.

"Hello?"
"Mrs Clarke? It's Detective Sergeant Peters. You agreed to see me."
"Oh, yes. Come in."

A buzzing sound indicated the door lock was released. He pushed the door open and entered, watching with satisfaction as the door closed and locked itself automatically after he'd entered. He followed the numbered signs along the corridor towards the rear of the building and knocked on the door of number 24 and waited, his ID card in front of the spy hole, until Mrs Clarke opened it.

"Good afternoon, Mrs Clarke. Thank you for seeing me."
"Come in. Would you like a cup of tea?"
"No, thank you."

Mrs Clarke was evidently in her sixties, well-dressed, with spectacles hanging on a cord round her neck. Her flat was nicely furnished and warm. She seemed happy and comfortable in her surroundings, with photos of what he guessed were her family on almost every flat surface.

"Please sit down."

She indicated towards the sofa, while settling in an armchair opposite.

"Thank you, Mrs Clarke. As I mentioned earlier, I've been handed the file concerning your neighbour's death. As you may know, it's still an open case, and I've been asked to take a fresh look at it. So, it means I'll have to ask you some questions, which, I know, you've been asked before, but it's just possible that you'll mention something which was omitted previously because it seemed irrelevant or trivial. Is that OK?"
"Yes, of course. But I don't think I can tell you anything I didn't tell the other police chap."
"Well, just talk me through everything you remember about that night. Anything you saw or heard. Anything at all."
"Well, as I told the other gentleman, I had spent the whole day inside – it was quite cold – but I stayed up until midnight. I always have done on New Year's Eve. Then I had a small sherry and went to bed."
"Did you hear or see Miss Braithwaite at any time of the evening?"
"No. I've no idea whether she stayed in or went out. I can't hear her door entry buzzer from here, not with the TV on, but sometimes visitors slam the door and I can certainly hear that."
"But not that night?"
"No."
"Did you see or hear anything suspicious outside at any time?"
"No. I don't open the curtains at night. You never know who might be out there."
"True. I noticed cameras covering the grounds, Mrs Clarke. Do they work?"

"I don't think so. I think they're just for show. But there's an address in the entrance hall for the security company which installed them. They might be able to help you."

"Thank you, Mrs Clarke. I won't take up any more of your time. Thank you for speaking to me. And if you remember anything which might be of use, please give me a call on this number."

He handed her his card, which she placed under the clock on the fire surround.

"I'll let myself out."

At the door, he made a note of the security company's details and arranged to see the manager as soon as he could get there. Punching in the postcode in his satnav, he followed the route to an industrial estate off the M606 and arrived within twenty minutes. The general manager, Billy Chapman, a stout man in his late forties, was waiting for him, and took him straight through to the office. There were piles of folders, and paper, everywhere.

"Thank you for seeing me, Mr Chapman. I won't take up more of your time than is necessary. I've just visited a flat in Eccleshill. Your company apparently provided the door security system, fire and smoke alarms for the entire block, and also installed the CCTV cameras on the outside of the building."

"Let me just check. I think I know the one you mean. I'll just pull up the details on the computer. Yes. Here we are. Is this the one?"

He turned the screen so Brian could see the photograph of the building. He nodded in confirmation.

"Yes. Door security, fire alarms and smoke detectors. We have a maintenance contract for them all."

"What about the CCTV?"

"They're dummies, I'm afraid. We installed them, but the management company weren't prepared to pay the maintenance cost and for the twenty-four-hour monitoring by our operatives. So, they were never used, unfortunately."

"Pity."

"Yes. I heard there was an incident over New Year. It's only when something like that happens that people realise the importance of security. Dummy cameras might deter criminals, but live ones help catch them."

"My sentiments exactly. Well, thank you for your time, Mr Chapman."

"No problem."

Brian Peters had seen some untidy desks and offices in his time in the police force, but Chapman's office was the worst he could remember. Back in his car, he pondered over his next move. He was unable to speak to Victoria, the dead girl's flatmate, until the following morning, but still had a couple of hours to kill before he could sign off for the day. He got out of the car and returned to Mr Chapman's office.

"Sorry to bother you again, sir. Do you by any chance have the address of the management company which looks after the Eccleshill flats?"

"Yes, I'll have it here somewhere. Just hang on a second. Ah, here it is."

"Thank you for your help, Mr Chapman."

"No problem."

Just hang on a second, he'd said. How on earth did he find what he needed so quickly under all those piles of documents? Peters shook his head in wonder and drove off towards Idle, where the management company, actually an Estate Agent, Bateman and Robinson, was located. He was able to park quite close, but unfortunately for him, there was only a receptionist, or Junior Salesperson, as she titled herself, in the office, and she was not authorised to give out the sort of information he requested without express permission.

"I'm sorry, sir, but both the partners are out on sales calls at the moment. We're very busy at the moment."

"If you're so busy, why don't you employ more staff?"

"That's not my decision, sir."

"Will they be long?"

"Mr Bateman should be back before five, sir. Mr Robinson will go straight home from his call."

"I'll wait. Do you mind if I look at some property details? My wife and I are looking to move to Bradford."

"Please do, sir. We have an extensive selection of properties, both in the city centre and more urban. Period dwellings and new-builds. Are you looking at any particular area?"

"No. A lot will depend on the local amenities, but I'd like to take some details back to my wife. Ultimately, she'll be the one who makes the decision, as long as it's fairly near to where I'm based."

"Well, just feel free to look through the displays. If you need any help, just give me a shout."

"Will do."

He spent almost an hour looking at, and discarding, details of several dozen 'desirable residences close to all amenities', before selecting a couple he quite liked the look of. Semi-detached, on the outskirts of Idle, but close enough to walk into the village for a pint, should he wish. He remembered his last visit to the Idle Draper, John Braden's local, and promised himself he'd become a regular there should they move into the area. He checked his watch. He'd waited long enough. He called the Junior Salesperson.

"Excuse me."

"Yes, sir."

"Do you have access to the partners' appointment diaries?"

"No, sir. Sorry."

"OK. Will you please let them know that DS Peters from Bradford CID has called and he will be back in the morning. He requires a list of all the residents of the apartment block in Eccleshill they manage. If he has to come back with a warrant, he will, but he is currently investigating a murder case and will not be very happy if he is made to wait unduly for the information he needs to do his job. Is that clear?"

"Yes, sir."

"Thank you. Goodbye."

Another jobsworth, he said to himself as he walked back to his car. Then, more charitably, he considered that she was only acting within the parameters of her responsibilities. Not her fault. It was just frustrating for him. He drove home. Another fruitless day over. He was looking forward to his new partner, Lynn, joining him. He didn't really know her well, but realised he worked more effectively when he had someone he could bounce ideas off. Ideally, someone with a sense of humour.

CHAPTER 5

He arrived for work early on Wednesday morning hoping to make some progress on his case, but Muesli soon extinguished all hope of that. Due to the flu epidemic currently sweeping the country, Bradford CID was experiencing a high level of absenteeism, and since Brian Peters was, as yet, without his own full case load, he was temporarily assigned to work as part of Hardcastle's team. He was not enamoured by the news but was unable to find a convincing excuse to refuse the assignment. Yet there was something about Hardcastle he disliked, something intangible, something he couldn't quite put his finger on. His old boss in CTU, Don McArthur, had always advised him, 'Unless you have hard evidence to the contrary, always go with your instincts. Trust your own judgment. You'll be right most of the time'. Sound advice. He would be wary of Hardcastle, but his professionalism forced him to do his best to hide his feelings and just do his job to the best of his ability.

Hardcastle, on hearing the news, was none too keen either.

"I hope you're up to it, Peters. Just because you were in the Glory Brigade doesn't mean you don't have to do the hard yards like the rest of us."
"I'm fully aware of what's expected of me. Whether I like it or not, we're working together for now."
"Well, let's hope it's not for long, eh?"
"It's for as long as Muesli says, so get used to it. So, what's today's job?"
"Petrol station in Cullingworth. Ram-raided late last night. See what we can find out. And I'll be lead on this one. I outrank you and I've been with the section a lot longer than you."
"No problem."

They drove in silence to the site of the incident. SOCO were already in attendance and the petrol station had been cordoned off and closed. Peters interviewed the manager. There were no eye-witnesses as such, due to the fact that the raid occurred in the early hours of the morning, but Peters was able to speak to local residents who were woken by the commotion and told him everything they had seen and heard. He thanked them and returned to confer with Hardcastle.

"Here's what we've got. Three local residents all gave very similar accounts. At approximately three-fifteen am, they were woken by a loud noise. Two people independently saw a dark-coloured, probably black, SUV driving away at speed in the direction of Bingley. Nobody saw the occupants, nor were able to tell how many persons were involved. One of the witnesses thinks the vehicle might have been a BMW, but he's not sure. What have you got?"

"CCTV more or less confirms the story. The camera display at 03.16.28 shows a black BMW X5 smashing through the front of the building. Two masked men get out, grab what they can and are gone within ninety seconds. It seems like a bit of a screw-up. The till was empty, as it is every night, so all they got was basically alcohol and cigs. I've got a copy of the images but I doubt whether they'll be any use in identifying the thieves unless we get suspects into custody. Might as well pack up and file our report."

While driving back to base, a call came through to inform them that the vehicle had been found. Hardcastle immediately performed a U-turn and headed towards Harden moor. Fifteen minutes later they pulled off the road into a makeshift car-parking area. In the corner was a collision-damaged BMW X5. They waited in the car until the Scene of Crime van arrived. They were not surprised to find that the scene offered little useable evidence, apart from the confirmation that the car was the one involved in the ram-raid, and that the criminals had switched to another vehicle, probably another SUV, judging by the tyre tracks left. Satisfied that the vehicle would be taken back for further forensic analysis, they drove back to base.

"If we're lucky, they'll get fingerprints, but my betting is that the car was stolen just prior to the robbery and any prints we get will belong to some businessman who was asleep in bed at the time of the crime. We'll just file it with all the others."

"All the others? You mean unsolved?"

"Yep. This is the fifth in the last four months. Same pattern. Little of any value taken. I'm thinking small-time criminals still waiting to make the step up to the big time."

"Any suspects at all?"

"None."

"OK, what's the next job?"

"We'll go back and write this up, and see if anything new has come in. What about you? Making any progress on the Eccleshill death?"

"The young woman in the flat?"

"Yeah."

"No progress. Still stuff to check."

"What sort of stuff?"

"Odds and ends. Just make sure I've done a thorough job to keep Muesli happy."

"Well, don't let it take up too much effort. It's at a dead end."

"You never know. Fresh pair of eyes and all that."

"Believe me. There's nothing more to find."

"If you say so."

They drove in silence, but Brian couldn't help wondering if Hardcastle was concealing something from him about the case. There had to be more to it. He was sure of it. Eventually, Hardcastle spoke.

"Look, Peters. I don't expect us to ever become friends. I don't care about that. I just do my job. OK?"

"What makes you think we'll never become friends? What have I done to upset you?"

"Well, nothing. It's just. I don't know. You just don't seem to trust us guys."

"I don't know how you've got that impression. As far as I'm concerned, you can't have an effective team without being able to trust every person in that team. So, why shouldn't I trust you?"

"No reason at all."

"OK. That's it, then. I trust you. OK?"

"OK."

Except he didn't. 'Trust your instincts', his old boss had said. That was good enough advice for him. The conversation went no further, though the mood between the two men never lightened. After lunch, they sat apart during the weekly briefing and reporting of local crime figures. Brian made notes. None of the other officers did, waiting instead to receive the written handouts at the end. Brian was particularly interested in the rise of low level crime in the area, which if not brought under control, could eventually escalate to a point where it became CID's business. As the meeting broke up, Brian was summoned to DCI Moseley's office.

"Come in, Brian. Take a seat."

"Thank you, sir."

"How are you settling in?"

"Fine, sir. No problems."

"Really? I've heard you don't see eye to eye with Hardcastle."

"I can work with him. But I don't think we'll ever be the best of friends."

"He's a good officer, Brian. Has got some good results in the past."

"Pleased to hear it, sir."

"Yet, I hear you don't like him."

"I don't know where you've heard that from, sir. As far as I'm concerned, it's the other way around. He seems to resent the fact that I'm one of the 'Glory Boys', as he puts it. Look, sir, I asked for a transfer to CID. It's where I want to work. I've proved I can work effectively in a team. If Hardcastle and I can't work together, then perhaps Hardcastle's the one with the problem."

"Very well, Brian. For the rest of this week, you'll work with young Gary Ryan. I'm sure you'll get along with him."

"I'm sure I will, sir. Thank you."

"And I'll remind you, Brian, you're still under probation here."

"Yes, sir."

That was a rap on the knuckles, he thought, walking back to his desk. He could feel eyes on him but ignored them. He could hear laughter from the far side of the room, where Hardcastle's desk was located. He could feel the colour rising in his cheeks but took a deep breath and opened his desk drawer, taking out the notes he'd made of the Eccleshill death. He remembered he needed a list of residents, and phoned the managing agent's office, hoping desperately he'd be able to speak to one of the partners rather than the office assistant. He was lucky. This time, Mr Bateman was available, had got his message and had the information to hand. Brian asked him to fax it to Mrs Shackleton, from whom he collected it ten minutes later. Again, she was very pleasant and polite with him, and he continued to wonder how she ever got the nickname 'Mrs Semtex'. He decided it would be prudent to wait until he got to know her a little better.

He spent the rest of the afternoon working his way through the list of names he'd acquired. Many were out, but a few were happy to speak to him over the phone. Others asked to speak to him in person, not because they had anything to hide, but simply because they were wary of giving out information over the phone to someone who simply purported to be a police officer. Brian understood. There were quite within their rights. You can't trust anyone these days, he told himself, and made appointments to visit and speak to them in person. These were tasks he'd booked for the following day. It would keep him nicely out of Hardcastle's sight. Before he left the office, he checked his mobile for messages. There was one from his wife.

"House for sale close to Idle. Looks great. Price OK. If you get chance, drive past on way home. See what you think."

He noted the address and locked his files away for the night as Gary Ryan approached his desk.

"Time for a quick drink tonight, Brian?"
"No, Gary. Sorry. I've just got a message to go look at a house."
"OK. See you tomorrow. I understand I'm with you for the rest of the week."
"That's right. You OK with that?"
"Of course. It'll make a nice change from the morons."
"OK. See you in the morning."

Driving towards Idle so he could take a quick look at the house Sarah had recommended, he realised he would soon be passing the retirement housing complex he'd visited earlier in the week. At the time, it had seemed like a clear case of accidental death, but on reflection, Brian wondered if he should take another look at it. It wouldn't do him any harm and it would keep him out of the office. He promised himself he'd go back with Gary before the week was out.

CHAPTER 6

Brian was reviewing the notes he'd made at the DCI's briefing the previous day when Gary approached his desk.

"Morning, Brian. What have we got lined up?"
"Morning, Gary. The Eccleshill death. We're seeing her flatmate. Victoria Armstrong. She's got a day off today, so let's get straight over there. I also want to speak to the dead girl's parents. And if we've got time, I'd like to have another look at the retirement housing complex in Idle. I've got a feeling about that. Something's not right."
"OK. Let's go."

They took Gary's car, a nondescript hatchback handy for house-calls, particularly on the estates where some of the residents could automatically sense a police car and make sure they stayed out of sight until it left the estate. They parked up and Gary pressed the button for the flat they required. He noted that the name of the dead girl, Amanda Braithwaite, had already been inked over, so the occupant was now listed only as 'Armstrong'. Following an audible 'click', a voice called,

"Hello?"
"Morning, Miss Armstrong. DS Peters and DC Ryan from Bradford CID. We have an appointment to talk to you this morning."
"Come in."

They heard the buzz as the door lock was released and walked along the corridor to number 25. Vicky Armstrong was at the open door, waiting for them. She showed them into the lounge.

"Would you like a cup of tea?"
"Please. That would be nice. Milk, no sugar for me, please."
"Milk and one sugar for me, please."

Although they didn't particularly want a drink, the fact that Vicky went into the kitchen left them free to take in their surroundings without raising any undue suspicion. Gary noticed a large untidy stack of CDs, but of more interest to Brian was the fact that one of the lounge windows had a crack across one corner. He nudged

Gary, indicating the window. Vicky returned with the teas on a tray. Brian spoke first, motioning towards the window.

"Been having a party, then?"

"That? No. Kids, I expect."

"Have you reported it, Miss Armstrong?"

"Not yet. I'll do it today."

"When did it happen?"

"Some time during the night. I noticed it this morning."

"How do you think it happened?"

"A stone, probably. Or an air-gun."

"Has this sort of thing happened before?"

"Not to me, no."

"Any idea who might have been responsible?"

"Kids from the estate, I guess. They can be a bit of a nuisance."

"In what way?"

"They tend to congregate in the alleyway round the back. Smoke, drink, probably do drugs. Basic anti-social behaviour."

"When you say 'drugs', do you mean Class A substances?"

"No. I don't think they do any of that stuff. It's just dope, and what they regard as the 'legal highs'. There's always a pile of those metallic canisters on the ground."

"Nitrous Oxide."

"Is that what it is?"

"Yes. Laughing gas. Have they ever threatened anyone in this building, to your knowledge?"

"No. They're all mouth. Just bravado."

"You've never confronted them?"

"Never. If you ignore them, they get bored and go away. That seems to be the best way to deal with them. Don't provoke them."

"Would you be able to recognise any of them?"

"I doubt it. They all wear hoodies. All the time."

"Have any of them, to your knowledge, ever managed to get into the building?"

"Not to my knowledge, no. I don't think they're that interested. I mean, if the door was open, they'd probably come in and see if they could nick anything. But I don't think they've got the balls to break in. They're only kids. Twelve, maybe fourteen at the most."

"Don't underestimate them, Miss Armstrong. These kids are a different breed to when you were that age. Anyway, to return to the unfortunate death of your flatmate, would you mind going over with us what you remember about New Year's Day?"

"I already made a statement to the other policeman. I can't remember his name."

"I realise that, Miss Armstrong, but sometimes people remember things at a later date. Something they might have thought trivial at the time."

"I understand. I'll go through everything I remember."

She made a lengthy statement while both men took copious notes, never once interrupting her for clarification. Finally, they thanked her and left. Once outside, they discussed their findings.

"Well, that was pretty clear. No deliberation, no repetition. In fact, it's almost word for word identical to her initial statement. She's either got a perfect memory, or she's rehearsed it very well."

"In which case, she's lying."

"Exactly."

"Let's split up and go door-knocking."

"OK. I'll start at the top and work down."

An hour later, they were back in Gary's car comparing their findings. By now, all but four occupants had been interviewed. Nothing significant had emerged until Gary revealed that security at the flats was not as strong as they'd been led to believe.

"During my conversation with Mrs…, just a second while I find it, ah, here it is… Mrs Davies, she mentioned that her neighbour in number 43 has a bad habit of releasing the door when anyone presses her number. The old lady at 43, Mrs Thompson, never mentioned it when I spoke to her, but that's not surprising, as Mrs Davies told me that she, Mrs Thompson, that is, suffers from early-stage dementia and doesn't even remember doing it. It's just become automatic for her."

"Interesting. So, there could have been a security breach. Wait there. It's not that I don't believe you, I just want to check it for myself."

Brian walked back to the entrance of the flats, pressed number 43 and waited. Seconds later, there was a buzz and the door swung open. No conversation. No check on the caller's identity. Just release the lock. He wondered if her behaviour was common knowledge. He walked briskly back to the car and got in.

"Let's take a break from this, Gary. I want to go through Muesli's briefing notes. Let's grab a sandwich."

They sat in a small café on Eccleshill's High Street, drinking from mugs of hot tea while munching on bacon sandwiches, poring over the crime briefing notes issued by Muesli and supplemented by Brian's own scribbled and cryptic notes.

"There's nothing we can work with here, Gary. I think there's still something out there somewhere. We just haven't found it yet."

They sat there for over an hour, tossing ideas back and forth. But none of it made any sense. There were still no discernible patterns to be found, apart from the fact there were two deaths, and some rampaging teenagers bent on causing a nuisance. At the moment, all they could do was react as the crimes were reported. Gary took a call on his mobile.

"Sorry, Brian. I've been re-assigned again. I have to get straight back to the office. Duty calls."

****

Brian worked alone during the afternoon, ploughing through as much as he could manage until he noticed the office was empty apart from him. He locked his notes away and left, faced with the prospect of continuing the task alone the next day.

He was at his desk late on Thursday afternoon when a call came through from Mrs Shackleton.

"Brian, I know how busy you are, but the DCI has taken a call from an irate Police Commissioner, who in turn was contacted by a member of the public outraged at the level of car theft from our patch. He's asked you to investigate."
"OK, give me the details."
"A Terry Stanton had his car stolen and wrecked a couple of weeks ago. The recovery driver told him he'd had to recover six or seven cars in the last six months, all stolen locally and all driven to the same spot where they were driven to destruction."
"Give me his number and I'll talk to him. Thanks, Teresa."

At least there's a pattern to all this, he thought as he dialled the number. He arranged to see Mr Stanton that evening after hearing how annoyed he was that nobody had caught the culprits after several crimes over a period of six months. Brian agreed that his complaint was a valid one and promised to give the case his full attention, although, of course, he already had other cases equally demanding of his full attention.

Once he'd spoken with Mr Stanton, he decided it required further investigation. First thing the following morning, he would ask Mrs Shackleton to get the reports from all the incidents. As soon as they were on his desk, he'd be able to get to work on them, and with Lynn joining them on Monday, he hoped they'd make quick progress. In the meantime, however, he had an interview with the dead girl's parents pencilled in for Friday morning.

****

He arrived at their detached house in Hawksworth at ten and was ushered in to the kitchen. Mr and Mrs Braithwaite were both in their early fifties, and neither had yet returned to work since the death of their daughter. They were clearly still very distraught, but kept their composure throughout, answering all Brian's questions civilly and calmly. Just before he wound up the interview, without having uncovered any new facts, Mrs Braithwaite casually made a comment that made his heart skip a beat. She'd said,

"At least we spoke to her. At least we've still got the memory of her voice wishing us a Happy New Year."
"She phoned you?"
"Yes. Just after midnight. She did every year, without fail."
"Well, thanks very much for your time. I know this must have been very distressing for you, but I'd like to reassure you we are still working the case. By the way, have all your daughter's belongings been returned to you?"
"Yes, I think so."
"Including her phone?"
"Yes. We've kept it because there are a lot of photos of Amanda on it. You know, selfies. Funny stuff."
"Would it be possible for me to borrow it for a few days?"
"I suppose so, as long as we get it back intact. But I don't know why you want it. The police examined it before they passed it to us."
"I've just been assigned this case. I like to double-check

everything."
"I'll just get it for you."

Before she handed over the phone, she made a point of expressing her view of her daughter's death.

"I'd like to make it quite clear that my daughter would never willingly take drugs of any description unless her doctor prescribed them. She just wouldn't do it. I *know* my daughter."

Once in his car, he couldn't wait to get back to the station. Then, he changed his mind and headed for Bradford University instead. He didn't want anybody else to know anything about what he'd just learnt. It was a breakthrough. He was absolutely certain. He'd read through the initial report thoroughly time after time and he was adamant it clearly stated that Amanda's phone was checked and that the last call was made late in the evening of December 31st.

Brian Peters parked in the staff car park at the university, as he always did, courtesy of his police pass, and headed straight up to the Lab, where Dr Martin Riley was waiting for him. An out-and-out 'geek', Riley was the go-to man for all the various technological issues or queries that his previous department, CTU, encountered.

"What is it today, then, Brian?"
"A mobile phone, Martin. I believe some data may have been wiped and I'd like you to see if it's retrievable. I'm particularly interested in any calls made or received on New Year's Eve and early on New Year's Day."
"No problem. Go get some breakfast and I'll call you when I've had a look at it."

As usual, Brian went down to the canteen, leaving Riley to examine the phone. It was not long before he got the call.

"Come on up, Brian. I've got some news for you."

He quickly finished his bacon sandwich, wiping the grease from his fingers with a napkin as he headed upstairs.

"What have you got, Martin?"
"Loads, Brian. Androids are easy. A bog-standard recovery program will retrieve most stuff. Mine goes a little deeper. Come

over here and have a look."

Brian walked around the desk and peered at the large screen of Martin's PC, where the display showed a directory of recovered files, organised by data type.

"These are the ones you'll be most interested in; Call History and Message Log, but there may be some useful stuff elsewhere. I'll copy the lot to a USB stick for you."
"Let me see the calls first, please."
"There. Only one recent. Time and date stamped. Tells you the duration of the call, and more importantly, the number dialled."

Brian took out his phone and checked his contacts list. The number Amanda had called was also logged in his phone. Amanda's parents.

"That's what I was looking for. Thanks, Martin."
"No problem. Just give me a couple of minutes and I'll copy the lot. There are loads of photos. There may be something useful there."

Brian was feeling quite pleased with himself as he drove back to HQ. At least now he had some progress to report to Muesli at his scheduled afternoon meeting. On a whim, he changed course and headed towards Bierley, to the Public Mortuary, calling ahead to make an appointment to speak to the head of the forensic science team, Dr Black.

Dr Martin Black was a white-haired, bespectacled man in his early sixties, with many years of experience in the field of forensic pathology. He was also the author of a number of books on the subject. Indeed, he was probably the most highly-respected authority on the subject in the north of England. In the course of his work, he had met Brian a number of times, and welcomed him into his office.

"Good to see you again, Brian. Now, what can I do for you?"
"Good to see you, too, Martin. I'm here about Amanda Braithwaite. Died on New Year's Day in the early hours. Cocaine overdose?"
"Ah, yes. I remember. I thought at the time that she didn't seem the type to be involved in that sort of thing, but one never knows these days."
"Can you take me through your findings, please? I've seen the

official police SOCO report, and the investigating officer's notes, and also read the coroner's findings. But I'd like to hear it directly from you if that's OK."

"Certainly. Let me get the file."

"Just one more thing, Martin."

"Yes?"

"Are all academics and technical, scientific types called Martin? A guy called Martin Riley at Bradford University provides technical services to us."

"Martin Riley? I know Martin. His team knocked us out of the Bradford Quiz League semi-final a couple of weeks ago. A clever man, like most people called Martin."

Twenty minutes later, Brian Peters was driving back to HQ. He now certainly believed foul play had occurred. During the post mortem examination, traces of powder had been removed from Miss Braithwaite's nasal cavity. Upon analysis, the powder was identified as cocaine cut with Benzocaine. The tested purity of the mixture was less than twenty percent. Dr Black's opinion was that Miss Braithwaite had suffered cardiac arrest after snorting cocaine which had been cut with Benzocaine. Even in those proportions, added to the fact that she had previously drunk alcohol, to the extent that she would have failed a breathalyser test, ingestion of the drug was sufficient to cause a cardiac arrest.

"The thing is, Brian, there is no definition of what should be considered a lethal dose. It depends totally on the individual. What will be a small dose for one person will be lethal for another. It's quite likely she was a first-time user, and so had no tolerance to the substance. This is borne out by examination of her hair, which retains a trace amount over months. When I examined her hair, it showed no trace of previous drug use. Nor did her nasal cavity show any sign of damage, which again can indicate long-term use. I think she was experimenting. Or else, she took it under duress. And the real puzzle, in the SOC report, is that there was no evidence of cocaine residue on any surface, which you would expect if she'd died alone. It's as if someone cleaned it all up."

Dr Black's words gave him cause to investigate further. He was convinced a crime had occurred and evidence had been covered up or destroyed. He still had time to write up his report, have some lunch, and prepare himself for the meeting. Perhaps Muesli would agree that he had reason to be satisfied with his first week's work.

He presented himself at the door to DCI Moseley's office promptly at three o'clock and went in when invited.

"Good afternoon, sir."

"Afternoon, Brian. Please sit down."

"Thank you, sir."

"So, how has your first week gone?"

"Quite well, sir. Some progress has been made on the cases I've been handed."

"Would you like to elaborate? The Eccleshill death?"

"Something interesting there, sir. I only uncovered it today, but it's a promising lead. Her phone, which was supposedly checked at the time, had had some files deleted, sir. It could be that the victim herself deleted them just to clear some space. But I think it's more likely that someone else tried to wipe anything which might be incriminating."

"And how did you discover this?"

"The victim's mother, sir. I went to see her parents, and her mother let slip in conversation that she'd received a call from her daughter after midnight, shortly before she died. The police report stated there were no recent calls or messages either to or from her phone, sir. So, I took it to a contact I have at Bradford University, and he retrieved a great deal of deleted data for me. I haven't yet had time to look through it all, sir."

"This 'contact' has, I presume, been authorised to carry out this sort of forensic work on our behalf?"

"He does all the forensic work for CTU, sir. He's the best there is."

"I have to remind you, Brian, that all forensic requests should be channelled to our own resources."

"With respect, sir, our labs always have a backlog of work. Dr Riley performs the work immediately. He's cleared by CTU and Scotland Yard to work on highly classified cases."

"In future, Brian, come to me before taking anything to your chap. Must follow protocol."

"Yes, sir. Sorry, sir. I didn't want to waste any time, sir. The other thing, sir, is that security at the flats is not as good as it should be. One of the residents has a tendency to let in anyone who calls her flat number without checking who they are. And it seems that a lot of youths tend to congregate in the alley at the back. Oh, and the CCTV cameras are just blanks."

"Hmmm. What about your other cases?"

"Nothing yet on the retirement housing death, sir. SOCO thinks it's accidental. I'm not so sure. I'll be able to look deeper into it when

Lynn joins us on Monday."

"Anything else?"

"I'm also looking into a spate of cases of vehicle theft, sir. Joyriding. No progress as yet."

"Ah. The issue the Crime Commissioner alerted me about. This one needs to be resolved, Brian."

"Yes, sir. I've already spoken to the most recent victim, and I'm waiting for reports on all the previous incidents to be forwarded to me."

"OK. DC Ryan will be back working with you on Monday for a few more days, until Lynn Whitehead is up to speed. Then I want to see some real progress on these outstanding cases."

"Yes, sir."

Brian left the meeting without disclosing the evidence he'd just received from Dr Black. He wanted to probe a little further first.

CHAPTER 7

It had taken almost two weeks for the cheque to arrive from the insurance company, and in that time, Ronnie had kept up the pressure on Terry Stanton, constantly criticising his work, and his timekeeping. There was some justification, for on the first Saturday his taxi was late, half an hour late, with the result that, even though he'd allowed himself plenty of time, he still clocked in at five minutes past six, with the result that he was docked fifteen minutes pay. Apart from that, his timekeeping was excellent; even on the third week when he was on the early shift he was often at work by twenty to six, having found a more reliable taxi company. The trouble was the late shift. Because of the bus services, it took almost an hour and a half to get to work. And since there was no fixed finishing time on the late shift - he had to stay until the final orders were packed - he was at the mercy of the limited bus schedule, one an hour, from the village close to the factory. He found it impossible to get a lift during the first week and on that Tuesday evening arrived at the bus stop just in time to see the rear of the bus disappear into the distance. It had been a hard day. Ronnie had been constantly on his back. And he felt so annoyed at the prospect of standing at the bus stop exposed to a cold, whipping wind that he decided to walk home. And after an hour, the rain came lashing down, but still he plodded on. There was no point in doing anything else. He was over half-way home. He was thoroughly soaked from the knees down, and though his waterproof coat afforded his upper body some protection, it was so waterproof that the rain filled his pockets. His lighter wouldn't work, and his cigarettes were soggy. Cold, wet, uncomfortable and tired. And he couldn't even have a smoke!

When he finally arrived home an hour and three quarters after clocking off, he just stripped off silently and ran a hot bath. He stretched out in it, closing his eyes as the hot water eased the tiredness from his legs and aching feet. And even after his legs had warmed through and his circulation returned, he noted the blue colour of his knees. Dye leaching from his jeans. He scrubbed hard, but the colour remained. He lay back, trying to blot out his anger and frustration. And Linda brought him a mug of hot tea and washed his back, massaging his shoulders, relieving his tension. She tried to talk him into taking out a loan, to buy a car, but he would have none of it. He hated debt. He'd been brought up with what he called 'old-fashioned values', the credo that said 'if you can't afford it, you do without'. And the way things were at work at the moment, there was no guarantee he'd keep the job long enough to repay a loan. He'd either get the sack, or walk out in anger, after telling Ronnie where to stick it.

But things did improve slightly. Soon, the gangmaster of one of the contract crews started to give him a lift most of the way home whenever they finished at the same time. Terry appreciated the gesture. He knew the gangmaster was breaking the rules by carrying a passenger in his minibus who wasn't a member of his crew. On top of that, the gangmaster had to face criticism from other workers for showing sympathy for a QC who was responsible for limiting their bonus by rejecting sub-standard produce. But the gangmaster was a fair-minded man, who reasoned that Terry was only doing his job, like the rest of them. And Terry, by way of appreciation, would quietly slip him a couple of packets of cigarettes at the end of the week.

The trouble really started when the cheque arrived.

Terry and Linda were up early on the Saturday morning. The cheque had been banked early in the week, and Terry inserted his card into the cashpoint to get a statement to ensure it had been cleared. It had. But as usual, there was no money in the cashpoint machine. It seemed to be permanently out of service, or out of order, and the most that customers in the shopping centre had come to expect was the facility to check their bank balance. Never mind. They were going into town anyway. He could withdraw cash from one of the main branches for his deposit.

On their limited budget, they weren't exactly spoiled for choice. Though there was no shortage of used car dealers, there was nothing by way of a bargain. All overpriced, clapped-out old bangers. And Terry was looking for something specific. Not a specific make or model. But something with an obvious and highly visible deterrent - an alarm. One with a light which blinked its warning that it was armed. That, coupled with a new and expensive Krooklok, the type which fitted over the steering wheel, would, Terry reckoned, be enough to deter all but the most determined thief. But at the end of the day, they'd drawn a blank. They'd visited over a dozen used car lots - showrooms were beyond their budget - and covered several miles on foot.

The argument which erupted that night had been brewing all day. They'd both had a bad day, an unproductive day, a wasted day. And when Terry poured himself a whisky as soon as he'd finished his meal, Linda snapped.

"Oh, that's great, Terry! You just sit there and relax. Leave me to clear away and wash up."
"I've had a hard day, Linda."
"I know! I know you've had a hard day. I was with you! Remember? Walking alongside you all those miles. That wasn't your shadow. That was me! My feet are sore! I'm tired too. But there's still washing up to do."
"You didn't have to come."
"I was trying to give you some moral support. You know? Be there with you. Like partners should be. Doing things together. Helping each other. And it's our money. Our car we're buying."
"Is it? Is it really? And whose money bought the Focus? Whose job was it that paid for that?"

He almost spat out the words. And instantly regretted it as tears began to well in Linda's eyes. She turned away in silence and walked into the kitchen from where he could hear her muffled sobs as she filled the sink. He put his hands over his eyes and rubbed his temples. What the hell was he playing at? They hadn't argued for years. He didn't know why he'd said it. It was stupid. Yes, it was true that he'd earned a lot more than Linda. But that was years ago. And she'd always pulled her weight. And when times were hard, it was she who kept things ticking over. She, who did the overtime, and freelance work on top. He put the glass down and walked slowly into the kitchen. Linda was staring blankly out of the window, holding a tissue tightly in her hand. She heard him approach but kept her back to him.

"Linda. I'm so sorry, love. I... I'm so sorry."
"I was only trying to help. I don't need reminding how you used to have a good job. And how you paid for everything. How it was your money, out of your bank account, which paid the deposit on our first house. Your wages which paid the mortgage. And bought all the furniture. Your money that paid for the fucking car!"
"Linda. I didn't mean it. I'm sorry."
"Don't you think I've put anything into this marriage? Have I just sponged off you all these years? Lazed about at home all day while you were out earning your fantastic wage? No, of course not.

I didn't stay at home, did I? I had a little job, didn't I? In an office. Didn't pay very well. More of a hobby, really. Not a real job, like you had. But I worked! And every penny I earned, I earned for us. Not for me! For us! So, thank you for your kind appreciation of my efforts."

"Please, Linda. I'm sorry. So sorry. Come on, please. I need you. Please give me a hug. I... I haven't been thinking straight. Everything's getting to me. Winding me up. I need you. Please, Linda. I love you. I need you. Please forgive me. I'm sorry. I'm really sorry."

She turned to face him, her head lowered. But he could see how he'd hurt her. Her eyes were red, and puffy, her mascara smeared. Her cheeks were still wet. He put his hand tenderly under her chin and raised her face to his. He kissed the salt tears from her cheeks and she clung to him, sobbing softly against his chest as he caressed her hair and held her close until the sobbing subsided. He took her by the hand and led her into the lounge. He made her sit down and put the glass of whisky in her hand.

"You need this more than I do, Linda. You relax for a while. I'll wash up."
"No, Terry. This is a partnership. We do things together. We share. You wash, I'll dry."
"It's a deal."

He took the olive branch gratefully. He knew what he'd said could never be unsaid. He cursed his stupidity, his thoughtlessness. Linda meant everything to him. He didn't want to hurt her. Didn't mean to. But things were starting to go wrong for him again. Things beyond his control. But this time it was nothing to do with market forces. Or the strength of the pound. Or his employers 'rationalising' their management structure. He was losing his grip on his job, and possibly on his close relationship with his wife because someone had stolen his car. Wrecked it. And pissed in it. He was determined to get even.

The crisis over, they finished the washing up and settled together on the settee, arms round each other. Physically closer than they usually were, but emotionally a rift had opened between them. A deep chasm, spanned by a rickety bridge built from and underpinned by their love for each other. And they were equally aware that unless they both worked together, continually, to keep the bridge intact, one day, sooner or later, it would start to crumble. And eventually collapse into the chasm, taking one or both of them with it.

****

The following day, they covered a different area of town. They walked hand in hand, uneasily silent for most of the time except when they arrived at a car lot. Then Terry would immediately ask Linda if there was anything she fancied. He was trying hard to involve her in the decision-making process, seeking her opinion, and if he disagreed, he tried to explain why without sounding patronising. The mileage on this one doesn't seem genuine considering its age and condition. That one would cost too much to insure. Wings are rotten on this one. And so, it went on, until they finally agreed they'd had enough. Linda wanted to go back to the first place, where they'd seen a battered old Fiesta, at a reasonable price. Terry wanted to check out just one more place, and if there was nothing there, they'd go for the Fiesta.

Linda saw it first. A 2009 Astra, dark blue, parked in a corner. They squeezed their way between the cars crammed into the small compound to make a closer inspection, as the owner eagerly tried to join them but found it difficult to compress his huge beer-belly through the narrow gaps. In the end, he gave it up, and went back into his cabin, emerging seconds later with several bunches of keys. He tossed one set to Terry and proceeded to shunt cars around so that the Astra could be driven out. Terry had already unlocked it, opened the bonnet, and started the engine, which caught at the third attempt. It sounded sweet enough, though running fast. The owner came over to add his sales pitch.

"Been stood a while. Needs a good service, but we do that anyway when we sell a car. Full service."
"How much MOT?"
"It's expired. But we'll put it through its test before we sell it. No point in testing it while it's just stood here in the yard. You might as well have it with a full twelve-month ticket. Nice car, this. Been well looked after. Good nick for its age."
"It's overpriced."
"So, make me an offer."
"How about a test drive?"
"No problem. Take it out of the compound while I lock up and get

some trade plates. I'll just be a minute."

The Astra handled quite well, and fifteen minutes later they were back at the compound where the owner showed Terry how the alarm worked. Terry was impressed. This was what he was looking for; an alarm which could only be switched off by use of the key. Otherwise the car was immobilised, and the lights flashed and the horn sounded, a feature the owner was only too pleased to demonstrate. Terry checked out the bodywork. The sills. The inner wings. The tray which contained the battery. He opened the boot and lifted the carpet. He took out the spare wheel and checked it and checked the well beneath. He pronounced himself satisfied, while trying not to sound overly enthusiastic. After all, there was still some bargaining to do over the price. He pointed out every spot of rust he could find but had to admit that all were superficial. The car was solid. He looked at Linda, who nodded her agreement.

"I'll give you eleven hundred, if you pay for six months tax on it."
"Sorry, sir. Think about it. It's a sound motor. Good condition. Runs well. You're getting a full service and a full MOT. Give me twelve, plus the road tax, and it's yours. And I'll throw in three months warranty. What do you think?"
"I'll give you twelve. You pay for the road tax."
"OK. Let's go into the office and sort out the paperwork."

They left a cash deposit of two hundred pounds and agreed to pay the balance in cash as soon as the car had been taxed and tested. They walked happily back to the town centre to catch a bus home, chatting animatedly, holding hands and discussing how to organise the collection of their new car. Linda clung to Terry's arm all the way home, seeming genuinely happy, as if the events of the previous night were forgotten. Terry was glad. It looked as if everything was going to be OK. They laughed at how the fat man had got wedged between the bumpers of two cars, how he'd prised himself into the back seat when they went for a drive. And Terry brought a smile to Linda's face by saying the car would fail its MOT because the rear suspension had just collapsed under his weight.

"His phone is more mobile than he is."

****

Brian Peters and his wife and child had spent a busy Saturday checking out a number of properties in and around Bradford. So far, a few had been marked as 'suitable', but only one had stood out as 'ideal', and even then, it was rather more expensive than they would have wished. They decided they would express an interest with the Estate Agent and wait until they received an acceptable offer for the house they currently occupied.

Back at work on Monday morning, he was pleased to see Lynn had already been signed in and was currently in the office with Muesli, receiving her pep talk. Teresa had bundled together the reports he'd requested concerning the car thefts; they were piled high in the middle of his desk. As soon as Gary Ryan arrived, the pile of reports was divided more of less equally between them. They worked silently, making copious notes until lunch. Brian noticed at one point that Lynn Whitehead was being introduced to the rest of the officers in the office.

She's a sensible woman, he thought. Wearing trousers at work was a sensible move with lechers like Hardcastle about. He could clearly see him craning his neck, watching her as she walked away. He knew exactly what Hardcastle was thinking. Then again, he was sure Lynn knew too. She'd been in this kind of male-dominated environment for long enough to be able to deal with it.

Lynn was able to join them in the canteen for lunch. Brian rose as she approached the table.

"Good to see you again, Lynn. This is Gary. DC Gary Ryan. He's been working with me. It seems he's one of the few good guys round here."
"I'm glad I'm able to sit with you two. Some of the others have made me feel distinctly uncomfortable this morning."
"You'll be fine with us, Lynn. My boyfriend would kill me if I so much as looked at a woman."

Lynn didn't bat an eyelid.

"In that case, your boyfriend is a sensible man. Have you been together long?"
"Six months or so."
"Well, don't let these buggers get to you. If they do, I'll sort them out."

"Thanks. At least now there are two people on my side."

"So, Lynn. We've got a number of cases ongoing. I'd like you to work with Gary on sifting through all the files we've been sent regarding car thefts. I believe a great number of them have been committed by the same person or, more likely, persons. Sort through them and put aside all those which don't fit the pattern. That is, those stolen from other areas of Bradford, or those disposed of in other areas around Bradford. The common traits we're looking for are, cars stolen from this area, wrecked and dumped in the fields up by the airport, and those which have been pissed in."

Lynn raised an eyebrow.

"Pissed in?"

"It seems to be their signature."

"Left-handed or right-handed?"

"If their cocks are relative to their brains in size, I guess they hold them with tweezers So, come on. I want to check these deleted phone messages."

Lynn and Gary worked quietly throughout the afternoon, talking only occasionally to question some point or other in the various reports. Brian was checking each phone number he found, compiling a list of everyone who had called Amanda and everyone she had called in the week before her death. He noted the duration and frequency of each call and wrote brief details on a whiteboard, trying to find connections between the contacts, finding out whatever he could about everyone whose phone number was on his list. After a few hours, by way of a change, he checked the images.

Before he finished work for the day, he copied the information he'd written on the whiteboard on to A4 sheets of paper. Then he wiped the whiteboard clean.

CHAPTER 8

A couple of days later, Terry returned to the car lot. In his inside pocket, he had a wad of cash, a thousand pounds altogether, in twenty-pound notes. The dealer had insisted on cash, but Terry wasn't concerned as long as he got his car, a receipt for the money, and the log book, MOT certificate, and tax. He gazed proudly at the Astra, which had been washed and moved to the front of the lot.

The transaction completed, he drove to the nearest petrol station and filled the tank to the brim. Almost forty quid. He reset the trip-meter and took it for a drive round the dual-carriageway which skirted the city, testing the acceleration, the brakes, and the general handling. He pulled in outside a discount motor accessories supermarket, where he bought an expensive Krooklok which practically enveloped the entire steering wheel, and which the salesman assured him was the best on the market. He was pleased and couldn't wait to get home so he and Linda could go for a drive together. Shopping, perhaps. Or maybe take it down the motorway. Down to Sheffield, maybe. They'd often talked about going there. And now they could. Things are going to improve now, he thought.

They covered over a hundred miles that weekend, driving around, visiting the small market towns in the north Yorkshire area. Sightseeing, like holidaymakers. It was a luxury they'd never allowed themselves when they'd first moved into the area; apart from their holiday, they'd spent most of their weekends, and their money, decorating the flat. And though the weather was cold and damp the whole weekend, they walked arm in arm like young lovers through the streets, window-shopping the way tourists do. They were happy together, recent events forgotten as they rediscovered their love.

Life for Terry quickly returned to its previous routine. Ronnie still gave him a hard time, but he ignored her threats and jibes and knuckled down to his job with a diligence he hadn't displayed before. He lightened up in his approach, too, and as a result, his working relationship with production staff improved. He was a little surprised, and highly delighted, when, at the end of the month, his pay packet showed his hourly rate had increased by fifty pence. It wasn't the extra money so much as the fact that he'd been put on the full rate, the qualified rate, for the job. His probationary period was over. They were satisfied with him, and he felt a little more secure about his future with the company. He'd take Linda out for a meal to celebrate that evening.

****

At six-thirty, when Terry was clocking off, a car transporter was loading up across the city at the car lot where he'd bought the Astra. The fat man had sold his last car there - a black Corsa to a young lad who'd recently passed his test - and he was well pleased. The young lad had no idea about car prices. He'd paid well over the odds for the Corsa because he liked the look of it and the throaty sound of the engine. It was no more than a basic model, but the lad had been seduced by the sporty body kit and spoiler fitted by the previous owner before he was banned from driving. And the fat man had picked it up cheaply at auction and made a tidy profit. Now the lease on the car lot had expired and it was time to move on. He'd already negotiated a new short-term lease in Doncaster and was moving his remaining stock there. On Monday morning, he'd be back in business under a new trading name. He felt no sympathy for the punters who'd recently bought cars from him. His three-month warranties were worthless because if the punters came back to complain, all they'd find would be a vacant plot. But that was business. 'Fuck 'em!' That was his motto.

****

Daz and Andy were restless. Things had been quiet recently. The nights had turned cold, and their mother, the lazy cow, hadn't made much money in the past few weeks. She said she'd been poorly, and in truth she hadn't looked well, but Daz put it down to the fact that her consumption of Special Brew had increased. She was turning men away some nights now, and even her regulars were of the opinion that the quality of 'service' had deteriorated. Nobody, least of all their mother Sheila, yet knew about the tumours eating their way through her body.

Daz and Andy had committed the odd opportunist theft. Handbag-snatching from old ladies was easy. So was conning their way into the houses of pensioners living alone and stealing their meagre savings. But Andy had stumbled across a more lucrative line of business. Drugs! The previous week the two of them had been in the Thorn, a public house frequented by petty thieves, shoplifters, drunks and drug users. They were playing pool, hustling for beer money, when Andy had spotted Dean, a lad who had been in his brother's class at school. They were never friends, but Andy had a little respect for Dean due to the way he constantly disrupted classes before he was expelled for physical violence towards the teaching staff. Andy remembered his brother telling him about the incident, that final day the police and an ambulance were called to the school. Dean had 'lost it' and attacked the English teacher with a chair, breaking his arm as he desperately tried to ward off the repeated blows. The whole class eventually got in on the act, turning over desks, smashing windows and setting fire to a waste paper bin. Daz had contented himself with kicking the unconscious teacher repeatedly about the head until his face was a bloody mask. Dean was expelled, and the teacher had never returned, but the rest of the class got off with a warning. And now, inevitably, Dean was back on his old patch, having served a short time in a young offenders' unit. It was there he'd begun using drugs. Cannabis and amphetamines at first, then anything he could lay his hands on until he finally graduated to heroin and cocaine. He was now an addict, financing his habit through theft and by dealing in cannabis and ecstasy, heroin and cocaine.

Dean joined Daz and Andy at the pool table as Andy once again sank the black to collect the last fiver from his opponent, who finished his pint and left immediately having lost most of his jobseeker's allowance during the brief lunchtime session.

"How you doin', Andy?"
"OK, Dean. You?"
"OK. Need any stuff?"
"What sort of stuff?"
"You name it, man. I got it, or I can get it. You want E? I got plenty on me."
"How much?"
"A ton, for thirty tabs."
"Too much. I'll give you fifty."
"Fuck off, Andy. You can sell these for a tenner each."
"So, why don't you?"
"Need the money now, man. I'm hurtin' bad. I can't wait till the clubs open tonight."
"Tough."

"Come on, man. Well, how about lending me a ton till tomorrow. I'll give you it back and twenty on top. How about it?"

"No chance!"

"OK, OK. Look, give me fifty quid for fifteen tabs and I'll throw in some smokes. It's good stuff. Honest."

"Twenty tabs."

"Done."

"Plus the smoke."

"OK. Toilets."

Andy made a tidy profit that night, selling ecstasy tablets in the city centre clubs. Easy money. The easiest money he'd ever made. He started by approaching people he knew, but soon strangers were approaching him as word got around and he could have sold twice as many. But he knew if Dean could afford to sell them to him cheaply then Dean must be buying them even more cheaply. He resolved to find out who Dean's supplier was and get them directly from him. There was a ready market out there and he was going to exploit it. This was his patch and he'd easily persuade Dean to go elsewhere. Backed by his brother and a variety of weapons - knives, baseball bats, crowbars; he'd used them all - he had a very persuasive manner about him. And as he grew older he was getting what he wanted, what he craved. Respect. That's what it was all about. Respect on the street. Nobody would mess with him and Daz. They feared nothing and nobody. And soon, with money in his pocket, he'd be number one round here. Make no mistake.

****

Terry clocked off at the end of his shift. The shifts were getting longer now as business picked up. It was six forty-five. He hung his hat and white coat in his locker and pulled on his outdoor coat. He took his watch from the inside pocket and strapped it on. Saying goodnight to the production line workers hurrying to collect their belongings, he walked briskly through the door to the rain-lashed car park.

The car park was inadequate for the number of workers at the site and Terry was dismayed but hardly surprised to find he was blocked in by a minibus. He recognised it. It belonged to one of the gangs of casual workers who had just started the evening shift. He turned and walked back into the building to put a call out for the driver before returning to sit in the car and wait. He lit up a cigarette and then cursed as he saw Ronnie driving slowly past, staring straight at him. The entire site was a no-smoking zone, and though most of the staff disregarded the rules, it was still a disciplinary offence to smoke within the compound. Ronnie had seen him smoking and, Terry was sure, she would have taken note. Another act of misconduct to add to her ever-lengthening list.

Ten minutes later, the minibus driver came loping across the car park, dodging the puddles. He gave Terry a cheery wave as he moved into a vacant space, shunting back and forward in a gear-crunching manoeuvre. Terry pulled out of the car park and drove slowly up the road to the main gates where the security guard raised the barrier to let him out on to the main road. As he waited at the exit for a gap in the traffic, the engine cut out. He started it again immediately, giving it plenty of gas, but the engine was running a little unevenly, misfiring. He put it down to the weather. It had been damp all day. It would be fine as soon as the engine warmed up.

The drive home took longer than normal. Traffic was heavy and slow-moving. The weather didn't help. Neither did the fact that traffic was being diverted due to an accident. A convoy of cars heading towards the football stadium swelled the evening commuter traffic coming from the west, and Terry was relieved when he finally reached the slip road for his turning. As he pulled into his parking space a few minutes later, the engine cut out again. He started it up and revved the engine briefly before allowing it to tick over. Satisfied it was running smoothly, he switched off, engaged the heavy Krooklok in position, set the alarm, locked the driver's door, and walked towards the back door of his apartment block. He stopped, turned and walked back to the car, checking all the doors were locked, peering through the window to see the reassuring blink of the alarm light before finally leaving it for the night. He decided not to mention to Linda that the car was misbehaving. No point in worrying her unless it became worse. And if it did, he'd book it in for a service with Salim. It had been a hard day, and he was looking forward to putting his feet up after dinner. Maybe even having a small glass of whisky. And then, perhaps an early night, if Linda was in the mood.

******

Brian Peters had spent the last couple of days phoning the

telephone numbers which had been recovered from Amanda's phone. Most were innocent enough; work colleagues, friends, hairdressers, nail bars, taxi companies – the sort of contacts many people would routinely have on their phone. He crossed them off his list as he cleared them of suspicion. But there were a few others from which he received no response, or the call was closed as soon as he spoke. He took a list of the outstanding numbers upstairs.

"Mrs Shackleton… "
"Call me Teresa, please, Brian."
"Of course. Sorry, Teresa. Would it be possible for you to find out who these phone numbers belong to? It's really important."
"I'll do my best. Could you leave them with me for a day or two?"
"Of course."
"Let me have a quick look."
"There are quite a few. They were all deleted from a dead girl's phone. It's possible the killer's number is among them."
"Right. The land-line numbers will be easy enough. The mobiles will take longer, and it's possible some will be untraceable. But I'll call you when I've done all I can."
"Thanks, Teresa. You're a gem."
"There are not many here who think so."
"I know better. Thanks again."

Walking back down the stairs, he found Hardcastle on his way up.

"Been to see old Mrs Semtex, have you?"
"I've been to see Mrs Shackleton."
"Like the gays, do you?"
"What are you inferring by that?"
"Well, you seem to get on well with the gays. Gary, Mrs Semtex."
"I like them both, yes. I like them because they get on with their job, and they both do their job very well. Whether they're gay or straight is immaterial."
"It's just that people will soon be talking about you the same way."
"I couldn't give a toss, Hardcastle. Now, if you don't mind, I've got work to do. I don't have time for idle gossip."
"How are you getting on with the Eccleshill case?"
"Making progress."
"Anything specific?"
"No."
Brian walked away. Was he just imagining it, or was Hardcastle

taking more interest in the case than he should? Maybe he's just making polite conversation, he thought, but then re-considered. Hardcastle was not the type to make polite conversation. Maybe he didn't want Peters to unearth some detail he'd failed to spot in his initial investigation. Or maybe he's covering something up. Whatever the reason, Brian was determined to get to the bottom of it.

Back in the main office, Gary and Lynn were still actively working the car thefts case. Together, they discussed progress, which was, in fact, minimal. During the course of their conversation, Lynn said,

"We followed one lead and spoke to one of the victims, but all he gave us really was a tale about local kids causing all sorts of problems in the area. Just idle gossip, really."

Brian's ears pricked up at the last phrase. Idle gossip. He'd used the same phrase a few minutes earlier during his conversation with Hardcastle. He had an idea.

"It's nearly knocking-off time. Anyone fancy joining me for a quick drink?"

They both nodded assent.

"Anywhere in particular?"
"The Draper. I want to see if we can pick up some Idle gossip."

There were already several customers, mainly standing at the bar, but Brian immediately spotted the man he was looking for. He motioned to his colleagues to sit at the adjacent table and went to the bar for drinks. The barman, Nick, recognised him immediately.

"Nice to see you again. What can I get you?"
"Two pints of Gold and a half of lager, please."
"Any preference?"
"Whatever's the lowest ABV, please. We're all driving."

As soon as he sat down with the drinks, the man at the next table spoke.

"Alright, la. I know you. You were here when we had John Braden's send-off party. This lady was here too. You were with the police."

"That's right, Billy. We still are. You've got a good memory."

"I never forget a face. So, what brings you back now?"

"We were just in the area. We're working a case around here."

"Arthur Williamson?"

"Yes. Did you know him?"

"I knew him well. He used to come in here regularly. Every other Friday he'd go to the Post Office around the corner and draw his pension. Then he'd come straight here for a couple of pints. We'd often sit together and have a chat. He was a nice old fella, was Arthur."

"Was he ever the worse for wear when he left?"

"Never to my knowledge. He'd normally have two or sometimes three pints, then go up to the Co-op for a bit of shopping, and then go home. I never saw him out at night. He was a tea-time drinker. Just liked a natter."

"You said he collected his pension before he came in here. Did he throw his money about?"

"God, no! In all the time I've known him, I've never seen him buy anyone a drink. I'm not saying he was tight; he just made sure he kept control of his budget. He wasn't short of a bob or two, though. On the Fridays I saw him, he'd just drawn £300. He told me he kept £200 in the flat and used the rest for shopping."

"He kept £200 in his flat?"

"That's what he told me. He let it build up. In case his daughter needed a loan or something. A bit of a hoarder, he was. For emergencies, and the like."

"Was it common knowledge, Billy?"

"I don't know. I never heard him tell anyone else. When he came in here he used to sit at the next table to me. He liked a chat. I don't think he knew any of the other customers very well."

"Would his neighbours have known about it?"

"I don't know. But he had a cleaner in a couple of times a week. And it wouldn't have been the first theft at that place."

"Really?"

"Oh, aye. A couple of years ago an old lady went to the police when some money went missing from her flat. She kept it in a biscuit tin in the kitchen cupboard, and somebody nicked around five-hundred quid."

"Anybody charged?"

"I don't think so. They couldn't prove anything. The old lady had a regular cleaner, and a carer every day, and often it was a different carer, apparently. And the warden was questioned about it as

well."
"The same warden that's there now?"
"The very same. Drives a BMW, she does."
"Thanks, Billy. Can I buy you a drink?"
"I'd rather you didn't. No offence, but I don't want people thinking I'm a police nark."
"What if I just leave a fiver on the floor when we leave?"
"Fair enough, la. People will think you dropped it by accident."

As they walked back to the car park across the road, Gary said,

"That was a stroke of luck. Meeting somebody who knew about Mr Williamson's money habits."
"That's exactly why we went. The chap we were talking to is called Scouse Billy. He's also known locally as the Town Crier. Knows every bit of local gossip. Now we need to get hold of Mr Williamson's daughter to see if she can corroborate what Billy told us. I'll ring the warden, sorry, Court Manager, in the morning."

CHAPTER 9

Mark Bell, Ding-Dong to his mates, had just celebrated his nineteenth birthday. He still lived with his parents, in a semi-detached in Eccleshill, where he was born. He was one of the few teenagers among his small circle of acquaintances who had a steady job - with a firm of shopfitters - and earned enough to pay his housekeeping money and save for the car he had craved.

Mark was happy with his Corsa. He'd fitted new fog lights and his uncle had helped him apply a sporty-looking red stripe down each side. He'd had the radio taken out and a three-hundred-pound sound system installed. He drove every evening up and down the local A-roads, then round the estates where more people would be able to hear the thump of music from his full-volume hi-fi. It turned people's heads. And even in cold wet weather he drove around with the driver's window down, his right arm resting casually on the frame, his fingers drumming lightly on the door. But on this coming Friday night the windows would be closed tight. Because on Friday night he and his new girl, Sharon, were going to do it. They'd decided. They'd been together since he got his car. He'd picked her up that very night when he'd pulled up alongside as she was chatting with a group of her mates. They went for a drive. He stopped in a quiet lane and they indulged in a little heavy petting. She'd finished him off with a hand-job, but, mercifully, it hadn't stained the upholstery. And this Friday they were going all the way. He'd already boasted to his mates that he'd poked her, but now he was really going to do it. He had an erection just thinking about it and took his hand from the door frame to stroke himself gently.

****

Linda Stanton wasn't in a good mood. In fact, she was in a terrible state. When Terry got home from work he could tell she'd been crying.

"What's up, love?"
"Your mum rang. Not long ago. It's your dad, Terry."
"What's happened?"
"He's had a heart attack."
"Bad?"
"He's in hospital. Intensive care."

"What's his chance?"

"It's critical, Terry. But at least he's in hospital. He's still alive. He's got to have a chance."

"I'd better ring mum."

"She's at the hospital. She said she'd ring you in an hour or so."

Terry could only pick at his dinner. He had no appetite, and his mind was elsewhere - one hundred and twenty miles away, in a hospital ICU, where his father was fighting for his life.

The call came just as Terry was dressing after his shower. He ran into the hall as Linda handed him the receiver, her eyes moist with imminent tears.

"Mum? How is he?"

"Still fighting, Terry. You know what a stubborn old sod he is."

"But what are his chances? What do the doctors say?"

"Not good, Terry, love. They don't expect him to last the night. He's had a massive heart attack. You should prepare for the worst."

"Oh God! What about you? Is anyone there with you?"

"No. But I'm all right. Don't worry about me. I'll be fine. It's your dad you should be worrying about."

"We're coming up. We'll set off as soon as we can."

"Thanks, Terry. Your dad would want you to be there when..."

"I know. We'll see you soon."

"Bye."

By nine o'clock, they were speeding up the A1. They had covered no more than fifty miles when the engine started to misfire and lose power. Terry cursed under his breath, indicated left and pulled off the road into a lay-by. As he pulled to a halt, the engine cut out. He switched off the lights and the ignition and counted mentally to ten before turning the ignition key again. The engine caught immediately but would not tick over. Instead, Terry had to keep pressing the accelerator hard. He engaged first gear, released the handbrake, switched on his lights and slipped the clutch to move jerkily and noisily back on to the road.

At around ten forty-five, Terry pulled off the road into a service station. He didn't really want to stop. They were only about twenty miles away, but Linda desperately needed a pee. Fifteen minutes later, they were still there. The bonnet was open and Terry was checking the plugs and HT leads. He didn't really know what he was doing. He wasn't a mechanic, but he knew enough to be able to eliminate obvious problems. It was times like this that made him wish he'd joined the AA.

At eleven fifteen, they were back on the road, and making good progress. Whatever Terry had done beneath the bonnet seemed to have done the trick as the engine was running as smoothly as ever. They were about half an hour's drive from the hospital.

At eleven thirty-five, Frank Stanton suffered a second major heart attack and was pronounced dead.

****

The drive back home was a nightmare. They were both in low spirits. They'd spent a couple of hours with Terry's mum, but she'd assured them she was fine. She had things to do, things to organise. She could cope. And she wanted to be alone, for a while at least. Besides, she reasoned, she could always phone her son and daughter-in-law if she needed anything, or if she just felt like talking. But for now, she didn't want to share her grief and she'd urged Terry to drive home and go back to work. She knew he was having problems and didn't want to compound them by causing him to break time, knowing he'd have to ask for time off for the funeral. So, reluctantly, they left.

The weather was foul. Lashing rain and a cold, biting wind. Lorries and trunkers thundered past, sending up showers of spray which obscured his vision as his wipers struggled to keep the screen clear. Linda was asleep. She wasn't aware that the car was running on three cylinders, with the fourth occasionally firing and producing unexpected bursts of power.

It was a little after four-thirty when Terry eased into the car park. He felt drained. Exhausted. Physically, the drive had been tiring enough. But his father's death had sapped his mental energy. He just wanted to sleep. He thought about calling work and asking for the day off and tried to weigh up the reaction and the possible consequences. Ronnie was unlikely to be sympathetic. She had no heart. No compassion. He decided he'd go to work, inform Ronnie his father had died, and ask for time off for the funeral.

Linda went to bed. She was having the day off. Her employer

would understand. Terry made a mug of coffee, changed into his working clothes, and settled in the armchair. He enjoyed a cigarette although he knew he'd smoked far in excess of his usual amount during the last twenty-four hours. Now wasn't the time to worry about the dangers of smoking to his health. He stubbed out the butt and immediately lit another. His eyes felt heavy. He struggled to remain awake. He finished the cigarette and drained the mug of coffee. Within fifteen minutes he'd lost the struggle and was hard asleep.

He was lying on the beach. It was warm. He could feel the heat of the sun through his closed eyelids. He was relaxed, with not a care in the world. He was on holiday. In fact, he was permanently on holiday. He didn't work. He had no need to. Money wasn't a problem. He was a millionaire. Life was a dream. He could feel Linda's hand on his shoulder shaking him gently. Then more persistently. She was beginning to annoy him. Probably wanted him to get her another drink. Why couldn't she just click her fingers like he did to catch the waiter's attention?

"Terry!"

He tried to ignore her. Tried to dismiss her from his thoughts and concentrate on re-forming the mental image of the young hotel receptionist. The one with the thick jet-black hair and laughing eyes. The one into whose willowy body he wanted to push his erection. To explode inside her.

"Terry! Terry! Come on, wake up! Wake UP!"

Startled, he opened his eyes and blinked at his surroundings. No sand. No sea. No sun. Only the cold light of another day.

"Terry. It's ten o'clock, love. You're late for work. Get a move on."

He splashed his face and neck with cold water in the bathroom sink. He brushed his teeth and combed his hair, cursing its reluctance to stay in place due to his sleeping position. His body ached. Pulling on his coat and boots and picking up his keys, he kissed Linda and walked briskly towards the car park. He stopped at the car, realising he hadn't got a pack-up. He checked his pocket for change. Enough to buy a couple of rolls and a coffee from the vending machines in the canteen. That would have to do.

As he pulled on to the main road, Linda was already trying to explain to an irate Ronnie that her husband was on his way.

How dare she tell me to fuck off? Ronnie was seething. The nerve of the woman! Just wait till Terry gets here. He's in for the bollocking of his life. No one talks to me like that.

Linda was shaking. She'd lost her temper. She couldn't believe the insensitivity of that woman. How the hell did Terry manage to put up with her? Linda had answered the phone but before she had the chance to explain what had happened she was subjected to an intense verbal assault. She couldn't get a word in edgeways. In the end, she lost her temper. She shouted "Fuck off, you old cow" and slammed down the receiver. Without thinking, she picked up Terry's pack of cigarettes and lit one. She hadn't smoked for months. Angry with herself, she moved to stub it out, then stopped. Terry's cigarettes! He'd gone to work without his fags. And without any breakfast. Or pack-up. She instantly felt sorry for him. On top of his father's death, he was now about to have a very bad day.

Terry was relieved to clock out that evening. He was amazed he'd managed to survive it. He'd needed all his willpower to avoid throttling the damned woman. All he wanted to do was to tell her where to stick her job. But he knew that was exactly what she wanted him to do. He refused to give her the pleasure, taking comfort in the fact that he was stronger and more bloody-minded than she'd anticipated. He refused to rise to the bait. Why should he give her any pleasure? If he did, he reasoned, he'd be the only man in town who would give pleasure, willingly or otherwise, to such an ugly, hard-faced bitch. But he'd held his temper in check, apologising for his father's lack of consideration for having a fatal heart attack at such a busy time of year. He didn't mention the funeral. He'd wait for mum to ring with the date before asking for more time off. But at least he'd got through the day, and some of his workmates had been sympathetic, offering him sandwiches and cigarettes to keep him going. And he would never forget the look of rage on Ronnie's face when she'd told him his wife had told her to fuck off. Nobody had ever said that to her before. Not to her face, at least.

He'd rung mum at lunchtime. The battery of his mobile had run flat, so he'd used a payphone near the locker room. It had taken all his change but he daren't risk using the phone in the QC office. If he was caught he'd be sacked on the spot. Private calls were prohibited, though he knew for a fact that Ronnie often flouted the rule. One rule for some; another rule for the rest. Nothing unusual in that. Privileges came with seniority and length of service, and at this moment he was well down the pecking order.

Linda had a meal ready by the time he arrived home. They discussed travelling up to see his mum at the weekend and decided to go on Sunday, so that Terry could book the car in with Salim on Saturday morning. He'd phone first thing in the morning in the hope that Salim would find time to check it over. He was usually very accommodating. He looked after his regular customers

****

On Friday morning, Teresa had walked up to Brian's desk and waited patiently while he finished a phone call before handing him two typed sheets of A4 paper. It was what he'd been waiting for – the names, phone numbers and, in many instances, the addresses of the contacts recovered from Amanda Braithwaite's phone.

"Teresa, you're an absolute marvel. Thank you."

He said it loud enough so that Hardcastle would be able to hear it clearly at the back of the office. And he wanted to ensure that Teresa was aware that Hardcastle could hear it. He put aside the file he was working on and looked carefully at each name. Teresa had conveniently highlighted those which she thought would be of the greatest interest and added brief comments alongside them. One caught Brian's immediate attention. He dialled the number. No answer. He tried again. His calls were being refused. There was no home address recorded, but there was the phone number of Kenny Collins, his former probation officer. He punched in the number.

"Kenny Collins."
"Good morning, Mr Collins. My name is Brian Peters. I'm a detective sergeant with West Yorkshire CID. I'd like to talk to you about one of your clients, Dean Donachie."
"That little scrote. What do you want to know?"
"I'd rather discuss it face to face if that's possible."
"OK. I'm afraid I've quite a lot of work on at the moment, but I may

have an hour this afternoon. I have an appointment, but I'm fairly sure it will be a no-show. It's happened before with this client, so if he does miraculously turn up, I'd rather keep him waiting. Can you make two-thirty?"

"Yes. No problem. Thank you."

"I'm in Fraternal House on Cheapside. Just ask at the reception desk and they'll direct you."

"Thanks, Mr Collins. I'll see you then."

No sooner had he finished the call than his phone rang again. It was Teresa.

"Hi Teresa."

"Hello, Brian. I'm sorry to be disturbing you, but I just wanted to say thank you for publicly praising me in the office this morning."

"You don't need to thank me. You deserve it."

"Yes, but you made sure Hardcastle heard it. That *was* intentional, wasn't it?"

"Yes, it was. But the praise was because you earned it."

"Yes, but you didn't see Hardcastle's face. He didn't look happy at all."

"That's his problem."

"You know why he doesn't like me, don't you?"

"I've no idea."

"Isn't it obvious?"

"Not to me."

"It's because I'm black. *And* I'm a lesbian. Don't tell me you didn't notice."

"What difference does that make? You're a very vital member of this department. You do your job to the highest standard. You're invaluable to me and my team. And I'm sorry that another serving officer should take a dislike to you on the basis of the colour of your skin and your sexual preference. It makes me ashamed to be associated with him. To me, you're Teresa Shackleton. The woman who can provide the answers to my problems. And on top of that, a woman who is a lovely person."

"Thank you, Brian."

"My pleasure, Teresa. I'll have you on my team any day."

Brian held a short meeting in one of the interview rooms with his team. He made a point of inviting Teresa to attend. Unfortunately, she reminded him that her role was to provide a service to the whole department, so, reluctantly, she declined.

The purpose of the meeting was to discuss between themselves the progress made on the cases they were handling and decide on strategies for further investigation. Gary started the conversation.

"No progress on the car thefts, apart from a pattern which would suggest it's the work of kids."

"Go on."

"All the stolen cars were mid-range family hatchbacks, or town cars, or small saloons. Older cars. Nothing high-end was taken. Nothing of real value. Nothing with elaborate anti-theft devices fitted. So, my guess is, they have not been stolen for parts or to export. It's not an organised gang. These people are stealing cars purely for the fun of it. Purely for joyriding. They just want to wreck cars. I'm betting it's a couple of kids. In fact, they may not even be old enough to drive legally."

"OK, Gary. I think that's a fair assumption. It might be worth checking if any minors have been picked up in the last couple of years for criminal damage to motor vehicles. I'm thinking they learnt to enjoy wrecking before they learnt how to drive."

"Will do."

"Lynn?"

"As you asked, I got a mobile number for Mr Williamson's daughter this morning. She's still in the Canaries, but she's got a flight home tomorrow morning. I have asked her to let me know before she goes to the flat, as I need to accompany her since it's still officially a crime scene. I need to find out if any money may be missing."

"Are the premises secured? I know the warden, sorry, the manager has a master key."

"SOCO had it padlocked. It's secure."

"Good work."

"How about you, boss?"

"Well, regarding the Eccleshill death, I'm pursuing a line of inquiry, but I need to keep it under my hat for the moment. It's not a reflection on either of you. It's just that things could become a little awkward if I said too much at this stage and was later proved totally wrong."

"Sounds intriguing."

"It is. But as far as either of you are concerned, there's no progress. Understood?"

They both nodded, understanding that if Brian's line of inquiry led him into trouble, then the less they knew about it, the better.

After lunch in the canteen, Brian made his way across the City Centre. Not exactly sure how far up Cheapside Kenny's office was, he walked along Market Street towards the bottom of Cheapside, soon reaching Bank Street. He stopped for a second, remembering the last time he was there; the day the bomber blew his friend and colleague David Lee to small pieces. After a moment's reflection, he moved on to Fraternal House, where he was directed up two flights of stairs. Kenny's office was the second on the left. The door was open. As he was about to knock, the occupant looked up from his work, smiled and approached the door.

"You must be DS Peters. I'm Kenny. Please come in and take a seat."
"Thank you, Mr Collins."
"Please. It's Kenny. Everyone calls me Kenny."

Kenny was smartly dressed in a tweed suit with a yellow, open-necked shirt with a wide collar. He also wore a wide smile.

"OK, Kenny. The reason I wanted to speak to you was a client of yours, Dean Donachie."
"Actually, he's an ex-client. He's gone back to Armley Jail."
"Why's that."
"Breaking the terms of his probation. Several times. Lost count of the number of second chances he's been given. Missing appointments. Generally being an arse. There are some people who just don't want to be helped. They prefer to help themselves. Usually to someone else's property."
"I gather he was arrested more than once for dealing drugs."
"Correct. He's been doing it since he left school. Some of the kids round here think it's a great career to aspire to. Respect on the street, and all that."
"Did he deal coke?"
"He dealt anything and everything."
"Anything else you can tell me about him?"
"Usual story. Unmarried mother. Lives on benefits in a small rented flat. He's never done an honest day's work since he was expelled from school."
"OK. Well, thanks, Kenny. Can I contact you again if I need any further information?"
"Certainly. Make an appointment here, please. But if you want an informal chat, you can normally find me in a pub up in Idle at

weekends."

"Which pub?"

"The Draper. The Idle Draper."

"I thought you might say that. It seems that *everybody* goes to the Draper. Thanks for your help."

"You're welcome. One more thing. If you're thinking of talking to Dean in prison, do it quickly. I've a feeling he'll be back out on the streets on Monday after his hearing."

Sleet was stinging his face as he walked the windy streets back to base. He would normally use an occasion like this for thinking. But not today. Today all he thought about was getting back indoors before his frozen appendages dropped off. He had fifteen minutes or so to warm up in the office and make a quick phone call before he was back out, in his car this time, for the short trip out of town to Leeds Prison, Armley.

Against the backdrop of the grey sky, the Victorian prison was an impressive, foreboding building, which had worked hard to free itself from its past reputation for having the highest recorded level of drug users and the second highest suicide rate of prisoners in England and Wales in the first decade of the twenty-first century. However, so far in the second decade there were still eleven recorded deaths of inmates, the second worst number of prison fatalities in the country. It made Brian wonder why so many repeat offenders found their way back there time after time. He parked up and made his way to F Wing, where he was expected and escorted to an interview room. Dean Donachie, and his solicitor, were already waiting.

"Sorry to keep you waiting, gentlemen. I'm DS Brian Peters, and I'd like to ask Mr Donachie a few questions if that's OK with you."

"You are aware, DS Peters, that my client does not have to answer your questions?"

"Of course, but I'm hoping he'll see there might be some personal advantage if he does."

"Such as?"

"Well, let's look at it a different way. If he *refuses* to answer, I may well think that he has something to hide, and in that case, I'll get the answers elsewhere, and charge him with anything I might think he's guilty of. I'd like to look on this as a friendly chat. OK?"

"Go ahead. Dean, don't answer any question you don't wish to."

"Mind if I begin?"

"Go ahead."

"OK, Dean. How much cocaine did you sell to Amanda Braithwaite?"

"I don't know what you're talking about. I don't know any Amanda Braithwaite."

"That's odd. She knows you. Your number is on her phone. She texted you a few times on New Year's Eve."

"I don't know what you're talking about."

"No? Then why did you text her back? This is one of the messages we found on her phone. B there about 12.30. Sum good coke 4 U. D."

"I didn't send that. I don't know anything about that."

"You're sure, Dean? You could put yourself in the frame for a murder if you don't tell me the truth."

"I've told you. I don't know anything about it. I don't know that woman. I never went near Eccleshill on New Year's Eve."

"I never said anything about Eccleshill, Dean. Why would you think it happened in Eccleshill?"

"My client read about it in the papers, officer. Plain and simple. Now, unless you have any more questions, my client would like to return to his art class."

"What's that? The art of lying? I'll be back. Thank you for your time."

He stood up and waited until the prison officer unlocked the doors and escorted him back to the Governor's office. There he produced the warrant and waited until the box containing Dean Donachie's confiscated possessions was brought out of secure storage. Dean's mobile phone was on top. Brian took a deep breath, switched the phone on, and scrolled through the contacts. Amanda Brathwaite's name was not there, neither was there any record of her number under any other name. He signed for custody of the phone and took it with him. He intended to take it to Martin Riley, at the University. It would have to wait until Monday. He was stuck in rush hour traffic. Then it occurred to him that he should perhaps check with Muesli about using Martin Riley's services again, remembering the previous rebuke he'd received. He pulled off the road and called him.

"DCI Moseley."

"Sorry to bother you, sir, but I have a new piece of evidence concerning the Eccleshill case, and I'd like your permission to take it to the University for analysis."

"What is it?"

"A mobile phone belonging to a drug dealer."

"You think he may be involved?"

"I'm sure of it."

"Where did you get it?"

"From storage at Armley. He's on remand, so it was confiscated. It's all above board, sir. You signed the warrant."

"Not if you take it to the University, it isn't. They're not authorised. Anything they unearth could be challenged in court. Bring it in and sign it into the evidence locker. Chain of custody, and all that."

"Yes, sir."

Brian cursed himself for forgetting that, unlike his previous department, CID were obliged to follow the rules.

He pulled back into traffic, heading for HQ. He knew how long it took to get anything achieved through official channels but consoled himself with the fact that there were plenty other cases to occupy his time. And if Muesli complained that progress on the Eccleshill case was too slow, he was the one to blame for the delay.

CHAPTER 10

Straight after lunch on Saturday, Brian Peters, Sarah and young Daniel were in the car on their way to Bradford with a short list of addresses to visit. Brian had planned the most efficient route, which, conveniently for him, ended in Idle.

The first two were plainly unsuitable, the third more promising, but lacking sufficient garden space, but the final one, a detached house in a cul-de-sac off Westfield Lane, seemed ideal. For once, it had everything Sarah deemed to be essential for the house where she wanted her family to grow up. As far as Brian was concerned, it was just about affordable, needed minimal re-decoration, and was close to a cricket club. Even more important, it was within walking distance of the Draper, even though it was an uphill hike back. As soon as they had left the premises, Sarah suggested they drive around the area to get a better perspective and look at the local amenities.

"Tell you what, love. Why don't you and Daniel do that, then do your shopping at the Morrisons we passed? And just at the side of the road back down the hill from Morrison's car park, there's a mobile shop which sells eggs fresh from the farm. I think they call it 'Cluck and Collect', or something. If you don't mind, I'd like to pop into the Draper for a word with a couple of the customers about an ongoing case."
"Never stop working, do you? OK. I'll call you when we're coming down to pick you up. Make sure you're outside. I don't want to take Daniel in. He might pick up bad habits from his dad."

Sarah was well aware that Brian simply fancied a couple of pints and was happy to play along with his little charade. He worked hard. He deserved a little free time. She dropped him outside the pub, executed a three-point turn in the car park opposite and drove back along Westfield Lane towards Wrose.

The Draper was crowded but Brian was able to squeeze his way to the bar and order a pint. Nick, behind the bar, acknowledged him.

"Hello again. How are you?"
"Fine, Nick. You?"
"Good. What can I get you?"

"A pint of Draper's Gold, please."

"John Braden's favourite."

"He had good taste."

"He certainly did. We all miss him."

"Me too. He was a good man."

"Here's Jim."

Jim, the owner, had just walked through the back door carrying a box full of bottles to put in the cellar. Seeing Brian, he stopped for a chat. They shook hands.

"Nick told me you were in a few days ago. Thinking of becoming a regular?"

"Possibly. We've just been to look at a house off Westfield Lane. I've left CTU. I'm with Bradford CID now, so we're looking to move closer to my work. And one of the criteria for our new home is that it must be close to a good pub."

"Well, you're always welcome in here. As long as you're off-duty, that is."

"Thanks. Can either of you tell me anything about Arthur Williamson?"

"Arthur? Quiet bloke. Teatime drinker. A couple of pints. Didn't speak much but sometimes he'd have a chat with Scouse Billy."

"Yes. I've already spoken to Billy. Did Arthur ever tell anyone about his financial affairs?"

"Not that I know of. He always had cash in his pocket. That's all I know."

"Ever met his daughter?"

"No. I didn't know he had any family. Always on his own, was Arthur."

"OK. Thanks for your help. I'll call in for a pint next time I'm in the area. I like it in here."

"Well, that's nice to know. You know, I still find it hard to believe we once had a suicide bomber in here. Yeah, we get the odd drunk and occasional moocher. But a terrorist! That's hard to believe. I mean, it's just not that kind of pub!"

****

It was Linda who took the car in after dropping Terry at work. It should have been his Saturday off, but when Ronnie asked him to work he agreed. He had little choice. Whenever Ronnie asked him to do something it came over as an order rather than a request.

Besides, he would still need time off for the funeral, so it was counterproductive to antagonise his boss at present and anyway the extra few hours at overtime rate would be useful.

It was a long shift, fraught with problems caused by the unusual inconsistency in the quality of the raw material. As a rule, each full batch was either totally good, bad or indifferent, but today it was simply totally inconsistent in quality, and Terry had to remain on his toes, ensuring the graders were diligent. He was happy to see Linda waiting in the car by the main gate at the end of the shift. As he approached, she got out and walked round to the passenger side. Terry always did the driving when they were together

"Hi, love. Everything all right?"
"Well, Salim wasn't sure. The car's running fine, but he's not sure if he's solved the problem. The trouble is, it's been running fine since I dropped you at work this morning. So, Salim had nothing to work on really. He's cleaned the carb, checked the plugs, points and something-or-other else. It's all on the invoice."
"How much?"
"Fifty."
"Hell, that's not bad."
"He said he didn't like to charge for any replacement parts because he couldn't be sure what was wrong. It could be the fuel pump, or something else he mentioned that sounded a bit expensive. You'd have to talk to him yourself for the technical details. He just said, if the problem recurs, take it straight in so they can have a look at it while it's failing."
"Fair enough. I'm whacked. Early night tonight, I think."
"Early to bed, but don't put your money on an early night. I've got steak for dinner. And a bottle of wine."
"Oh, you're a darling."
"And I'm horny."
"Not sure I can help you there, I'm afraid. I could always ring for a Shagagram."
"Fine by me. As long as you pay."
"Oh, no. You get the pleasure, you foot the bill."
"OK. As long as I can have the black donkey."

They laughed. The black donkey was the name Linda had given to an actor, if that was the right word, in a porn film they'd once watched together. Linda couldn't believe how long and thick he was, and how he used it. Terry had teased her that it was all done with computer enhancement; that in reality it was only the size of a cocktail sausage. But she knew that low-budget porn films didn't employ that sort of expensive technology. What you saw was what you got. Or at least what the actresses, if that was the right word, got. The memory of some of the scenes turned her on, and she surreptitiously tightened and relaxed her fanny muscles all the way home.

Dinner was a hurried affair. Linda's bare foot caressed Terry's inner thigh under the table throughout the meal. Both gulped their wine. Terry eased one foot from his slipper and slid it under the hem of her skirt. Her legs parted, and he rested his toes on her moist hot crotch. She closed her eyes as he wiggled his toes against her dampness, feeling for her opening, rubbing his big toe against her swollen clitoris.

They made love on the dining room carpet. Not even wasting time by undressing completely, they fulfilled their lust eagerly, greedily. His orgasm was intense; hers, all of them, were overwhelming. And as they lay there afterwards, whenever he touched her, wherever he touched her, her whole body tingled. They went to bed, leaving the washing-up piled by the sink for the morning. They felt light-headed and happy, and slightly drunk.

****

Eddie was more than slightly drunk. He was the same every Saturday. He went to the pub at lunchtime and watched the horse racing on TV, nipping next door to the bookies at regular intervals. The afternoon had started well. Two races, two winners. And by the end of the afternoon, he'd won close to seventy quid. But Eddie was a soft touch, and the regulars knew it. By the end of the night, he'd spent the lot, buying drinks for all his 'friends', the ones who only appeared when he had money in his pocket. But he was a lonely man. A widower, living in a small rented flat, he needed company, and was a sad, pathetic figure without it. With money in his pocket, however, and drink in his belly, he was popular, and everybody in the pub knew him and spoke to him and laughed at his jokes and enjoyed his company. Now, his wallet empty, he was walking home, as he did every Saturday night. Staggering across the car park, he stopped by the bushes and unzipped his fly, unaware of the fox hiding deep in the undergrowth, unseen, and out of reach of the hot spray of urine. Finished, he shook his dick and tucked it back in his underpants, forgetting to zip himself up again. He lurched across the tarmac in the general direction of home knowing full well that it would take well over an hour to cover the distance of approximately one mile. One mile, that is, in a straight line. He paused to light a cigarette, using all his concentration to keep his hand, or was it his head, still, so that contact could be made between cigarette and lighter. He inhaled deeply, then let out a racking tubercular cough, and continued on his haphazard way. He didn't see the Astra in his path. Alternately coughing and inhaling, staggering left and right, he fell hard against the bonnet.

"Bastard."

He pulled himself to his feet and eyed the car which was blocking his path. Steadying himself, he aimed a kick at the wing mirror, missed and found himself once again flat on his arse on the tarmac. He grabbed the mirror to raise himself, and once he'd achieved some kind of unsteady balance, drove his fist into the reflective glass. It cracked immediately, then shattered with the second blow. Breathing heavily, yet still demanding retribution from the vehicle for barring his path, he extracted his house keys from his trouser pocket. Gripping them firmly in his right hand, he inscribed a long wavy line through the paintwork, from bumper to bumper. Not yet satisfied, he pulled the wipers away from the screen and bent the blade carriers so the ends were almost touching. Finally, he kicked in the rear light clusters, and, having successfully negotiated the obstacle barring his path, meandered home.

The closed-circuit TV camera remained motionless, its lens pointing at the parked delivery trunkers, as the control room operator flipped through his well-thumbed copy of a porn mag and ate his sandwiches.

****

Mark Bell was on cloud nine. He'd done it with Sharon on Friday night, in the back of the Corsa, and they'd just done it again. She was a real goer! More experienced than he, but then again, he'd been a virgin. But not any longer. Twice in two nights! He couldn't wait to tell his mates. Of course, he'd embellish it a little. He wouldn't mention the fact that the first time he'd ejaculated as soon as he put it in, and the second time he'd lasted only about thirty seconds. That didn't matter. At least he'd done it. Now he had some real experience to fantasise about while he masturbated, and he was driving home now to do just that. He'd had his pleasure. He was now a man. He wondered if he was in love.

Sharon had no such illusions about the nature of their relationship. Still only sixteen years old and already two months pregnant, she saw Mark as a potential parent and breadwinner for her unborn child. She knew he had a job and had saved to buy himself a car. His parents both worked, and they lived in a large semi-detached house far from the council flat which she inhabited with her mother and infant brother. She wanted a better life for herself and her child, and though Mark was far short intellectually to be a candidate for membership of Mensa, he was nevertheless a hard worker. Besides, she knew how to manipulate him. The promise of a blow-job was enough to make him accede to her every wish.

****

Terry was annoyed. Very annoyed. He'd rung mum on Sunday morning to tell her they were coming up. They'd had a good breakfast, then showered together, indulging in a little soapy foreplay. But the moment they saw the damage to the car, their joyous mood evaporated.

It was mid-afternoon before the car could be deemed roadworthy, though Terry had taken the risk of driving to a scrapyard knowing full well that if the police stopped him he'd incur a hefty fine. At least the weather stayed dry so he could manage without the wipers. He eventually picked up the required parts and set to fitting them. By the time he'd finished, it was too late to consider driving up to Newcastle. He phoned his mother to apologise.

Terry felt bad. His mother sounded distraught. She said she was coping but the hesitancy in her voice suggested otherwise, as if she were on the verge of tears. He promised they would be there on Monday, for the funeral, and hung up. He stayed by the phone for a while. In the hall, he was out of sight of Linda, and with the TV on, she couldn't hear him sobbing.

****

The Monday morning drive north for the funeral was without

incident, although the mood was sombre. The funeral service went smoothly, though not without tears. Frank Stanton was a popular man, and there was a good turnout of friends to see him laid to rest in the rain-soaked ground. Margaret Stanton maintained an air of dignified composure throughout the proceedings. She'd grieved silently and in private up to that point and would grieve later. But not now. Terry was immensely proud of the way his mother conducted herself, though it seemed to him she was somehow smaller than before, and her hair greyer. As he stood beside her, his thoughts returned to the night his dad died. Fifteen minutes earlier, and he could have said goodbye. That damn car! If only he'd had the Focus.

"The bastards pissed in it!"

He became aware of Linda's hand squeezing his. Looking round, he noticed the quizzical and disapproving looks on the faces of those close by and realised he'd expressed his thoughts out loud. He felt embarrassed and could feel his face reddening despite the cold wind. He coughed nervously and self-consciously and tried to banish all thoughts of his wrecked car. But one day, he'd get even. He promised himself that much.

****

Monday couldn't come soon enough for Brian. Once at work, he went straight to the evidence room to arrange the secure transfer of the mobile phone to Forensics in Wakefield. He signed the necessary forms and countersigned the sealed evidence bag, and before he left, he asked the duty officer how long it would take before the results came back.

"Sorry, sir. It's difficult to say. Depends on their workload."
"Can't you tell them it's top priority?"
"They determine their own priorities, sir, as far as I'm aware, based on their resources and the workload."
"Have you got their number?"
"Yes, sir. It's on the bag."
"Of course. Thank you."

He noted the number and returned to his desk. His first task was to call Forensics. To his dismay, he was told by a member of staff they were overloaded with work, due to staff absences – the flu epidemic again – and he couldn't really give an estimate, and, yes, he understood how important it was, and they'd pull out all the stops and give it top priority, etc. Brian had heard it all before. Claptrap, just to get the caller off the phone so they could get back to their technical problems in their own good time. The annoying thing was that Martin, at the University, would have the work done in an hour at most. He turned to his two colleagues in the hope that their cases were proceeding more smoothly.

Gary was still cross-referencing criminal records for minors who'd committed offences of criminal damage, particularly to motor vehicles. He had a long list to check.

Lynn, though, had some positive news. Arthur Williamson's daughter had already been in touch about clearing her dad's flat, and Lynn was meeting her there at 10.15. Brian decided to tag along.

They were waiting in the car, sheltering from heavy showers of rain, when they saw a white SUV pull into the car park. A stout woman, probably in her late fifties walked quickly towards the door of Mr Williamson's flat.

"She's a bit blowsy," Brian thought, though that was rather a flattering description.

They got out of the car and joined her at the door of the flat which she was attempting to push open despite the padlock.

"Just a moment, please, miss. Could I ask who you are?"
"Doreen Gibson. Arthur Williamson's daughter."
"Could we see some ID, please?"
"Driving license OK?"
"Fine."

He checked the license and handed it back.

"I'm sorry about your father. Just let me remove the padlock and we can go inside. Please don't touch anything without one of us present."
"Why not?"
"We haven't yet ruled out the possibility of foul play. We'd like you to go through his possessions methodically and tell us if anything

of value is missing."

"I don't think he owned anything of any value. But there should be quite a lot of cash in the flat, plus a bank card."

"Then let's have a look."

Doreen went straight to the drawer where she knew her father kept money. The A4 envelope which usually contained bundles of twenty-pound notes was practically empty. Doreen was apoplectic with rage.

"Sixty quid! Shit! There should be over a grand in there! I saw him with it just before we went on holiday, and it was full then. He gave me £500, and there was a lot more left in it. So, where the hell is it?"

"When exactly did you last see your father with this envelope?"

"The beginning of January. I called to see him before I went on holiday. Just to make sure he was OK and to see if he needed anything."

More likely to see if she could get some money from him for her holiday, Brian thought.

"Could you please check to see if anything else is missing?"

The two officers followed her as she checked every cupboard and drawer in the small flat before declaring,

"There should be a coffee tin in the back of this drawer. Under the socks. This is where he kept the bulk of his savings. It's gone."

"Any idea how much he would have kept there?"

"A couple of thousand at least."

When she'd left, Lynn and Brian locked the flat securely before leaving. As they pulled out of the car park, they almost collided with a car pulling in. Lynn stopped their car abruptly and let the other car, an Audi, pull into the space they'd vacated. They watched as the manager got out of the Audi and walked to her office.

"That's odd. Scouse Billy told me she had a BMW."

"Perhaps she's come into some money."

"Exactly what I was thinking. Let's talk to her."

Brian knocked on the office door and they walked in.

"Sorry to disturb you again, Mrs Cunliffe."
"Oh, hello again. I thought it was you in the car park."
"Yes. Just called to apologise for almost colliding with you. Wouldn't want to damage your new car."
"No harm done."
"You must earn a good living here to afford a car like that, though."
"It's on lease."
"Still, the monthly payments must be high."
"Quite reasonable."
"Well, my wife has a good job, but she'd struggle to afford one of those."
"My husband left me some money. When he died."
"Sorry to hear about that, Mrs Cunliffe. I didn't know. Was it recent?"
"A couple of years."
"We won't take up any more of your time."

Back in the car, they were both in agreement.

"She's lying."
"I agree. What struck me is the fact that, if it was my husband who'd died, I wouldn't be so vague. Instead of answering 'a couple of years', I'd give the exact date. I wouldn't be able to help myself."
"Let's get back to the office and do some digging. And look through the pathologist's report again. Something's not quite right here."

Before the afternoon was over, Lynn had unearthed enough of Mrs Cunliffe's background history, with help from Teresa, to pull her story to shreds. She could hardly wait for Brian to end his phone call to the forensic pathologist to tell him what they'd discovered.

"Thanks for that, Martin. Can you please fax or email the full report to me? Yes. Thanks for all your help. Goodbye."

Turning to Lynn and seeing the wide grin on her face.

"I take it you've got some good news for me?"
"I have. First, Teresa called all the local Audi dealers. A company in Halifax leased her that car for £349 per month, over three years. Nothing unusual there, if she'd had a windfall, but, get this! I had a trawl through public records but couldn't find any record of a death

of any male between forty and seventy named Cunliffe in the last three years in this area."

"Interesting, but it may not have been local. And Cunliffe may have been her maiden name."

"I haven't finished. Wait for this. What I did find was a record of a divorce decree absolute a couple of years ago. I managed to trace him – he lives in Skipton with his new wife – and I spoke to him on the phone. He's definitely Mrs Cunliffe's ex-husband, and he's definitely very much alive. There was no financial settlement. They were both always short of money, so just divided up the assets and walked away."

"That's good news, Lynn."

"So, tell me what you've found."

"I spoke to Martin Black, who examined the body of Arthur Williamson. He's adamant that the blow to the head was the cause of death but was unable to rule out the possibility that Mr Williamson may have been pushed from behind, causing him to stumble. We can't prove that, but what we *can* prove is that Mr Williamson's examination showed evidence that he'd engaged in some form of sexual activity in the hours before he died. Martin found traces of seminal fluid in Mr Williamson's otherwise clean underwear."

"He might have had a Barclay's."

"He might. But have you seen the state of his hands? He had arthritis. Martin Black confirmed if he did it himself it would have given him more pain than pleasure. Let's assume someone else did it for him."

"And you think that person might have been Mrs Cunliffe?"

"Precisely. Let's imagine I'm right. She gave him a hand-job. Maybe it was a regular thing. But maybe this time she asked him for extra money. He refused, she pushed him. He fell and smashed his head and died. She left him there, took his money and locked the flat behind her."

"It's feasible."

"She's lied to us. She's suddenly got a new car. The deceased had sex, and unless he managed to give himself a hand-job, whoever he had sex with locked the door behind her when she left. And as far as we are aware, Mrs Cunliffe is the only other person with a key."

"I think we can call that a good day's work."

"Me too. We'll take it to Muesli in the morning. Well done, Lynn."

Brian was in a good mood by the time he arrived home, and in an even better one when Sarah informed him she'd accepted an offer for their house, at the asking price, and had immediately made an offer on the property near Idle.

****

Andy had been busy throughout the evening. While his brother hustled at the pool table at the Swan, Andy was trailing around the city following Dean. Dean was up to something. He was edgy and furtive, but unaware he was being followed. In truth, he couldn't care less. Having just been released from Armley, he needed to score. He was already less than pleased that his phone had 'been misplaced' while it was in storage at Armley, so he had no access to his contacts. He was trying places where he expected to find them. Andy watched from a safe distance as Dean knocked on the door of a run-down terrace house. Andy guessed it was a squat. He lit a cigarette and waited.

When Dean emerged, he looked calmer, less agitated. He was unaware of Andy's presence until he felt the knife against his back.

"Jesus, Andy! What's the problem, man?"
"Who's in the house?"
"Just a friend, Andy. That's all."
"Your supplier?"
"Yeah. Don't tell him I told you. He'll kill me."
"How many are in the house?"
"Two. Just the man and his girl."
"You lying to me?"
"Honest, Andy. I swear."
"Now fuck off."

Andy took out his mobile and called Daz, who got a taxi straight away and met his brother across the road from where he'd been keeping an eye on the house. They walked up to the front door and knocked loudly.

"Who is it?"
"Dean sent us."

A bolt slid back and an unshaven face squinted at them round the half-open door. Daz slammed his full weight against it, knocking the man backwards and off balance. They were in. Andy closed the door behind them. He wanted to make sure there were no witnesses.

They emerged a half-hour later, leaving the occupants to pack and clear out before midnight, at which time they threatened to return and burn down the house. The threat was taken seriously. The girl's thin needle-scarred left arm had been fractured by Daz's multi-purpose iron bar - his 'persuader' - and the man had a deep gash in his cheek, and right through his upper lip, courtesy of Andy's knife. Andy smiled, revelling in the terror he was able to generate, enthralled by his power. And he now had the contact details of the man who supplied the street dealers. That man would be their next target.

****

On his way home, Brian stopped outside a Polish off-licence. He felt like celebrating and was aware that his supply of malt whisky at home was dangerously low. He went into the shop and bought a bottle of Glenlivet.

Later that night, after they'd eaten, and put Daniel to bed, Brian opened the bottle and poured a glass for himself. He was immediately aware that, somehow, it wasn't right. He'd got quite used to the taste of Glenlivet since John Braden died, and this tasted different. The flavour was only subtly different, but he was convinced it just wasn't right. He examined the bottle closely. It looked authentic enough, a twelve-year-old, not a special release, but then he saw it. The mistake. How could he not have noticed? Now he'd seen it, it stood out like a sore thumb. It was the label. The error was an elementary one. Amateur even. The address of the distillery clearly stated 'Banfshire', instead of Banffshire. He put the bottle back in its box and placed it in the kitchen to pass on to Trading Standards in the morning.

The lesson is, he thought, don't be a counterfeiter unless you can spell.

CHAPTER 11

Brian's first task on Tuesday morning was to present his evidence on the Williamson case to his superior and get his approval to bring Mrs Cunliffe to the station for questioning. Muesli agreed there was a good case to proceed based on the evidence but reminded Brian to do it by the book.

"This is not CTU, Brian. No strong-arm tactics. Follow the rules, inform her of her rights, etc."
"Yes, sir. I'm fully aware how to proceed."
"Very well, Brian. Go ahead. Good work."
"It wasn't just me, sir. It was Lynn, Gary and also Teresa Shackleton. It was a team effort."
"Well, tell them all they did a good job."
"Yes, sir. Thank you, sir."

Brian returned to the office with a smile on his face, having first stopped at Teresa's desk to give her the news and thank her. Later, he and Lynn drove to collect Mrs Cunliffe, leaving Gary to work on the motor vehicle thefts and pass details of the sale of counterfeit whisky to Trading Standards.

By lunchtime, Mrs Cunliffe, her solicitor at her side, was nervously seated in an interview room, waiting for DS Peters to begin the interview. He formally introduced himself and Lynn, and acknowledged the presence of the solicitor, for the benefit of the recording. He informed her of her right to silence. Then came the questions.

"Mrs Cunliffe, will you please take us through everything you remember of the night Arthur Williamson died."
"I was at home, all night. Alone."
"Alone?"
"Yes."
"Of course. I almost forgot. You told us about the unfortunate death of your husband a couple of years back."
"Yes."
"You remember telling us that?"
"Yes."
"Mrs Cunliffe, my colleague DC Whitehead spoke to your husband yesterday. He's very much alive."

It was obvious Mrs Cunliffe was startled. Her face went white and her head dropped.

"Why did you tell us your husband was dead, Mrs Cunliffe?"
"As far as I'm concerned, he's dead."
"But, actually, the two of you divorced?"
"Yes."
"So, there was no windfall?"
"No."
"Would you like to tell us how you paid for your new car?"
"Out of my wages."
"You didn't have any little side-line? Any income from other activities?"

Her solicitor jumped in.

"My client doesn't have to answer that."
"Then let me come more to the point. Mrs Cunliffe, this is what our evidence tells us occurred. Mr Williamson had a couple of pints in the afternoon after withdrawing money, £300, from the post office. He returned to his flat, made a meal, and drank a little whisky. Later that night, he had a visitor, who performed a sex act on him. It seems there was then a dispute over payment for the sex act during which Mr Williamson received a head injury which caused his death. Does that sound about right?"

Norma Cunliffe burst into tears. Brian handed her a tissue and sat silently until she was able to respond, hesitantly.

"I didn't kill him. He fell."
"Please state exactly what happened."
"You're right. I was there. We had an arrangement. I'd go to his flat once a week, outside working hours, and give him a hand-job."
"How long has this been going on for?"
"A few months. Since his arthritis became worse. He begged me to help him. I refused at first, until he said he'd pay me."
"How much?"
"Twenty pounds."
"And you agreed to that arrangement?"
"Yes."
"Go on."
"That night, I did it for him as usual. Then I told him in future it would cost him fifty. He wasn't happy. He called me a dirty tart and

threw a twenty-pound note at me. Then I told him that would be my last visit and he'd have to find somebody else to wank him off. I took the money and turned to leave. He got out of his chair – I didn't know he could move so fast – and tried to grab my shoulder. But he lost his balance and fell over. His head hit the corner of the table. And he was out cold. He was dead. He had no pulse. He wasn't breathing. I took his money. I knew where he kept it. I think I left a few notes, maybe sixty pounds, something like that. Then I locked the flat and went home. That's it. That's all. I didn't kill him."

"Is there anything else you would like to add?"

"No. Just, I'm sorry."

"Didn't you think about calling for an ambulance, or the police, at that time?"

"He was dead. There was nothing I could do. I panicked and left."

"You were in such a panic to leave, but you stopped to take the time to steal his money?"

"It was no use to him."

"But what about his family?"

"His daughter only visits when she wants money."

"This interview is ended, at one-fifteen pm. Thank you, Mrs Cunliffe. We'll prepare a report for the CPS, and I expect you will be charged with theft, at least. I would think it quite unlikely there will be any other charges, but that's not our decision."

"What happens now?"

"You will remain in custody until a hearing decides if you can be released on bail pending a trial. Thank you for your co-operation."

Brian spent the rest of the afternoon completing his report, filing it, and sending copies both to CPS and his boss, Muesli. Then, out of courtesy, he made a call to the head office of the housing association which employed Mrs Cunliffe. Courtesy, however, was not his prime concern. The retirement flats housed some vulnerable people who needed the security a manager should provide. Not surprisingly, those at head office were shocked to hear his news. Brian wondered how often they came across incidents of elder abuse. Often, he imagined, but not often resulting in a death. Yet the ways in which people acted to extract personal gain from the misfortune of others never ceased to amaze him. Still, it was only his job to deal with it, not to understand it.

****

On that Tuesday morning, Terry had reported back at work having been allowed one day off for the funeral, and even that one day was granted reluctantly. Walking into the QC office, he was surprised to find Ronnie talking to a young man wearing a QC's white coat.

"Oh, you've turned up at last. Terry, this is Philip. He's joining the QC team."

"I didn't know we were recruiting,"

"It's been decided we need more cover on the production lines. What with business picking up, and your frequent absences."

"I've just been to my father's funeral, for Christ's sake!"

"Whatever. I want you to show Philip the ropes. The procedures, paperwork, the lot. You're going to be working together."

"On the same shift?"

"Yes."

"There isn't enough work for two."

"That's your opinion. But it's not your decision."

"Fine."

"Philip, I'll leave you with Terry. I'll see you later this afternoon. If you've any problems or complaints, just let me know."

She left them. Philip was nervous, apologetic almost. Terry was angry and confused.

"I guess I've put you in an awkward position, Terry."

"That depends. Have you been taken on permanently?"

"Yes."

"That means I'll be getting the boot as soon as you're trained up. If not before. Bastards!"

"Sorry, mate. But don't take it out on me. They offered me the job, and I accepted. They said they had a vacancy. Someone was leaving. But I never realised someone would be leaving without his knowledge. They've put me in an awkward position as well."

"Like you say, Philip. It's not your fault. This is how they operate. If you can keep on the right side of that old cow, you'll be fine."

"Ronnie? She seems all right."

"Don't believe it. She's a vindictive old slapper. Be warned."

Despite the awkwardness of the situation, Terry and Phil hit it off immediately, and in different circumstances could have become friendly workmates. Towards the end of the shift, Ronnie summoned Philip to her office, and after he emerged, Terry got the call. He knew what was coming and accepted his written warning without protest. Protesting to Ronnie was a futile exercise.

The news didn't go down very well with Linda, but she resigned herself to the fact that she'd have to earn some extra income to make up for the shortfall if, or rather when, Terry got the push. She made a mental note to call some of her contacts in publishing to see if they could use her services as a proof-reader. Terry, to his credit, responded to the crisis by behaving impeccably at work. He trained Philip in all aspects of the job, whilst performing his own duties diligently and with enthusiasm. He was determined to make it difficult for Ronnie to find the final excuse she needed to sack him. And for the next two weeks he succeeded.

****

Brian and his team spent the rest of the week checking, and re-checking, statements from a list of owners who'd reported their vehicles had been stolen and wrecked. They had shortened the list slightly by identifying two individuals whose claims were already being investigated by the Fraud Squad as being 'highly suspicious'.

On a whim, Brian decided to call Kenny Collins, only to be told he was absent with flu. He left a message for him to get in touch on his return to work. At least, though, he got one piece of good news – a call from Trading Standards to thank him for the tip about the counterfeit whisky, which led to a raid on the premises and the likelihood of a successful prosecution.

When he finished work on the Friday, he decided to take a drive around Idle and Eccleshill before heading home. He'd heard that large groups of youths tended to congregate at various points in the area and thought he'd take a look for himself. He drove into Idle and pulled into the public car park. At the entrance were a group of about a dozen youths. He walked towards them. They stood their ground, blocking his path. He had no intention of walking around them. They, in turn, had no intention of making way. Brian knew who would give first. He walked right through the middle, noting that some of the younger, smaller lads grudgingly stepped aside, while the older ones stood fast. That is until Brian barged the one he guessed was the ring-leader with his shoulder. Hard. The youth squared up to him, but Brian was ready and had him in an arm lock in a second, tightening the pressure as the youth squirmed.

"Listen to me. I'm Brian Peters. Detective Sergeant Brian Peters. Remember my face. Next time you see it, get out of my path. Or else, I'll make life very difficult for you. Understand?"
"Yes, sir."
"Good. Now clear off."

They dispersed, grudgingly, as Brian heard sounds of applause. He looked across the road where a number of customers were standing outside the Draper. He graciously acknowledged their applause and walked around the corner towards the retirement complex, where he bumped into Mrs Carr.

"Oh, hello again, officer."
"Hello. I'm sorry. I know we've met, but I can't remember your name."
"Mrs Carr. I live at number 46."
"Ah, yes. Mr Williamson's neighbour."
"Yes. I know it might all be rumour, but they say the manager was arrested. I think it's so sad what happened to Arthur. He was a lovely man. The really sad thing is, if I'd known that all he needed was a bit of hand relief, I would have done it for him, for free. Just for a bit of company."

CHAPTER 12

There had been a sizeable crowd at the football match, considering it was a midweek game. The visiting side won one-nil, thanks to a late penalty, and their supporters were ecstatic. After the final whistle, the roads leading out of the city became gridlocked. Dennis and his two football-mad friends made a snap decision to pull off at the next exit, find a pub, and relax for an hour until the traffic had eased. As they drove slowly down unfamiliar roads, Dennis noticed the illuminated sign of the Cross Keys. He indicated and pulled into the car park. The lads removed their scarves, and anything else which would betray their allegiance to their team, wary of the fact that they were on enemy territory. They entered the pub, ordered their drinks and sat quietly in a corner, huddled together, talking in whispers about the game. Dennis wasn't too happy about sitting in a pub drinking coke, but it was his turn to drive, which meant he paid for nothing. It was the same system they'd used for years; the passengers paid for the driver's match ticket and the petrol, and his soft drinks. In return they were free to drink as much as they could hold, and tonight they were celebrating. Neither of them had a great deal to spend, but they pooled their cash, and Dennis took twenty pounds for petrol, before they spent the rest over the bar and pushed coin after coin into the fruit machine. At closing time, they decided to start the journey home, after first relieving themselves.

As Dennis walked into the Gents, he bumped into a tall thin youth, who apologised, brushed past him and left.

They drove back towards the dual carriageway and, seeing the petrol filling station was still open for another half-hour, pulled in and stopped by a lead-free pump. Before filling up, Dennis felt for his wallet to check how much he could afford. It was a habit of his. He'd once filled the tank before realising he'd left his wallet at home. But this time, he knew he had his wallet. He'd put twenty pounds in it in the pub. The lads had given him twenty pounds between them. He'd picked it up. And put it in his wallet. He was absolutely certain. But now he couldn't find his wallet. It wasn't in his inside breast pocket where it should have been, where it always was. He checked his other pockets, the glove compartment, under the driver's seat, the side pockets, everywhere. Until the penny finally dropped. The young lad. The one who bumped into him by the toilets. Who made a great fuss of apologising and patting him to ensure he was all right. Who picked his fucking pocket!

Between the three of them, they had less than three pounds in cash and no plastic. The car's petrol gauge was already on the red. Billy, in the passenger seat, pointed out the supermarket car park through the trees to the left, where wagons were parked up for the night. There were also one or two cars visible through the trees.

They drove into the car park. Billy noted the CCTV and motioned for Dennis to park up out of its line of sight. They sat in the car for fifteen minutes, during which time the camera never moved. Billy indicated the Astra parked alone close to a block of flats. They drove slowly towards it and parked alongside. Dennis switched off the ignition and silently handed the keys to Billy. He got out of the car and opened the boot, taking out an empty petrol can, a heavy-duty screwdriver and a length of tube. He knelt at the side of the Astra and prised open the petrol cap cover exposing the cap to the long-bladed screwdriver. It soon succumbed to the pressure and he prised it off. Now for the unpleasant bit. He pushed the rubber tube into the tank, braced himself for the taste of petrol, and sucked. He removed the tube from his mouth, covered the end with his thumb and guided it into the empty can on the ground by his feet, spitting to clear the taste of fuel from his mouth. When the can was full, he emptied it into the tank of Dennis's car, repeating the operation three times. They drove off, leaving Terry's Astra standing in a rainbow pattern of spilt petrol on the tarmac.

****

Andy had already made his move. He'd persuaded the small-time dealers to reveal their suppliers, and he was making his way up the chain of supply towards the big players. He waited nervously with Daz, watching as the dark Mercedes pulled in at the back of the unlit municipal Sports Centre. The four occupants got out and walked towards them. Daz fingered the iron bar tucked under his jacket, knowing that in all probability, if things turned nasty, he'd have to use it. And knowing that it wouldn't be enough. These people would kill him. These people carried guns. He drew a deep breath. He didn't want his little brother to know that for the first time in his life he was genuinely frightened.

"So, you're the guys who've been causing the trouble. Disrupting things on the streets."

The owner of the voice stepped forward into the light. He was powerfully built, expensively dressed, and meant business. Daz attempted to speak, but no sound issued from his dry throat. Instead, Andy stepped forward.

"That's right. This is our patch. If you want to work this area, you deal with us. Nobody else."
"You got money?"
"Enough?"
"You got contacts?"
"Like I said. This is our patch. We control what happens here."
"I like your style. Here's the deal. You buy only from us. You distribute via users. Drip-feeding. Never give any street dealer enough. Make them come back to you. If you find anyone else selling on this patch, eliminate them. You pay me top price, and you get good quality. What you do with it is your concern. Cut it, whatever, that's up to you. In the first month, you buy a Monkey's worth of high grade heroin or coke. Anything else is negotiable. In your second month, you buy seven-fifty's worth of H or C. After six months, if you're not taking three grand's worth then you've failed, and we move you out of the marketplace. Deal?"
"Deal."
"One final thing. If I find out you're buying from anyone else, my boys will come over and surgically remove your arms. Without anaesthetic. Understood?"
"Understood."
"We meet here a week from now. Bring the money."

They watched the Mercedes drive away. Daz was worried. The expression on his pale face showed he was out of his league.

"Christ, Andy. Call it off. You don't want to mess with people like these. They don't take prisoners."
"Neither do I. I'm moving into the big league."
"Get real, Andy. You're not up for this! You're only seventeen, for fuck's sake."
"I'm going for it. I know what I'm doing. Are you with me?"
"I'm not happy about this."
"You will be when you see the sort of money we pull in."
"Just be careful. And don't cross these people."

"Everything's going to be fine. They're businessmen. Once they see we're the works, we're made for life."
"Life imprisonment."
"The easy life!"

He could see Daz was far from convinced. But he needed his big brother on his side. And he needed his assistance to raise the finance for the first deal. He had already formulated his plans, targeting the shopkeepers among the Asian community. Small off-licences and mini-markets, the ones which hadn't installed any security devices, the ones often staffed by one person at particular times; prime targets, easy money. He had made a mental list of likely hits. He and Daz put their plan into action without delay

****

Terry swatted at the alarm clock as it roused him from his deep sleep, eventually managing to press the correct button to silence it. As usual, Linda slept through it, or at least pretended to. Thursday mornings always seemed to be the worst somehow; not quite near enough to the weekend for him to relax and sleep well in the knowledge that he could soon have a lie-in, yet far enough into the week for him to feel totally exhausted. He lay quietly for a while, feeling as if he hadn't yet had enough sleep. Wondering how long he dare lie there, how long it would be before his eyelids closed and he drifted off. It had happened before. Several times. But Linda had always come to his rescue, waking him, reminding him he had to get up. Though she always seemed to be asleep, it was as if some sixth sense alerted her if he was still in bed five minutes after the alarm had rung. Then she would suddenly wake, rouse him, and promptly go back to sleep. But he knew it wasn't fair to rely on Linda. The alarm clock was set early to wake him. To make sure he was up early enough to get to work on time and so avoid any further warnings about his timekeeping. Reluctantly, he got out of bed.

He was half an hour late for work. It could have been worse, but he knew it was bad enough. He'd got in the car and switched on the ignition, staring incredulously at the fuel level dial as it refused to move out of the red. Was it stuck? Or had he actually run out of petrol. That wasn't possible. He'd filled the tank the previous weekend, and it normally lasted a fortnight. He got out of the car and walked around it, noting the petrol spill and the wrecked fuel cap lying under the rear tyre. He was then faced with the decision whether to risk driving straight to work and possibly running out of petrol on the way or driving a couple of miles in the opposite direction to the twenty-four-hour service station. Either way, he was running late, and if he ran out of petrol on the way to work, then potentially he could be very late. He chose the lesser of two evils, going back to the flat to take a ten-pound note from the housekeeping jar in the kitchen. He was glad he did. With the fuel gauge showing empty, he had to free-wheel the final twenty yards or so down the slight incline to the services. But that wasn't the end of it. The engine misfired and lost power several times on the way to work, cutting out when he stopped at junctions. He guessed that sludge and debris from the bottom of the petrol tank was blocking the filter. He'd have to take it in to Salim's again at the weekend. By the time he clocked in, he was thoroughly pissed off, and the summons to Ronnie's office was as expected as the outcome was inevitable. A second written warning. Dismissal was now just a matter of time.

****

It seemed to Brian Peters to have taken an age, but that morning he finally got back the phone he'd sent to Forensics for data recovery, along with a USB stick bearing the recovered files. He inserted the memory stick into a spare port on his PC and watched impatiently as the files downloaded. When the download was complete, he copied the entire file to another memory stick and put it in his jacket pocket. Suspicious by nature, he'd cultivated the habit from years of working in a profession where he habitually encountered dishonesty, lies and treachery, and where he'd learnt to trust nobody until they had earned the right to be trusted. He printed the list of numbers both called from the phone and received, and the flow of messages back and forth, in the twenty-four hours over the New Year. He took the list to Teresa who was more than happy to put it on the top of her pile of work to do.

"Hardcastle's stuff can wait. Yours is more important, Brian."
"Thanks, Teresa. You're a gem. What's he working on?"
"Armed robberies. Off-licences and shops."
"I'm sure he won't be in any hurry."

****

A spate of robberies had started the previous evening and would continue over the next few weeks, the targets being mainly Asian-owned off-licences. The amounts stolen were small, between two and five hundred pounds, but in every case the shopkeeper was threatened with a knife. From descriptions given by the victims, police were sure the same robbers were responsible for each incident. Police patrols were stepped up, and shopkeepers warned to be extra-vigilant. However, the robberies ceased, as suddenly as they'd started.

Andy had his stake money, and more. The robberies had been easy. He'd enjoyed them. The fear in their victims' eyes. The way they had stammered when confronted with the knife. The way one had even wet his trousers. It was Daz who'd persuaded Andy to stop, Daz who'd had the sense to realise that eventually they'd get caught. And Daz who reminded him that the robberies were a means to an end, not an end in themselves. So, they lay low for a while, staying in the flat, and occasionally visiting the pub for a game of pool, but keeping a low profile all the same. Both had their hair cut and dyed and removed their earrings. Andy threw away his beloved baseball cap. He was growing up fast.

"C'mon, Daz. Let's have some fun. Let's do a car."
"No. We do nothing to draw attention to ourselves. From now on, the only time we'll be in a car is when we're doing the delivery rounds."

****

The following morning, Teresa delivered a list of names alongside the associated numbers she'd taken from Brian the previous day. Again, she'd underlined the numbers she thought were significant.

"Messages to and from the deceased girl. And later, a call to his mother. Looks a bit suspicious to me."
"Thanks, Teresa. I'll look at these straightaway."
"And then go and arrest the little bugger."
"Hope so."

Dated New Year's Eve, there were three messages from Dean Donachie's phone, and three responses from Amanda Braithwaite. Brian read them out to Lynn and Gary.

"8.15pm – from Amanda
have u got it yet?
8.20pm - reply from Dean
going for it now.
8.22pm – Amanda again
OK. soon as u can. she's gone out.
10.57pm – Dean again
got it
11.00pm – Amanda
how long?
11.35pm – Dean
B there about 12.30. Sum good coke 4 u. D."

Brian had that smug look he always wore when one of his hunches had been proven correct.

"There we are. There's a positive link between the deceased and her drug dealer. A link that Dean Donachie denied existed. Now, here's where the plot thickens."

He read out the text of another message.

"she wants some coke from u."

"That message was sent from her flatmate's phone to Donachie early on New Year's Eve. Her flatmate, who denied Amanda took drugs, had acted as go-between. Bring her in and get a statement. Frighten her a bit. The usual. Just find out what she knows."
"OK, boss."
"What about you?"
"I'll find Donachie."

Before his colleagues had left the office, Brian was on the phone to Kenny Collins. No response. He tried the number for reception, and was informed Kenny was still off sick, but was expected back on Monday. He looked frantically through his case notes, found what he wanted and scribbled down Dean Donachie's address. Then, before he left the office, he pored over the list Teresa had provided. There it was. An address for Donna Donachie, Dean's mother. He phoned his wife to tell her he'd be late home.

Dean Donachie had a flat in Undercliffe. It was part of a larger Victorian property which had, in its heyday, been occupied by a wool merchant and his family. It had once been a highly desirable property, with views over the park, and beyond, over the whole city. However, it had seen better days, and had eventually been bought by a property developer who'd converted it into four flats to rent in the 1960s. It had undergone further cosmetic changes over the years and been bought and sold several times. Dean had Flat 1 – the basement. Brian rang the bell several times but got no response. He squatted to look through the uncleaned windows but there were no lights shining from within. He could see nothing. As he stood up, a man emerged from the ground floor flat. Brian walked up to him, ID in hand.

"Excuse me, sir."
"Yes?"
"Do you know the young man who lives downstairs?"
"I've seen him occasionally. Never spoken to him. Why?"
"Just routine. When did you last see him?"
"A couple of weeks ago. He keeps funny hours. I don't think he works. Well, at least not in the conventional sense."
"Seen any visitors?"
"Only one."
"Could you describe him?"
"Early forties, I guess. Wearing a suit and tie. Dark hair. Clean shaven. About six feet tall. Medium build."
"Anything else you can tell me?"
"Not really. I keep to myself. Mind my own business."
"Thank you, sir. You've been a great help."

Brian was not convinced he had been of any real help. The description he'd given would fit a sizeable proportion of the male population. But, at the same time, it would *eliminate* a great number of people. Then he had a lightbulb moment.

"Just one last question, sir."
"Yes?"
"Who is your landlord?"
"I don't know who owns the building, but we all pay rent to a management company."
"Not by any chance Bateman and Robinson?"
"Yes, that's right."

Brian put Dean's phone in a padded envelope, sealed it and pushed the package through Dean's letterbox.

That was a long shot, he thought. But there's a link between the Eccleshill flats, where Amanda Braithwaite lived, and here, where Dean Donachie lives. And Dean and Amanda knew each other. He needed to find out who actually owned both properties. It was too late in the day to contact the Estate Agents, Bateman and Robinson. That would have to wait until Monday, unless, of course, he and his wife just happened to be in the Idle area on Saturday.

It was a long drive in heavy rain through rush hour traffic, but eventually Brian's Satnav directed him to take a right turn as he drove through Sandbeds. He sat in a queue of traffic waiting to cross the canal by the swing bridge as a couple of narrowboats chugged through. Finally, he was driving uphill through East Morton, wondering if the address was correct. This was not the sort of area he expected the single mother of a drug dealer to live in. He had envisioned a high rise on a council estate. But not this. He pulled up outside a stone-built detached house on the outskirts of the village, got out of the car and walked to the door. There was a two-year-old Mercedes on the drive, but apparently no-one at home. He went back to his car and waited.

Upstairs, in the back bedroom with the blinds drawn, Donna Donachie sat motionless, staring at the images on the screen, beamed directly from the CCTV cameras discreetly positioned around the house and garden. She didn't recognise the man in the car but would ensure the images were saved so her partner could look at them later. It was likely he would recognise the caller; he knew a lot of people, many of them bad people, which is why she never answered the door to unexpected callers.

Brian looked at his watch. He'd been there almost an hour. He got out of the car and knocked on the front door once more. No response. That was expected. That was not the reason he was standing at the door. He expected there would be security cameras on a property of this type and wanted to make sure that his smiling image was clearly captured for the benefit of the owner.

He returned to his car and drove off.

CHAPTER 13

Saturday dawned cold and bright. Just the sort of day, Brian mentioned to Sarah over breakfast, when they should take a look at some of the local home and garden businesses in the Idle area, after having another look around their new home and planning modifications to the layout of the garden.

"I don't understand why you've suddenly developed such an interest in gardening, Brian."
"I just thought it would be good for me. Help me relax."
"More likely you want to dump me and Daniel at some crummy garden centre while you work on one of your cases."
"You know how it is, Sarah. It's not a nine-to-five job."
"I know. You do what you have to do. Just try to be home before tea."
"It won't take long."
"But it can't wait until Monday?"
"I'd rather it didn't."
"Off you go, then."

Sarah knew there was no point in arguing. She knew the demands of the job. She also knew that it could be a marriage-wrecker but was determined that it wouldn't wreck theirs. Their relationship remained strong, and she accepted that, at times, the job came first. It was simply how it was, and over the years, she had learnt to cope with it. Besides, now heavily pregnant, she'd rather spend the weekend planning for their new arrival.

Brian wasted no time. He called the Estate Agent, waiting impatiently for an answer.

"Come on. Pick up!"

Then after what seemed several minutes, the voice of the Junior Salesperson with her far-too-cheerful greeting.

"Good morning. Bateman and Robinson. How can I help you?"
"DS Brian Peters here. Let me speak to one of the partners. Please."
"Oh, I'm afraid they're both out at the moment."
"When will someone be back?"

"Late afternoon, most likely."

"Give me their phone numbers, please."

"I'm sorry, I'm not authorised to do that, sir."

"I'm authorising you now."

"I'm sorry, sir...."

"Listen. Give me their numbers. Do it now, or else I'll have you arrested for obstructing a police officer in the execution of his duty."

"Oh. Just a minute, sir."

And after a short silence.

"Eric Bateman here. How can I help you, DS Peters?"

"You were in the office all the time?"

"Yes. I ask not to be disturbed at times, I'm afraid."

"Well, sir. I'm sorry if I'm disturbing you but I require some information about some of the properties you manage."

"What do you need to know?"

"Who owns the Eccleshill flats?"

"The block you asked me about last time?"

"Yes."

"They have a number of different owners, sir. Most are owner-occupied."

"What about the rented ones?"

"Again, some were bought from the developer, and sold on, or rented out."

"Braithwaite and Armstrong. Number 25."

"Let me have a look. Here we are. That one is owned by a company, DPH Holdings, plc."

"What about Webb Drive. Flat 1, number 24?"

"Let's have a look... Same again, DPH."

"OK. Can you print me a list of the properties you manage on behalf of DPH?"

"I'm not sure if that's permitted under our agreement with DPH."

"I'm permitting you now. I also want a copy of any documents relating to your relationship with them. And before you say anything, if you don't produce them, I'll have you arrested for obstruction."

"Do you have a warrant?"

"No, but I can soon get one. Then I'll be back with a shitload of officers. We'll come in the middle of the day when plenty of people will be able to see us raiding your premises and tearing the place apart. I don't think that will be very good for business, do you?"

"I'll just get copies printed for you."

"Thank you for your co-operation, sir. I'll be there within the hour."

True to his word, Brian set off immediately and was pleased to find the documents he'd demanded were ready for him to collect. He thanked Mr Bateman for his compliance, took the file of papers and drove down to HQ. Arriving there, he was happy to note the absence of cars in the car park, meaning he was unlikely to be disturbed. Sure enough, the office was empty. He switched on his PC and logged on. While waiting for the system to load, he flicked through the A4 sheets. As soon as his system was ready for input, he opened the Criminal Records Database and searched for DPH. There were no results.

That doesn't mean they're clean, he reminded himself. It just means they've not been caught yet. He tried Google.

Bingo! DPH Holdings, Inc., importer and exporter. Registered at Companies House. No financial figures recorded for the past two years. Registered business address, Broadway House, York. Managing director: D Donachie. He made notes of the details he'd gathered. And underneath, wrote

Shell company? Money laundering?

He found himself doodling on his notepad, absent-mindedly, as he thought. He'd written the names 'Amanda Braithwaite' and 'Dean Donachie', with a thick black line linking them. Then he added 'DPH'.

"Amanda and Dean knew each other. The phone records established that much. Dean was a drug dealer. In all probability, he supplied the cocaine which caused Amanda's death. Dean then rang his mother, Donna, who lives in an expensive house. Unless Dean is a big-time dealer, someone else is paying for that house. Who?"

He underlined 'DPH' on his notepad, then typed 'Donna Donachie' into the database. There was quite an extensive history, but all low-level crime. Shoplifting, prostitution, drug use, drunk and disorderly, right from her teenage years. But nothing at all for the past five years. Turned over a new leaf? He didn't think so. She was still getting money from somewhere. He made a note to ask

Teresa to look up Donna's employment history and her benefits record on Monday. Then, he'd head off to York to call on DPH Holdings. He wanted to find out if D Donachie, the director, was Dean or Donna. Not that it really mattered. He would have bet his life on it. D Donachie is just the name on the registration form. Someone else is running the business.

He hoped Monday would bring him some answers.

****

Mark was confused. His vision of love, the naive way in which he'd mapped out his future with Sharon, had started to undergo subtle changes. He hadn't changed, but Sharon had. She was moody. It wasn't just sex now; their relationship, or at least that was how he saw it, had moved on, reached a higher plane. He didn't know whether this was how things were supposed to be. He still loved her. He was sure he did. And she loved him. He was sure of that too, despite what some of his mates were saying. What did they know? They hadn't been through it. Some of them were still virgins, for Christ's sake. However much they boasted, they'd never had more than a wank. He was sure of that. Never mind what all the surveys said about teenage sex. The statistics were compiled from interviews with teenagers. And how many teenage lads would admit to their virginity? And how many would greatly exaggerate the extent of their sexual experience?

But Sharon was moody. The focus of their relationship had shifted. It wasn't fun anymore. Sharon had hinted they should get engaged; not publicly, not with a blatant display of undying commitment to each other, but simply by a mutual vow to stick by each other, whatever the future may hold. He'd agreed, figuring that when two people were in love, whatever decisions they took together were a matter for them only. He guessed his parents would disapprove. They didn't know the extent of his relationship with Sharon. They didn't even know it was a sexual relationship, only that their son was dating a girl called Sharon. So, they were unlikely to sanction a hugely expensive engagement bash for a girl they'd never met.

And then she'd dropped the bombshell. She was pregnant. She'd told him immediately after handing him a tissue upon the conclusion of a quick blow-job. Mark's emotion swung wildly between elation and despair, and now, a week later, he was in torment. His friends, and some of hers, were urging him to back off. He was making a terrible mistake. It wasn't his! That was the overwhelming consensus of opinion. She's a slag! Stay clear, Mark. Cut yourself loose. It's not yours, Mark. It'll probably be black anyway, and how are you going to explain that to your parents? She's shagged everybody in town, Mark. Yeah, he thought, everybody but you. You're jealous, that's all. Because you're not getting it. And I get it regularly. And you're jealous! That's all there is to it.

All the same, seeds of doubt were now firmly planted in his mind, and the more he brooded alone, the more those doubts seemed to be taking root, growing, soon to burst into the light, spread their leaves, flower and propagate. It was no use. They'd have to talk. He'd have to put his feelings aside and be objective. Express his concerns, and those of his friends. And he was sure, absolutely certain, that his fears, his misgivings, would be unfounded. He paced his small bedroom, carefully rehearsing the words he would say when he saw her tomorrow. He was convinced she'd have an answer to his concerns. It was his. She'd tell him it was his baby, and he'd believe her. It was just a vicious lie which had been fed back to him that a practice nurse who'd examined her at the clinic had told Sharon's friend's mother how far advanced her pregnancy was. It was a lie. Or a mistake. Yet he had to admit that if it were true, then even he, with his supercharged teenage libido, would be hard-pressed to have impregnated his girlfriend two months before he met her.

****

Gary was already at his desk when Brian arrived at work on Monday morning. He couldn't wait to give his report.

"I spoke to Vicky Armstrong on Friday. She admitted she was a recreational drug user, and that she'd talked Amanda into trying coke. She says they were going to use it together, but then she got invited to a party in Leeds on New Year's Eve. She told me Amanda was upset because she'd nowhere to go, so decided to get high on her own. So, Vicky asked Dean to take her a fix. She says she had no idea it would do her any harm. She said Dean's coke was always cut. Actually, I believe her."
"OK, Gary. Thanks. When Lynn gets in, will the two of you try to

trace Dean and bring him in for questioning. I'm guessing he's in hiding. So, what I suggest is you get your friend Vicky to send him a text asking to meet and bring her some coke. And when he turns up, grab him."

"You're assuming he's picked up his phone from his flat."

"I hope he has."

"OK, I'll do that."

"Thanks. I'm going to York. I'll be back before lunch."

"What's at York?"

"The Minster, lots of museums. And the registered office of DPH Holdings, whose managing director is D Donachie."

"Not *the* D Donachie?"

"One of them."

By the time Brian had found a parking space within walking distance of the office block he was visiting, the light flurry of snow which had followed him from Bradford had blown itself out and the city was bathed in cold sunshine. The weather didn't seem to bother the hordes of tourists who came pouring out of coaches and blocking the pavements while they posed for their selfies. He managed to navigate a path between them without having to show his ID. Most of these tourists, many from the Far East, wouldn't know what it was anyway. They would probably think it was some novelty souvenir, grin widely, and ask 'How much?'

He looked at the board in the unmanned reception, and walked up to the third floor, the lift having a quickly-scribbled 'Out of Order' notice taped to the panel. He found what he had expected – an open office where large, locked mail boxes were stacked the length of the far wall. One of them bore a sticker with 'DPH Holdings, Inc.' typed on it. That was all it was. A mail drop.

Might as well act like a tourist, he said quietly, taking a snap of the box on his phone.

Before he'd got back to the car park at HQ, he'd heard the sound of a message reaching his phone and, expecting it to be from one of his colleagues, displayed it as soon as he'd switched off the ignition. He was pleasantly surprised to find it was from Sarah.

"Moving 6 wks on Wed. Book day off. Sarah xxx."

He went past his office and up the stairs to Teresa's desk.

"Morning, Teresa."

"Morning, Brian."

"I thought I'd better sort this before I forget. Can I book some time off, please?"

"You tired of us already?"

"No. Just got the date for moving house. Can you book me three days, please? April 11 to 13."

"I'll do it now and pass it straight to DCI Moseley to approve."

"Thanks."

"No problem. How are the open cases going?"

"Slow progress."

"Well, if you need anything, you can always count on my help."

"Thanks. I appreciate it. Actually, you could get me a number for the Fraud Squad."

"I didn't know you had any fraud cases open."

"I'd just like to know if they have anything on a company whose name has come up in the course of the Eccleshill case."

"Give me the company name and I'll make some enquiries for you."

"DPH Holdings, Inc."

"I'll see what I can find out."

Back in his office, he'd just sat down at his desk when Gary and Lynn walked in.

"Good news, boss. We spoke to Vicky and stood at her side while she texted Donachie. He responded. He's going to call at her flat this evening. Seven o'clock."

"Good work. Where's Vicky now?"

"Interview room. Don't worry. We've taken her phone."

"Good. Don't want her tipping him off. Cancel any arrangements you have for this evening. You'll both be on duty, I'm afraid."

"No problem."

"Me neither."

"I'll want the two of you outside the flats. When you see him enter, follow him in. I'll be waiting in the flat with Vicky."

"I'll be looking forward to this."

"We'll keep Vicky here as long as we can, then I'll take her home and stay with her. I expect her solicitor will want her released as soon as possible, but I want to keep an eye on her until we've got Donachie safely in custody. Now let's get Vicky interviewed."

The 'interview' was a sham, in effect, simply to ensure she didn't tip Dean off that he was walking into a trap. Brian, however, used the time to inform Vicky that they had the power to confiscate her phone and recover any deleted data should they believe it had been used to jeopardise the investigation, and she would face a charge of attempting to pervert the course of justice, which offence carries a maximum penalty of life imprisonment. Once Vicky heard that statement, her face drained of colour.

Shortly before five o'clock, Vicky was being escorted from the building as DI Hardcastle walked in. He stopped Brian in the corridor.

"Isn't that the girl who lives in Eccleshill? The flatmate of the dead girl?"
"That's right."
"I thought you would have dropped that by now. It's a dead case."
"New evidence."
"Really? Like what?"
"I'll tell you later. I'm in a bit of a rush just now."

So, he's still taking an interest in this 'dead case', Brian thought. Maybe it's not that dead yet.

They held their positions until a little after eight, Brian in the flat with Vicky, Gary and Lynn in the car out in the street. There had been no sign of Dean. Vicky's phone had been in Brian's possession since Gary passed it to him. She hadn't been able to use it since she sent the message to arrange for Dean to visit. Brian handed her the phone.

"Send him another text. Tell him you need the coke urgently. Ask him where he is."

Brian watched as she did exactly as she was instructed. He dismissed Gary and Lynn but stayed a further hour just in case. But there was no response from Dean, despite a further message sent at Brian's insistence. Finally, he admitted defeat.

"He's not coming. Either he hasn't got access to his phone for some reason, or someone is preventing him from coming. Or he suspects it's a set-up. I'm going home, Vicky. If he turns up, call me on this number immediately."

She nodded agreement, and he left. It had been a long day, but by the time he got home it was a little late for a full meal, so he settled for a chicken sandwich, washed down with a large glass of Glenlivet – real, authentic Glenlivet, purchased at the supermarket on his way home.

CHAPTER 14

Terry couldn't sleep. He glanced at the alarm clock on the bedside table. Two-fifteen. It was no use. He'd have to get up, just to set his mind at rest. He slipped quietly out of bed without disturbing Linda and tiptoed into the bathroom. He closed the door and felt for the cord. He blinked in the bright light, catching sight of his unshaven sallow face in the cabinet mirror. He dressed wearily and left the flat.

Hunched against the cold, he let out a long breath of relief. The car was still there. Now perhaps he could get back to sleep. He turned back towards the flats, then stopped, did an about-turn and walked towards the car. He wasn't satisfied until he'd walked right round it, checking the bodywork for fresh damage, checking the tyres hadn't been let down, checking the fuel line was intact, checking the doors were locked and the alarm was set. It was becoming an obsession. But getting up in the middle of the night was now an established ritual. It gave him peace of mind, even if only briefly. Something caught his eye. A movement. A dark shape emerging from the bushes. An animal, trotting across the car park some thirty yards away. It stopped and stared at him, then trotted off into the night. It was the first time Terry had ever seen a fox. He went back inside, undressed in the bathroom, laying out his clothes for the morning, and slipped into bed.

The car park was quiet now, but two hours earlier Daz and Andy, craving excitement, had broken a rear quarterlight of an old Suzuki, hot-wired the ignition and driven away, heading towards Oakland.

As they turned off the roundabout down the unmade road which led to the fields, the car's headlights picked out a Jag. A gleaming bronze XJ12, parked at the roadside. Daz knew nobody would have just left it there. There had to be someone inside. He drove past and turned around further down the road. He gunned the engine, selected first, raised the clutch and accelerated hard. The tyres spun, burning rubber, then gripped and the Suzuki snaked forward gathering speed as Daz changed up. He side-swiped the Jag, then brought the Suzuki to a skidding halt twenty yards away, slewing it round again so that its headlights shone directly on the Jag.

"Look at that, Andy. Fuckin' 'ell!"

A man's bald head appeared in the back window of the Jag. He looked confused and embarrassed. The reason soon became obvious, when a woman's head appeared next to him. Her hair was dishevelled; her upper body naked. Daz edged the Suzuki forward for a closer look and switched the headlights to full beam. As the Jag's passengers raised their hands to shield their eyes, Andy squealed with delight.

"Look at them tits, Daz!"

The woman's naked upper body was exposed to their gaze. She ducked immediately out of view, shaking with embarrassment and fear.

Daz reversed at speed back to the roundabout, executed a handbrake turn, and raced down the slip road to the dual carriageway.

Two miles further down, he brought the car to a halt, broadside on, across both lanes. Andy jumped out and plunged the blade of his knife into each tyre, while Daz gobbed a wad of phlegm on to the rear-view mirror. They scrambled up the embankment and hid in the bushes, watching as traffic came upon the abandoned Suzuki and took evasive action to avoid it. They slipped away in the darkness as a police car came on the scene, resisting the temptation to watch the two burly officers struggling to push the car off the carriageway, cursing its flat tyres.

Arriving home, they skipped supper, though reluctantly. The old whore was ill. She lay moaning on the ancient threadbare settee, holding her stomach and muttering obscenities. Beside her were four cans of cheap supermarket lager, three of them empty. Between them they drained the fourth, but their mood was subdued. Instead of their usual raucous behaviour in the flat, they sat quietly, watching their mother as she dozed fitfully. They were worried. Andy resolved to call a doctor if she was no better in the morning.

****

Linda woke suddenly, feeling a chill at her back. She turned over sleepily and felt for Terry. She was alone in bed, again. She looked at the clock. 3.45. She sighed, knowing where he'd be. What did they call it? Obsessive Compulsion Disorder. Compulsive Obsession Disorder. Whatever. She knew he'd got up again to check the car. It happened almost every night now. It was all he thought about. He didn't give a damn about his job, their deteriorating relationship - they hadn't had sex since before the funeral - or anything really. Linda had done her best. She knew he was under pressure, with problems at work compounded by his father's death. But his obsession with the car, well, she couldn't quite take it. The way she saw it, he was transferring his problems, his worries, his concerns, to his car. It was his way of dealing with his father's death. She'd have to let him get it out of his system. Be there for him. Help him deal with it. But he kept shutting her out, making it difficult for her to help. She pulled the duvet tight round her shoulders, turned over and snuggled deep into its warmth. To hell with him, she thought. Get a grip, Terry!

Terry was in the car park, fully dressed though shod in his slippers. He'd already checked the car. It was fine. The night was silent. Cold, and with a full moon in a cloudless sky, a heavy frost had formed on the car's glass. Nobody would steal a car on a night like this, he knew. Twenty seconds to break in and start the engine, then five minutes to clear the windscreen. It wasn't a viable proposition. Nevertheless, he strode back to the car, and walked round it to the passenger door, checking all the locks on the way. Finally, he bent close to the passenger window and breathed on the glass, rubbing away the frost. Eventually thawing a small round area of glass, he pressed his face against it, cupping his hands round his temples to blot out the moonlight. He relaxed and stepped back once he'd seen the reassuring rhythmic blink of the intruder alarm. He yawned and trudged back to the flat.

****

It had been gnawing at Brian all night. He'd slept fitfully. He had come to the conclusion that, for reasons best known to himself, Hardcastle had brought the investigation to a premature close. To Brian, though, there was clearly more to it, more unanswered questions. He was determined to chase the truth, wherever it led him.

He was at work early, again, but was pleased to note his two colleagues were already at their desks. His first job, though, after greeting Gary and Lynn, was to see if Teresa's research had brought any results. He phoned to ensure she was at her desk, then went upstairs for a briefing.

"Morning, Brian. Not much luck, I'm afraid. DPH Holdings haven't filed any accounts after a couple of years in existence. It looks very much like a shell company. Could possibly be used for money laundering. Fraud squad have nothing on it, but if you find anything, they'd be grateful if you could pass it on to them."
"So, no leads at all?"
"No. Sometimes, the company name gives some sort of clue as to its purpose, so I've been trying that angle. DP could be Data Processing, Digital Photography, Direct Parcels, that sort of thing."
"Well, thanks for trying, Teresa. Don't spend any more time on it. I guess it's a dead end."

He was walking away when Teresa's next words brought him to an abrupt halt.

"It could even be Daniel Patrick Hardcastle."
"What?"
"DPH. DI Hardcastle's full name is Daniel Patrick Hardcastle."
"Teresa, you're a genius! I could kiss you."
"Better not. It would be bad for my image. People would talk."

Back at his desk, he was deep in thought. This could be the breakthrough. It would explain a lot of things. Why Hardcastle was constantly telling him the case should be closed, but still asking if there was any progress. He took out his notepad and started a list.

1. Hardcastle had headed the initial investigation.
2. Crime scene was clean. If Amanda had been alone when she died, there would have been coke residue somewhere. None found. Who cleaned it?
3. Phone messages had been deleted from Dean's and Amanda's phones.
4. Vicky denied any knowledge initially.
5. Dean, Amanda and Vicky all did drugs.
6. Dean's mother in expensive house.
7. Link Dean and mother to DPH. Director?

He flicked back through his notepad till he found what he was looking for. There it was: Dean's neighbour's description of Dean's visitor.

"Early forties, I guess. Wearing a suit and tie. Dark hair. Clean shaven. About six feet tall. Medium build."

It was a tenuous connection, but the description certainly fitted Hardcastle. It would explain a lot of things.

He wrote again on his notepad the possible sequence of events surrounding Amanda's death.

Amanda was alone.
Dean brought coke and was there when she snorted it. If she *was* a first-time user, he would show her how to do it.
He panicked when she died and phoned his mother.
She told DPH. Was he with her at the time?
DPH went to Eccleshill and sanitised the flat. Destroyed evidence.
Deleted incriminating phone messages and went home.
Does he have a key?
Took charge of case and found nothing. Not surprising!
So, what is DPH's relationship with Dean's mother? Director – business only, or more?

Time for a team meeting, he decided, picking up the phone.

"Teresa, what time's your lunch?"
"One till two, normally. But I'm flexible."
"Good. Can you join me, Lynn and Gary for a meeting away from here?"
"OK."
"Good. I'll set it up with the others and let you know where and when. And Teresa, not a word to anybody."
"Understood."

Discreetly, he sent a brief text message to his colleagues.

They met in a coffee shop in the Broadway Centre, ordered sandwiches and coffee – Brian paid the bill – and sat at a corner table at the back where they couldn't be seen by anyone passing by outside. As they ate, Brian laid out his theory.

"I'm happy with the verdict of misadventure, but I'm certain there's been a cover-up. This is how I see it. Vicky told us that she and Amanda intended to do some coke together at New Year. Then Vicky was invited to a party in Leeds. Amanda decided to try it anyway. We know Dean Donachie was there and brought the coke. And since we are almost certain that Amanda was a first-time user, someone had to show her what to do. Dean would have arranged the lines for her to snort. When she died unexpectedly, Dean panicked and phoned his mother. She got someone to go around and clean up so that her son would not be incriminated. Hardcastle, I believe, was the man. He destroyed the evidence – there was no sign of any coke residue on any surface, as you would expect to find. No prints were found. Phone messages were deleted. And the door was locked. It is quite feasible that the owner of the flat would have a set of keys. It is also quite logical that a serving police officer would know what evidence you would expect to find at a crime scene, and therefore would be careful to remove it if it could possibly incriminate him or his 'acquaintances'.

I believe Hardcastle is the owner of the property, acting under the company name of DPH Holdings, which we believe is a shell company. A man fitting Hardcastle's description was seen entering Donachie's flat recently. At the moment, that's about it."

"So, where do we go from here?"

"We need to prove that Hardcastle and Donna Donachie, Dean's mother, are linked. We know that she is living in a large detached house in a rural area but doesn't work. The house is owned by DPH, and I would expect that Hardcastle stays there at least part-time, although Teresa informs me the home address on his file is in Allerton. I want him followed when he's off duty. I want usable evidence that he's seeing Donna. Also, I want Dean found. I think Hardcastle tipped him off. He saw Vicky at the station and guessed we were trying to lure Dean out into the open. That would explain why Dean didn't respond to Vicky's texts."

"What do you want us to do?"

"First and foremost, don't breathe a word of this to anyone else. This stays with the four of us. Understood?"

They all nodded agreement before Gary said what they'd all been thinking.

"Since this is highly secretive, then we can't claim any overtime, because that would mean telling Muesli the purpose."

"That's correct. When, and only when, we prove our case will you then be able to claim overtime retrospectively."

"Personally, I'll work for nothing if I can help put that bastard Hardcastle behind bars."

"I appreciate that, Teresa. But you will get paid. Eventually."

"Fair enough. I guess we're all in. I'm sure each of us has a reason to despise Hardcastle."

"Let's try to keep it professional. As far as I'm concerned, he's committed a crime, so he needs to be punished. But I've a feeling it's something bigger than just a matter of destroying evidence."

****

Teresa volunteered to be first on the surveillance rota. She successfully argued that her car would be difficult to identify as she was never allowed to park it at work, so few people knew what sort of car she drove. Since parking spaces were at a premium, only serving officers were given permits. As a civilian assistant, Teresa had to park in a public car park a few hundred yards away. Ten minutes before the official end of Hardcastle's shift, she was in position to see his car leave the HQ car park and head towards Allerton. She followed in her Mini at a discreet distance, stopping at the end of his road but keeping his car in sight until it turned into the driveway of his house, which, according to the notes she had, he occupied alone. She waited. A little over an hour later, she watched him emerge accompanied by a young man. She took an image on her phone and sent it to Brian Peters, then put the car in gear and followed Hardcastle and his companion as they drove away in Hardcastle's Vauxhall Insignia. They drove through Wilsden and Harden, before turning down towards Bingley and from there towards East Morton. Teresa knew where they were headed, having been well briefed by Brian. She managed to take another snap as they entered the house when its occupant opened the door for them. She sent the image to Brian and waited. In less than half an hour, Brian called her.

"Good work, Teresa. The images are clear. The young man is Dean Donachie, without a doubt. The woman bears a strong resemblance to the images on police file for Donna Donachie. You can go home. Job done. We'll talk tomorrow."

Teresa drove all the way home wearing the widest grin she could remember.

Sometimes, she thought, I *really* love my job.

****

The following morning, Brian plucked up the courage to take his suspicions to DCI Moseley. He wasn't sure what reception he would get, but felt obliged to inform his superior officer, and proceed as he instructed. As he passed Teresa's desk, she mouthed 'Good luck'.

DCI Moseley listened intently without interrupting as Brian detailed his findings, deciding it would be more prudent to get his superior's reaction to that before expressing his suspicions of Hardcastle's further criminal activity. Moseley's response was measured, and much as Brian had feared.

"These are very serious allegations, Brian. Hardcastle is a long-serving officer with a good record. I hope the fact that the two of you don't seem to see eye-to-eye isn't affecting your judgment."
"With respect, sir. I feel there is enough in this report for matters to be investigated further. Would you be prepared to pass it on to the Professional Standards Department?"
"Leave it with me for now, Brian. Let me think about it. Unless you are 100% correct in what you've told me, and also in your suspicions, you could cost a good man his career and his reputation, at the least."
"I understand, sir."
"And, Brian."
"Yes, sir?"
"Concentrate on the cases I have entrusted to you. You and your team have no right to go off on a tangent and follow your own agenda. This isn't CTU. We're a little less gung-ho here. We have to be. We're more visible in the way we deal with matters. We're more accountable."
"Yes, sir."

Brian was disappointed but could understand Moseley's reaction. The Professional Standards Department had ruined many a career of many a good officer. However, they'd also brought to account a number of corrupt officers. He needed a discreet team meeting. He sent a quick text for Lynn, Gary and Teresa to meet him in the Broadway Centre, as before.

It was a sombre meeting. Any euphoria they'd previously experienced rapidly evaporated as Brian related the story of his meeting that morning.

"The thing is, he's right. All the evidence we've uncovered so far, although it adds up to major criminal activity, is merely suspicion. A good lawyer could easily pick apart the individual elements as just that, mere suspicion. And there's always the fact that I used an unauthorised technician to recover data from Amanda Braithwaite's phone. That evidence could be deemed inadmissible. We need some hard evidence."

CHAPTER 15

The snow, which had started to fall the previous day, continued to fall heavily through the night. Brian studied the weather forecast and decided it would be time-consuming and stressful to join the commuters into Bradford. From his house, it was a shorter distance to the destination he had in mind, and as long as the roads were passable, he decided to give it a try. He called to arrange his visit, then left a message at HQ stating he was stranded due to the weather and hoped to be in later. He packed the boot of the car with his emergency kit – shovel, squares of old carpet for grip, blanket and a flask of hot coffee. He made sure his mobile was fully charged and dressed as warmly as he could. Then he was off, pulling out of the drive on to the road outside covered with undisturbed virgin snow. He was fortunate; his tyres gripped and he was able to drive away steadily in low gear and turn into the almost empty main road towards Wakefield. Progress was slow though, mainly due to the number of motorists who had set off ill-prepared and had to abandon their car at the roadside, but Brian continued with few alarms until, twenty-five minutes later, he pulled up on the road outside the bungalow. He changed into his boots and walked to the door which opened as he approached.

"It's good to see you, Brian. Come in and get warm."
"Thanks, boss. It's good to see you too."
"Less of the 'boss', Brian. It's Don now."
"Of course. Old habits. Let me take my boots off."

He followed Don McArthur into a warm lounge where his wife sat quietly by the fire, a blanket over her legs.

"Janet, we have a visitor. You remember Brian?"

She looked up wearily and nodded.

"Hello again, Janet. It's good to see you."
"Brian and I will go into the kitchen, Janet. We have business to discuss. We won't be long."

Again, she nodded. Don ushered Brian into the kitchen where they sat at the table.

"Don, I was really sorry to hear about Janet's stroke. Is she getting any better at all?"

"A little, yes. It's too early to say how far her recovery will take her, but it's scuppered our plans to retire to Spain, I'm afraid."

"I know the pair of you were really looking forward to it."

"We were. We were just on the point of booking a holiday when she took ill. It came out of the blue. Knocked us both for six. Anyway, Brian, what is it I can do for you?"

"Well, I'm wondering if you can call in any favours. I need to get hold of enough hard evidence to put away a dirty cop."

"I take it you've been to your new boss and he's told you your evidence is not sufficient for a successful prosecution?"

"Exactly. All it amounts to is suspicion. But, I *know*, Don. I just *know* he's corrupt. I just need one piece of hard evidence to tip the case."

"Give me his name. I'll make some inquiries. But first, tell me what you've got. Then we'll have a chat. I want to know how you're doing in your new environment. I believe Lynn's joined you?"

"Yes. She's doing well. I've also got a young officer, Gary Ryan. Very keen. He'll work out well. And there's a civilian clerical officer called Teresa Shackleton...."

"Mrs Semtex?"

"How do you know that?"

"I was once at a conference when I got into conversation with a CID officer from Bradford. He told me about her. Now, what was his name?"

"Hardcastle?"

"Hardcastle. That's the man. I didn't like his attitude. Too big for his boots."

"He's the man I want to cut down to size."

"In that case, I'll do everything I can to help, Brian. Tell me the full story."

An hour later, Brian shook Don's hand at the door, pulled on his boots and left the warmth of the bungalow in exchange for the fierce wind and driving snow. Don had agreed to call in some favours but reminded Brian he couldn't solve the case for him.

"I can probably get you more data, Brian. But that's all it is. Raw data. Hearsay, even. But it may take you further. You'll still have to connect the dots and make a coherent argument."

Brian took the rest of the day off. He had started to make his way back to Bradford but was getting nowhere fast so he went home and worked from there, keeping contact with the rest of his team electronically. Only Teresa had made it into work and was not surprised to find the office practically empty. However, without the habitual constant interruptions, she was able to get through a mountain of work unimpeded. She only picked up the phone whenever she recognised Brian's number; all others went ignored.

Brian was on the point of calling it a day when his phone pinged to indicate an incoming message. It was from Don.

"Martin R expecting u in morning. He's lending u D.E.G. Will tell u what to do. D."

What the hell is a D.E.G? Brian had no idea but was looking forward to a trip down to Bradford University in the morning all the same. Whatever it was, if Don had set it up, it had to be useful.

****

It had snowed again throughout the night, but nevertheless Brian was up early and fully prepared for what he was certain would be an arduous journey into Bradford. He was right, but fortunately only the brave, and none of the foolish, drivers seemed to have attempted the trip. Either that, he thought, or they would be setting off at their usual time, having failed to factor in the extra time required to cope with the conditions. As it was, he arrived at the University without incident, although driving at snail's pace. The car park was practically empty, though few spaces had been cleared of snow. It made no difference to Brian. He simply parked as near as possible to the entrance. He was impatient to see what Martin had for him.

But he had to be patient. When he reached the Lab, there was a message awaiting him. Martin Riley was making his way to work on foot and was not expected before ten o'clock. Brian waited in the canteen, warming his hands on a mug of tea. In time, a weary Martin trudged in, shaking snow from his boots.

"Sorry to keep you, Brian. It was a long walk."
"How far?"
"Allerton."
"Well, thanks for coming in. I appreciate it."

"So you should. I was informed in no uncertain terms that I was not authorised to undertake any work for you."

"Who told you that?"

"A DCI Moseley. Your new boss, I assume."

"Of course. I should have known. But this is off the record, Martin. I don't know what Don told you."

"Nothing, except for explaining a purely hypothetical situation where someone might want to see what's in another person's phone memory without their knowledge and without having to bring it here."

"And, hypothetically, it can be done?"

"Certainly! It's what I call a D.E.G. - a data extraction gizmo. I programmed it myself. Basically, it's a memory stick – with a difference. It's got interchangeable connectors, so it fits almost any phone, and once it's connected, it's programmed to read everything in the phone's memory and copy it on to the memory stick. Then you just disconnect it, plug the stick into a PC and it will show a menu, so you can download the data, or whatever."

"How long does it take?"

"To copy? Between five and ten minutes, depending on the phone."

"So, if someone left their phone unattended for ten minutes, they would never know their data had been read and copied?"

"Precisely!"

"And you've got one for me?"

"Right here. But please let me have it back once you've got the data you need. It's the only one I've got."

"I'll get it straight back. By the way, whereabouts do you live in Allerton?"

"Chapel lane. Why?"

"You don't have a neighbour by the name of Hardcastle, by any chance?"

"Four doors down, there's a chap called Hardcastle."

"Early forties, short dark hair, clean shaven. About six feet tall. Medium build?"

"Yes. I would say so."

"Do you know him well?"

"No. We've never had a conversation. Why?"

"He's in Bradford CID."

"A friend?"

"Just the opposite."

"Understood. I'll never mention the fact that I know you."

"Thanks. But if you ever see him doing anything you think is suspicious in any way, please let me know."

"Ah. The D.E.G is for his phone?"

"Hypothetically."

"I won't breathe a word. It's between you, me and Don McArthur. But you do realise, of course, that any information procured illegally in this manner may not be allowed as evidence in court."

"I understand that. But it might just lead me a bit closer to the answers I'm looking for."

Twenty minutes later, Brian was back at HQ. The office was virtually empty. Hardcastle was at his desk having a long and loud conversation on his mobile. Brian guessed that the rest of the staff were either in the canteen or were working from home or else out on jobs. He left the office and walked up the stairs to see Teresa.

"Morning, Brian. You made it in OK?"

"Yes. Had a call to make first. Can you do me a favour, Teresa?"

"I hope so. What do you need?"

"Hardcastle is alone in the office at the moment. He's on his phone. When he finishes the call, I'll let you know, and I'd like you to get him out of the office for ten minutes on some pretext. Get him to come up to see you to sign some forms. Anything to get him away from his desk. Can you do that?"

"Of course. Just give me the nod."

"You're a gem. Thanks."

Back in the office, Brian had to wait a further five minutes until Hardcastle finished his call. The wait was worth it, as Hardcastle immediately put his phone on charge. Quickly, Brian sent a discreet text to Teresa. Seconds later, Hardcastle took a call on his landline phone, cursed and walked out of the office. As soon as he'd left the room, Brian unplugged Hardcastle's phone from the charger, and attached the gizmo, praying nobody would come into the office and see what he was doing. The seven minutes it took to transfer the data seemed like an eternity, but once it had completed, Brian removed the gizmo, slipped it into his pocket and put the phone back on charge. He was walking back to his desk when the text came through.

"Arsehole on way down. T."

He smiled as Hardcastle came through the door, looking distinctly unhappy. Brian could hear him chuntering away.

"That bloody useless woman! Wasting my time."

He texted back,

"Mission accomplished. Thanks. B."

He watched as Hardcastle picked up his phone and checked the battery level. Still charging. He put it down and immersed himself in his paperwork. Brian made a pretence of working, but in reality, he was simply going through the motions. He couldn't wait to get home so that he could plug the data stick into his own, private computer, and read it without fear that anyone else could access it.

****

Lynn and Gary walked into the office. They had managed to get into work and had been in the canteen. Neither of the two looked particularly happy but soon cheered up when Brian whispered his news. Lynn had news of her own.

"I took a call first thing this morning from a Terry Stanton. He wanted to know what was happening about the car thefts we were supposed to be investigating. I told him work was ongoing, but he didn't seem very happy about it."
"Nothing else we can do. Any further progress on that one?"
"Still following up leads. There was an incident at the beginning of the week which might be linked. This time, the car was left in the middle of a road near the airport, with the tyres slashed."
"So, what's the link."
"Well, I'm thinking they were disturbed. They had already side-swiped a Jag and may have been worried that the occupant had phoned the police, so ditched the car fast. Because of that, they didn't have time to piss in it. But they did leave a gob of phlegm on the rear-view mirror. That's something that is mentioned in the files on some of the other cases."
"Good work. See what you can get from the driver of the Jag."
"Doing it this afternoon."

****

Over the weekend, Brian worked on the data he'd downloaded to his PC at home. There were a number of messages to and from Dean and his mother, which was what he had expected, but he was surprised at the content of some of them. He made copious notes and produced a file of contact numbers to pass to Teresa on Monday in the hope that she would be able to trace the owners.

****

On Monday, Teresa got to work straightaway on tracing the phone numbers Brian had entrusted to her. She took care to put them in her drawer whenever anyone approached her, and ensured they were locked away when she was away from her desk. During the morning, she received a positive response to a discreet enquiry she'd made the previous Friday. She picked up the phone on the first ring.

"Teresa Shackleton."
"Hi, Teresa. It's Dawn Rushworth in Traffic. You left a request concerning a car you wished to trace. A black Vauxhall Insignia, FG16 XXF?"
"Yes. Any luck?"
"I've been through the traffic cams in the area around the time you gave us. We've got the car travelling up through Wrose towards Five Lane Ends, at 1.15am, then in the Eccleshill area shortly after. Then at 2.35am, we get it leaving Eccleshill in the direction of Five Lane Ends, then again travelling through Wrose towards Shipley. The identity of the driver is not totally clear, but it's a white male, dark hair."
"That's fantastic! Thanks, Dawn. I owe you."
"No problem. I've copied the images to a DVD for you. It's all time-stamped and the venues are easily identified by the codes at the bottom which state the camera ID. It's on its way to you as we speak."

Teresa couldn't wait to tell Brian and composed a cryptic message to send him.

"Nice pictures of New Year Party to show you."

Brian was delighted at the news. The time the car was seen leaving the Eccleshill area corresponded with a message sent from Hardcastle's phone to his partner, Donna Donachie. It read –

"Job done. On way home."

To Brian, it was confirmation of his suspicion. He knew Dean was in the flat when Amanda died and that he called his mother. She then evidently passed the message to Hardcastle who drove straight over to clean the crime scene and return home undetected. Or so he thought. Here was evidence to the contrary, backed up by traffic camera images. Another nail in Hardcastle's coffin. But it was still not enough. He needed evidence which would actually put Hardcastle in that room. He had to find Dean Donachie and get him to talk.

Later that morning, he overheard the news that Hardcastle had rung in sick – a touch of flu – and would be off probably the whole week. Brian was not unhappy to hear it. It meant that nobody would be keeping tabs on him as long as he kept his enquiries low-key so that his behaviour didn't alert the other members of Hardcastle's team. He needn't have worried. They had plenty work to keep them fully occupied. He picked up the phone and called Dean's probation officer, Kenny Collins.

"Collins."
"Kenny, it's Brian Peters, CID."
"Hello, Brian. What can I do for you?"
"We're desperate to get hold of Dean Donachie. He's done a runner, it seems. Do you have any ideas where we might be able to get hold of him?"
"Let me look through my records. Can I call you back?"
"I'll be in the office all morning. But you can get me on my mobile at any time."
"I'll be as quick as I can."
"Thanks, Kenny."

He looked through the information Lynn had left for him. She'd interviewed the owner of the Jaguar, but all he was able to say is that the car which collided with his was a dark-coloured Suzuki. There were two occupants, both young males, as far as he could tell, since both were wearing dark hoodies. That was the extent of the information. Nothing to go on there.

****

The temperature had risen during the night. The recent cold snap had ended abruptly as the weather system rotated, pulling in warmer air from the south. The heating was still on full - the heat stored in the bricks of the Economy 7 was now being released into the bedroom where Terry was sleeping, turning and thrashing under the heavy duvet. His pillow was soaked with sweat from his neck and his brow. His semi-conscious brain tried to make sense of the sudden input of distant noise; a familiar noise, one that demanded investigation on a conscious level. Terry needed to know.

He woke, aware of the dampness of the pillow and the stifling warmth of the room. He was vaguely conscious of the sound, faint, far off, and he struggled to recognise it. He strained to listen more intently, trying to block out extraneous noises - the alarm clock's rhythmic ticking, the muffled hum of the fridge in the kitchen. And suddenly he realised what it was. A car alarm! He listened for perhaps a minute, comparing the sound with his recollection of that issued by the Astra's alarm. But he'd never before listened to his car alarm at such a distance, when it could be distorted by the blocks of concrete separating the car from his bedroom. He couldn't be sure. He had to check. He slipped quietly out of bed, stumbled in the dark to the bathroom and dressed.

Linda's brain had registered the sound of the alarm and had chosen to ignore it. She was also aware of the fact that the warmth of Terry's body had gone. She chose to ignore that, too.

Terry strode quickly down the stairs and along the corridor at the end of which was the door which opened on to the car park. The sound was fainter here, at this lower level where the trees and bushes around the car park acted as a baffle against noise, and Terry had to stop and really concentrate to ensure the sound was still there. But he could still hear it. Just. He opened the door to breathe in the night air and listened intently. The sound was clearer now, louder, and Terry knew immediately it wasn't his car alarm. Even without seeing it, he knew. This sound was slightly louder, slightly deeper in tone, and slightly more rapid in the frequency of its pulses of noise. The differences were subtle, but sufficient, and Terry relaxed a little as he stepped along the path, emerging into the car park. The Astra was there. Further along, fifty, maybe sixty yards away, stood a Mondeo with its indicators flashing on and off, its alarm sounding loud and intrusive from beneath the bonnet. And there was no-one in sight. Terry walked over to the Astra and inspected it closely, reassured by the hypnotic blink of the dashboard-mounted alarm light. He'd known all along but was unable to resist this strange compulsion to check. He knew it was irrational. He knew it was destroying him, destroying his marriage, his whole life. Yet he was powerless. He knew that one day, some day in the future, for once he'd forget to lock the car, forget to set the alarm. And if he did, the bastards would be there, hiding, skulking somewhere in the dark, just waiting for the opportunity to drive it away. And piss in it. And even when he knew he'd locked it and set the alarm, was absolutely certain of it, would have bet his life on it, he still couldn't resist reacting to the possibility that the sound of a far-off alarm in the middle of the night might, just conceivably, originate from his car. He breathed a sigh, shaking his head slowly from side to side, and went back indoors.

"All right, Terry, love?"

Linda shifted dreamily, aware of Terry's body nestling against her.

"Yeah. Somebody's alarm going off. Thought I'd better check."
"Suit yourself. If you want to be a car park attendant..."

Five hours later, though to Terry it seemed like five minutes, the hands on the bedside alarm ticked round to the pre-set position to sound the bell. Its loud persistent tone failed to rouse Terry. Instead, Linda had to react. She shook him gently by the shoulder.

"Terry! Come on, love. The alarm's ringing."
"Bastards!"

Terry leapt out of bed, ignoring the clock, and stumbled towards the bathroom for his clothes. Linda reached across and silenced the bell, quietly cursing her husband's disorientation. She slipped out of bed and donned her dressing gown. She padded wearily to the bathroom.

Terry was staring into the bathroom mirror. "You look like shit", he thought. The alarm had stopped ringing. But he still had to check it out. If he ever, just once, failed to check, then they'd have his car. He couldn't let that happen, not again.

"Terry? Why didn't you turn the alarm off?"
"It's stopped, love. I'm just going to check it out."
"Terry. It was the alarm clock. The clock, Terry. Remember? The

one you set to wake you up? The one that reminds you to get up and go to work? The one that goes tick tick tick all night until the hands move round to the right place and then it goes riiiiinnnngg? The one you're supposed to switch off when it's woken you, so it doesn't wake up the rest of the neighbourhood? Remember?"

Terry's early morning grey face turned a shade greyer.

"Shite!"
"OK, love. Look, why don't you make an appointment to see the doctor? Let him give you something to help you sleep properly."
"I don't want to sleep. I want to know what's going on."
"You know damn well what's going on! You're becoming obsessed! You're killing yourself with worry, Terry. Leave it, love."
"I can't."
"It's not that important, Terry. It's only a car. Metal and glass and rubber and plastic, for Christ's sake. It doesn't matter. It can be replaced."
"It matters to me."
"For fuck's sake, Terry! Can't you see what it's doing to you?"
"No."
"Terry, it's killing you. It's eating you. It's all you think about. You don't give a toss about me, our relationship, your job, our future. Or anything. And if you want the truth, you don't really give a damn about the car. All you want is the bastards who wrecked the Focus."
"So?"
"So, give it up. It's not worth it. You'll lose your job if you keep on sleeping in."
"It doesn't matter."
"Of course, it matters, Terry."
"It doesn't."
"Terry, you can't let it get to you like this. If you do, they've won. Don't you see?"
"They won't win."

Terry was staring at Linda through the bathroom mirror. The fluorescent light above exaggerated the shadows beneath Terry's eyes, made his grim, determined expression look demonic, maniacal. For the first time in her life, Linda actually felt a tinge of fear, just momentarily, of the man she loved, the man she married, the man she'd promised to spend the rest of her life with.

But this wasn't the same man. Things had changed, Terry had changed, and would never be the same again. Linda turned away, realising the futility of arguing or reasoning with her husband, and went back to bed, feigning sleep until she heard him leave.

Terry could see it too. He was losing Linda. Or rather he was freezing her out. He had to make a decision, and Linda didn't come into it, because her logical mind would try to reason with him, show him the error of his judgment, plead with him to move on, put it all behind them, and start again. But he'd seen the reaction on her face reflected in the bathroom mirror. He'd caught that look of horror. And he'd seen his own grim determination and the savage instinct to get even. He'd made his decision. Now he had to figure out how to accomplish it. He swore aloud as the engine cut out when he stopped at the traffic lights. Accustomed to it now, he switched the ignition off, counted three and fired it up again, giving it full throttle as he pulled jerkily away.

He was only five minutes late for work, but that was enough for Ronnie. It was all she'd been waiting for. She'd kept meticulous records, detailed enough to satisfy any personnel department, ACAS or industrial tribunal. She knew Terry had no defence - no length of service, no record of outstanding performance, in fact no record of anything apart from lateness and absenteeism. He was just another loser; the type Ronnie hated - people whose only reason for existing was their ability to cause her problems, to make her job more difficult.

Terry paid little attention as the charges were read. He'd waived his rights to representation and waited impatiently until the room fell silent and the form was pushed across the table towards him. He turned it round and read it without interest, and signed it immediately, without question. He stood, turned and walked out of the office, down the narrow corridor, up the gangway between production lines one and two. He ignored the comments from the line workers and continued down the steel steps to the end of the lines where he turned left to the QC office. Closing the door behind him, he leaned against it and shut his eyes, forcing an image of Ronnie to take mental shape on the back of his eyelids. As soon as the image became sharp, he screwed his eyes tight shut shattering the image which became obscured by deep dark black. He opened his eyes and blinked at the garish fluorescent-lit room. He tore off his white coat and hat and threw them into a corner, walked through to the locker room, grabbed his coat leaving the locker keys hanging from the open door, and walked out of the factory for the final time.

He managed to keep his anger in check until he reached the car park. He was blocked in. A Fiesta - he didn't know, or care, whose - was parked, or rather abandoned, across the front of his Astra and the car next to it. It didn't matter. Terry's normal reserve and consideration had evaporated. He manoeuvred the Astra back and forth until it became apparent that the gap was about six inches too narrow for him to squeeze the car through. He nudged forward until his front bumper made contact with the rear bumper of the Fiesta. Increasing the pressure on the gas, he gradually, though noisily, pushed the Fiesta sideways. Slipping the clutch and rolling slightly back, he eyed up the gap and nudged forwards again. This time the Fiesta resisted, its offside rear tyre having butted up against a ridge in the tarmac. Annoyed, Terry increased the acceleration, riding the clutch, pushing hard against the Fiesta's bumper until finally, with a resounding crack, it gave from its rusting mountings and buckled inwards. Sensing the lack of resistance, the Astra surged forwards, stripping a thin line of paintwork from its flank as it ground its way through the gap.

Terry drove straight into town, parked in a Pay and Display, and without stopping to inspect the damage to his car, walked away, hands in pockets, towards the Job Centre.

He was through the doors as soon as the office opened. He was seen quickly, filled in the forms, made his appointment to sign on, and half an hour later was back on the street. He called into a cafe and ordered a pot of coffee and a bacon sandwich, sitting in brooding silence for the best part of an hour. He toyed with the idea of returning to the Job Centre to check the boards for suitable vacancies but decided against it. There would be no 'suitable' vacancies. And even if there were, there would be a hundred applicants better qualified than he was. Instead, he called into the offices of two adjacent employment agencies, knowing full well that he'd be offered nothing but factory work. And knowing that in a matter of a few short weeks he'd probably be desperate enough to accept anything.

CHAPTER 16

In the CID office, none of the teams seemed to be making much progress on their allotted cases. There was a general mood of despondency among the detectives; each team going over and over the information they had about the crimes they were desperate to solve, in the forlorn hope that the solutions were there, and that somehow they'd simply overlooked something they'd previously considered trivial, but which could, in fact, be the key to opening up the investigation. DCI Moseley, in a bid to freshen things up, had proposed moving some personnel between teams, hoping that a fresh pair of eyes might provide a breakthrough, or at least some impetus. He'd already moved Gary into another team, but Brian firmly resisted a compensatory move of one of Hardcastle's men into *his* team. He had a heated discussion about it in Muesli's office.

"With respect, sir, it would be counter-productive to move any of Hardcastle's men to work with me. For my part, I would worry that anything which turned up in our investigations would be leaked back to Hardcastle, to the detriment of our case."
"You have no hard evidence of Hardcastle's involvement in any of the cases you're working."
"Just because we haven't yet proved conclusively that Hardcastle is involved doesn't mean he's totally innocent. Until we clear the Braithwaite case, we have to take all precautions to bring it to its conclusion without any interference. And if we are then satisfied Hardcastle has had no involvement, I'll personally get down on my knees, lick his boots and apologise."
"An apology will be sufficient, Brian. Leave the sarcasm out."
"Yes, sir."

Brian was seething as he left Muesli's office. He'd lost Gary and turned down the offer of a replacement on principle. He felt sure that the integrity of his investigation could be undermined by a mole in the team. That's how he thought of it. And why not? If one of his trusted team were moved into Hardcastle's, he would fully expect, even demand, any relevant information to be fed back to him. He broke the news to Lynn, who simply shrugged her shoulders.

"So, we just do our best and get on with it."

****

That evening, Mark Bell had picked up his girlfriend to take her out. They'd driven over to a pub on the outskirts of Otley where he was certain nobody would know them. Sharon's seventeenth birthday was approaching and he wanted to have a heart-to-heart chat with her on neutral ground. He was nervous. He wanted to do the right thing, but he also wanted to know if the child she was expecting was, in fact, his. He wanted her to tell him face-to-face. Then he reckoned he would be able to know whether she was telling the truth. If he came to the decision that she was lying, he still didn't really know what he would do.

****

With money in his pocket from their first two weeks of selling drugs, Daz had gone out and bought an old battered BMW saloon. With third-party insurance only, in his mother's name, but no tax, it was his first car, his pride and joy. With brother Andy in the passenger seat and a tank full of petrol, they'd gone out of Bradford towards Skipton and into the Dales, putting the car through its paces. He took care to avoid driving the way he drove stolen cars; there would be no handbrake turns in this, no side-swiping other vehicles. Only when they had driven deep into the countryside did he pull over and let Andy take a turn, warning him first to drive sensibly. Or else.

Daz allowed Andy to drive for fifteen minutes or so, then, sensing Andy was struggling with having to drive in a sensible and disciplined manner, ordered him to halt. He pulled into the next lay-by where they shared a spliff. They sat for a while, talking about their dreams, the money they were making from selling drugs, and how they wanted to move up to the big time. Daz's priority was to hire a driver. Andy's was to buy a gun.

****

Mark and Sharon had spent over an hour talking in the pub. Mark had drunk two cokes, Sharon two halves of lager and Mark had started to relax. They had enjoyed each other's company, and though Mark had not had the confidence to ask the question he really wanted the answer to, nevertheless he felt their relationship was on the right track. Before they left the pub, Mark had asked

Sharon to marry him; she, of course, had agreed enthusiastically. As he drove home, they talked excitedly about their future together. Even the rain which was falling heavily failed to dampen their spirits.

Mark could see the headlights in his rear-view mirror. He could tell the vehicle was travelling at high speed. He tilted his mirror as the full beam from behind was dazzling him as the car moved out to overtake him on the ascent up Pool Bank New Road towards Yeadon. Mark had his foot down hard to keep up his speed to take the hill. The car alongside him was matching his speed, its driver seemingly unable to comprehend the fact that the old Beemer didn't have the extra burst of power to complete the overtaking manoeuvre. The two cars were racing side by side as an oncoming wagon rounded the bend before them. The wagon flashed its lights as the two cars approached. At the last second, the BMW's driver wrenched the steering wheel to the left to avoid the oncoming wagon, but in doing so, the BMW clipped the front wing of the Corsa, causing it to veer wildly to the left. It mounted the pavement and struck the wall, demolishing it and careering on down into the wooded gully. The BMW stopped momentarily in the road further on, then screeched away at high speed.

The wagon stopped further down the hill. The driver put the hazard lights on and ran up the hill towards where the Corsa had left the road. As he approached, he pulled out his mobile and dialled 999. Making his way down through broken branches and foliage with difficulty, he wrenched open the driver's damaged door, unbuckled the seat belt and helped the dazed driver out of the car. He went around to the passenger side which had evidently taken the brunt of the damage. The passenger was slumped forward, seemingly unconscious, with blood oozing from a head wound. The windscreen was shattered, but the buckled door was jammed tight. He scrambled back round to the driver's side, reached over and released the seat belt, and tried to pull the injured body out of the car. He quickly realised why he was unable to move the girl's body. Her broken legs were trapped by mangled and twisted metal. There was nothing he could do except pray the emergency services would arrive before it was too late.

Daz didn't stop driving until they'd arrived safely home. They went straight to the flat where their mother lay sleeping on the sofa. They woke her, and told her that, if anybody asked, her two sons were home with her all evening. They made her promise, using the threat of violence. Satisfied, the boys shared a joint and watched some TV.

****

In the morning, Lynn took a phone call from a colleague in Traffic.

"Hi, Lynn. It's Dawn. I don't know if this is of any relevance to you, but there was a serious RTA last night. A car was forced off the road into a wall. The passenger, a young pregnant woman, died at the scene. The driver, a young man, survived with cuts and bruises."

"Why should that be of any interest to CID?"

"I heard you were looking into a spate of car thefts."

"Yes."

"Well, the driver was only able to give a vague account of what happened, but it sounds like the car which forced them off the road may have been stolen. It was being driven dangerously. The occupants were, he thinks, two young males. They were wearing hoodies, so he couldn't give a description. The driver of a wagon, who witnessed the accident, said the same thing. Two young males. They may be the ones you're looking for."

"Could be. Any description of the car they were in?"

"A BMW. Dark colour. They were unable to give the registration number, I'm afraid. Nor the model."

"Thanks. I'll circulate it. Do you think you can trace the vehicle through your traffic cameras?"

"Already on it. I'll get back to you."

She added the information to her case notes, found the incident report on the database, and made arrangements to interview the injured driver at his home. She left a note for Brian, asked Teresa to inform her if she received any reports of a stolen dark-coloured BMW, and left the office.

****

DI Hardcastle was not absent due to the flu. That was just a convenient excuse so that he could make time for something more important. As Lynn was on her way to conduct her interview, Hardcastle was in his parked car outside a motorway service station on the M62 close to Liverpool. He'd received the text stating the cargo had left Liverpool2 Container Terminal a short while ago without any problems and was on its way towards him. Seeing the two lorries pull into the service station, he got out of his car and walked towards them. As the driver of the first lorry got out of his cab, Hardcastle flashed his warrant card. The driver grinned.

"Hardcastle?"
"Yes."
"Let me examine your ID."
"Here."
"Thank you."
"Now show me yours."

The driver pulled his cargo manifest from his inside pocket and handed it over.

"All correct. Children's toys."
"No trouble?"
"None. Straight through, as promised."
"The other lorry the same?"
"Exactly the same."
"OK. Take the toys to the wholesaler, then take the real stuff to the warehouse. You'll get paid when the stuff gets unloaded and checked at the warehouse."

They shook hands and parted company. Back in his car Hardcastle smiled in satisfaction. This was the big deal he'd been working on for months. A cargo of three hundred kilos of cocaine had just entered the country illegally, stuffed behind false panels of the containers. Now it was on its way to a warehouse in Manchester to be cut for the first time. Its street value, once cut, was approximately fourteen – fifteen million pounds, maybe more, depending on how many pairs of hands it passed through on its way to the end-user. It made no difference to Hardcastle once he'd passed it down the line; he'd already made a massive profit. One more year, one more deal like this, and he'd be out of the country for good. He'd come a long way in a short time since he first arrested a small-time importer by pure chance. The man was in debt to a cartel and needed to complete the deal. Hardcastle saw his chance. He buried the evidence and let the criminal go, in return for a majority share of the profits. He learnt quickly, till he reached the point where he no longer needed the man who simply disappeared. The shallow grave on the moors would never be discovered. The man would never be missed. Hardcastle made his way up the supply chain, taking bribes where necessary, and eliminating his opposition when necessary. And now, he had people he trusted working for him right along the supply chain, and the profits, channelled through a shell company, were sitting in a safe place in the Bahamas. His position in CID meant he was kept informed about police investigations into the drugs business, and he was able therefore to stay one step ahead. Peters, though, was a potential problem. He seemed unable to accept there was nothing to be gained from digging into the Braithwaite case. Peters would need to be watched closely, but luckily Hardcastle had his trusted allies to do that for him.

****

Brian was pissed off. His cases seemed to be going nowhere, and he'd had to take over some of Hardcastle's cases in his absence. He'd spent most of the day in Wilsden, where another ram-raid had taken place overnight. A Co-op, this time, had been the target, and in addition to cigarettes and alcohol, the cashpoint had also been smashed open and emptied. Driving back to base, he decided to take a detour. Kenny had not yet returned his call. Brian had rung his office number and been informed he'd finished work for the day. Perhaps he could catch him in the Draper. He was in luck.

As soon as he walked through the door he caught Kenny's eye and moved towards him. Kenny excused himself from his present company and joined Brian at the bar.

"Nice to see you, Brian. Have you come looking for me, by any chance?"
"Yes. I was wondering why I hadn't heard from you."
"I called you on your office number. Didn't they tell you?"
"Who did you speak to?"
"He didn't give his name. He just said 'CID'."
"We're supposed to identify ourselves if we don't know the caller."
"I asked his name, but he wouldn't tell me. He just kept saying 'CID'. I asked if I could speak to you and he said you were out. And then he asked if I'd like to leave a message. I just told him I'd ring back. But I never got around to it."
"You did the right thing. Anyway, did you get anything for me?"
"Well, apart from Donachie's Undercliffe address, I found two

others he's used in the past. I wrote them down for you. They're in my pocket. Somewhere. Hang on a minute while I have a rummage."

Kenny went systematically through his pockets, emptying loose change and scraps of paper onto the bar, unfolding them, reading the contents and stuffing them back in his pockets until he found what he was looking for.

"Here we are. The top two addresses. Ignore the other number underneath – it's a bookie's."
"Thanks, Kenny. I'll give these a visit in the morning. Just now, though, what I need is a beer. Can I get you one?"
"No, thanks. I'm meeting someone over the road. I'll see you some other time."
"OK. Thanks for the addresses, Kenny."
"Yeah. No problem."

Brian stood at the bar, sipping a pint of Ruby Mild. He'd chosen it because it had the lowest ABV of the hand-pulled ales on offer and it turned out to be the right choice. Sam, behind the bar, asked him if it was OK.

"You look like you're really enjoying that. Is it OK for you?"
"It's really good. Which brewery is it from?"
"We brew it round the back. We've got our own micro-brewery."
"Well, if all your beers are this good, you'll do very well. I can see myself coming here every night when we move in up the road."
"Well, you'll be welcome. Is this your first visit?"
"No. I've been in a couple of times. I'm not in this area very often."
"Where do you live now?"
"Out Wakefield way."
"So, what brings you all this way over here."
"Business."
"What sort of work do you do?"
"CID."

Brian noticed a quick look of shock on Sam's face before he recovered his composure.

"Don't worry. This is purely a social call."
"Ah. So, it's nothing to do with the wrap of weed in my pocket?"
"No. I'm off duty."

"I was only joking anyway."

"I know."

Back home, Brian finally had time to talk to his wife. For the last couple of weeks, she'd been handling all the arrangements for their house move, packing items and disposing of some things they'd decided not to take with them. She'd spent hours on the phone arranging to register with a local doctor and dentist, filled out online forms to have post re-directed, arranged their broadband contract to be moved, and a host of other things on her checklist. Now, she wanted an evening off. Brian did his best to act the dutiful husband and father, but occasionally his mind drifted back to his work.

****

The following morning, Daz reversed his BMW into his newly-rented lock-up garage, a ten-minute walk from where he lived. He didn't want it out on the streets where a passing patrol car could see it. For a while, it would remain there. For a while, they would use taxis to sell their goods.

****

Brian had driven directly to the first address Kenny had provided. It was a run-down multi-occupancy building near Manningham. After trying all the door-bells in turn, he finally got someone to leave their bed and let him in the door. It was a sleepy-looking woman wearing a tiger-skin patterned onesie. If she'd worn a head to match, she'd have looked like an advert for Frosties cereal. It was evident to Brian that he had disturbed her day. She was sullen and uncommunicative, but at least she informed him that Dean had not been around for a day or two, which she thought was rude of him as most of the residents relied on him for their regular supply. The second address yielded no joy. Brian drove away with the distinct impression that Dean used the place only occasionally when he wanted to keep a low profile. Now it seemed that it was no longer safe for him. Someone had tipped Dean off and he'd gone into hiding. The only options left for Brian would be to try to get a warrant to search the house in East Morton, which would alert Hardcastle, or drop the search for now. He wondered, though, if he could get Moseley to approve the use of a phone-tracker to find Dean but wasn't sure he'd even heard of such a thing. He decided to keep that up his sleeve in case he needed to track Hardcastle at some point in the future.

He was still thinking about Dean as he pulled into the car park at HQ. His phone was ringing as he walked from the car towards the entrance. He checked the caller. Teresa. He answered immediately.

"Teresa. What's up?"
"Brian, sorry for calling you like this, but there's someone who's been trying to get hold of you. He needs a word on the quiet."
"Who is it?"
"A man called Alex Sinclair. Detective Inspector Sinclair. He works for the NCA."
"OK. How do I get hold of him?"
"Go back out of the car park. Across the road you'll see a silver-coloured Jaguar on a 2016 plate. Two male occupants. They're expecting you."
"OK."

He closed the call. NCA. The National Crime Agency, the guys who investigate serious and organised crime. Drug trafficking and the like. Brian was intrigued. As he approached the car, a man got out of the rear and held out his hand.

"Thanks for coming over, Brian. Is it OK to call you Brian?"
"Yes. You must be DI Sinclair."
"The very same."
"And can I please see your ID?"
"Of course."

He pulled his warrant card from his inside pocket and allowed Brian to examine it. The driver of the car did the same.

"Just give me a second, please."

Brian took out his phone and called Teresa.

"Teresa. Can you please do a couple of ID checks for me? A DI Sinclair. And a DS Chris Fox. Call me back. Thanks."

He turned back to the two officers.

"Sorry about this. Won't take long."

"No problem. I checked you out fully before we decided to approach you. Your old boss, Don McArthur, vouched for you."

"If I'd known you were coming, I'd have done the checks in advance."

"The fewer people who know about this meeting, the better. At the moment, there's just McArthur, and Teresa, who your old boss said could be trusted. We'd like to keep it that way."

Sinclair got back in the car. There was a minute or so of uncomfortable silence during which the two occupants looked idly out of the windows, avoiding eye-contact. The silence was broken by the ring-tone of Brian's phone.

"Yes, Teresa."

"They're genuine, Brian. Both check out. Sorry for the delay. I had to wait until there was nobody around who might see what I was doing."

"That's fine, Teresa. Thank you. Keep this to yourself."

"Of course."

"So, Chris and Alex. What do you want from me?"

"We understand you've been investigating a colleague?"

"You mean Hardcastle?"

"Yes. What do you know about him?"

"Why are you interested?"

"We believe he may be involved in serious criminal activity. We need to know exactly what you've found out. And then, we'd like you to leave him alone."

"You've just said he's crooked."

"Yes. But this is our job. If he finds out he's being investigated, he might bolt. This is why it's imperative that you back off. Don't make him suspicious. Let us do our job."

"OK, but there's a problem with what you're asking."

"Which is?"

"He's guilty of destroying evidence at a crime scene. He's covering up for someone else. It's my duty to investigate till I get to the truth."

"Look, Brian. We know you're a good officer. We've got Don McArthur's word for it, and that's good enough for anybody. All I'm saying is, Hardcastle is not just a corrupt officer, he may be involved in some big-time criminal activity, and I don't want someone scaring him off. We already know there's someone in

CID who's feeding him information. We've got one chance to nail him, and we need your help. Look, Brian, all I'm asking is that you put your investigation on the back burner. Let Hardcastle feel relaxed. Let us do our job."

"OK. What do you want from me?"

"Let's go somewhere for a quiet chat."

They drove away from the City centre, past St Luke's Hospital and turned left along Horton Park Avenue, pulling off the road at the entrance to the park. The driver, DS Fox, got out of the car, ostensibly for a smoke, but primarily so that he could check for any vehicle which might have followed them. DI Sinclair came straight to the point.

"OK, Brian. What do you know?"

"Actually, very little. But I suspect a great deal."

He paused, unsure of just how much information he should share. Eventually, he continued.

"I was asked to take a second look at a suspicious drugs-related death. Hardcastle handled the initial investigation and dropped it as he believed it was an accidental overdose. I was of the same opinion but felt there was more to it."

"Go on."

"Well, the initial report stated that the victim's phone showed no calls or messages in the hours before her death, yet her parents attested she'd called them. I had the phone checked and data recovered proved that calls were made. We were also able to identify a person who was with her when she died – a dealer who provided the drugs. We examined his phone and found that data had been wiped from it. Once recovered, we were able to prove he'd made a call after the girl had died. Shortly after, Hardcastle's car was identified in the vicinity of the crime scene and seen driving away from it later. I believe he'd been informed of what had taken place and had come over to remove any incriminating evidence. The crime scene had been sanitised."

"Can you actually put Hardcastle at the scene? Can you even identify him as the driver of the car?"

"No. Most of the evidence is circumstantial. But we do know that Hardcastle has a relationship, both business and personal, with the dealer's mother. And the three of them have been seen together."

"It's hardly conclusive."

"No, but on top of that, we have been able to link Hardcastle and the dealer's mother to a shell company which owns a number of properties. It's called DPH Holdings, registered with an address in York which is merely a post-drop. The letters DPH, by the way, in case you haven't made the connection, are Hardcastle's initials."

"Who else knows all this?"

"My team members, Lynn Whitehead and Gary Ryan."

"And that's it?"

"Moseley, the boss, knows the basic facts. I went to him with my suspicions."

"And what did he say?"

"Circumstantial, basically."

"And no-one else knows?"

"No."

"Sure?"

"Positive."

"OK. Well, thanks, Brian. Now what I want you to do, is just shelve it. Leave it inactive and don't pry any further. We're building a case here which makes what you've been investigating look insignificant."

"So, you expect me to just drop it? When he's committed a crime?"

"Don't sweat the small stuff, Brian. When we present our case, he'll go down for a very long time. We'll be sure to give you credit for uncovering the small stuff when everything comes out. We appreciate your cooperation on this, Brian. Can we count on it?"

"Yes."

"Good man. We'll give you a lift back and let you get back to work. I'm sure you've got plenty of other cases to work on. Leave NCA to look after this one, eh?"

"OK."

"And please don't let anyone else know you've spoken to us. OK?"

They dropped Brian outside HQ and drove off. He entered the building and went straight upstairs to Teresa's desk.

"Hi, Brian. How did it go?"

"I'm not sure, Teresa. I'm not really comfortable with all this."

"Is there anything I can help you with?"

"Well, for a start, you can explain to me how NCA knew I was investigating Hardcastle."

"I don't know. I hadn't really thought about it."

"Well, the information has come from somewhere."

"Brian. *I* haven't mentioned a word to anybody outside your team. I swear that on my life."

"I believe you. I trust Lynn. Which leaves Gary, my old boss, Don, and a techie at the University. Out of those, Gary is the only one I'm not one hundred per cent sure of."

"You're forgetting someone."

"Who?"

"DCI Moseley."

"Surely you're not serious?"

"I'd believe Gary before Moseley."

"Don't mention a word about this to anybody. Not a word, Teresa."

"Of course not."

"But if you can find time, find out everything you can about Gary."

"Will do."

****

After lunch, Brian walked up to DCI Moseley's office to update him on the Braithwaite case. It went against the grain for Brian to lie to a superior officer, but until he could be sure who could be trusted, he was taking no chances. He told Moseley that the files recovered from Donachie's phone yielded no useful information.

"Personally, sir, I don't think we can go any further with what we've got. I think it needs to go on the back burner for a while and if no new evidence turns up, we close the investigation."

"Agreed. In the meantime, perhaps you could take a look at last night's incident. A mill fire in the Manningham area. Looks like it may be arson. Get the details from Teresa and get down there with Lynn."

"Yes, sir."

On the way down to the site of the fire, a disused textile mill which had been boarded up for several years awaiting planning permission being granted for conversion into flats, the pair indulged in light banter, but neither mentioned the Brathwaite case. On arrival, they headed for Stephen Dunsworth, the leader of the SOCO team, who was engaged in deep discussion with the unfortunately named Geoff Burns, the chief fire officer. They broke off their conversation to greet the new arrivals.

"Afternoon, lads. What have we got?"

Geoff was keen to get his views in first.

"Arson, Brian. This is the seat of the fire. Combustible material was piled in this corner. We found cans of lighter fuel, probably the accelerant, and evidence of other petroleum distillates...."

Stephen, however, had a different take on it.

"While I broadly agree with Geoff's findings, it may possibly have been an accidental fire, almost certainly started by those accelerants, but we have to remember that this is the sort of place frequently used by squatters. Such people may well have tried to start a small fire simply for warmth. It *was* rather cold last night. And all of the canisters we found have a secondary purpose...."
"Which is?"
"To get high, Brian. People who can't afford alcohol have been known to sniff lighter fuel."
"So, which is it? Arson or accidental?"
"We'll let you know, probably in the next twenty-four hours."
"Were there any witnesses? Did anybody report the blaze?"
"There was a 999 call, but the caller didn't leave a name."
"OK. We'll let you get on with your ruminations. We'll go take a listen to the report down at the call centre."

As they walked away. Lynn asked Brian.

"What's your best guess, Brian?"
"No idea, Lynn. My first thought was that the seat of the fire wasn't the ideal place for an arsonist to choose. But, then again, not all arsonists are experienced. We'll wait for the experts to decide between them."
"You want me to organise a door-to-door? See if anyone has spotted any comings and goings? Squatters, druggies, that sort of thing?"
"Yeah. Get on to uniform. See if they can spare some manpower for a few hours."

As they reached the corner on their way back to the car, a passing car backfired. Lynn flinched and pulled back away from the roadside, her heart pounding. Brian noted her action, fully aware of its significance.

"OK, Lynn?"

"I'm OK, yes."

"Still attending therapy sessions?"

"Once a fortnight. You?"

"No. Not now. I'm self-medicating now."

"Alcohol?"

"Yeah."

"Is it working?"

"I don't think anything works 100%. It's different for everyone. We all react differently. It's nothing to be ashamed of. Only those who were there at the time can ever really understand the impact it has."

"I know. At least it's not as bad as it was. I rarely have nightmares now."

"You'll be fine, Lynn. If you ever want to talk about it, I'm always here."

"Thanks. Come on. We've a job to do."

Once they were safely back in their car, Brian silently reflected on their shared experience of the recent Bradford bombing which had killed their colleague. He'd attended therapy sessions, it was true, but soon quit. The truth was, he didn't want to be reminded of what had occurred. He didn't want to deal with it and move on. He was uncomfortable talking about it. He just wanted to forget it had ever happened. Alcohol helped him do that.

CHAPTER 17

When Brian arrived home, Sarah had some news for him. He could tell by the expression on her face it was bad news.

"Brian, I'm so sorry. I had a phone call from Don this lunchtime. Janet had another stroke late last night. She passed away this morning. Don's devastated and asked that we don't call him for a while. He said he'd let us know the funeral arrangements and hopes we will attend. We have to respect his wishes, Brian. I know you want to call him, but just leave it, please."
"Yes. Of course. Poor Janet. Poor Don. So much for a happy retirement."

****

A week passed before the funeral took place. With Hardcastle now back at work, having got over his 'bout of flu', Brian was allowed the afternoon off to attend. At least the weather held, and the burial took place under a dark, cloudy sky. At the crowded wake in the local pub, Brian took the time to speak to some of the people he knew and worked with previously in the CTU. In reality, he was waiting for the opportunity to talk to Don away from the crowd. His chance came when he noticed Don slip out of the Tap Room door into the car park. He followed and caught Don lighting up a cigarette. Don noticed the look of surprise on Brian's face.

"First one in over three years, Brian. Stress does funny things to people."
"It's your choice, Don."
"I thought for a second there you were going to say 'it's your funeral', but, of course, it's not."
"I'm so sorry about Janet, Don."
"Me too. But, to be honest, the last stroke was so severe, she would have been glad not to have survived it. It's a blessing. That's a cliché, but it's true."
"And what about you? Apart from smoking, how are you managing?"
"I'm OK. I'll get used to it. I'll miss her like hell, for as long as I live. But life goes on, as they say. Don't worry about me, Brian. How are *you* getting on?"
"Actually, if I'm honest, I miss CTU. I never thought I'd ever say

that. But CID work can be really frustrating. Too much red tape. Necessary, I know. But frustrating, all the same."

"Just stick at it, Brian. Think of the pension. And if you ever need anything, you can always come to me for advice. Just because I'm a widower doesn't mean I'm going to become a miserable, reclusive hermit."

"It's only right that you take time to grieve, Don."

"Yes, but I'm not one to wallow in self-pity. Now I sense you've got something on your mind. Am I right?"

Brian thought for a moment, trying to judge if this was the right time to bring up his suspicions about Hardcastle. He decided to bite the bullet.

"Last time we spoke, Don, you gave me the means to get hold of further incriminating evidence about Hardcastle."

"Yes. I remember. So, Martin Riley came up with the goods?"

"Yes. I believed I had quite a compelling case against Hardcastle. I'd previously spoken to my superior officer, but he told me to drop it. The evidence was circumstantial. In fact, he gave me a bit of a bollocking, to tell you the truth, for not following protocol. And with this new evidence, well, I just didn't feel it would be convincing enough for him. And now those two guys from NCA are investigating...."

"Which two guys?"

"The two you sent."

McArthur's face showed his surprise. He took a final drag at his cigarette and flicked the butt into the shrubbery.

"I didn't send them. Does anyone else know they've spoken to you?"

"Only Teresa."

"Keep it that way. And how many people know you were investigating Hardcastle?"

"Just my team. And you, and Teresa. I'm totally sure they're clean. And the only other person, apart from Hardcastle probably, is Moseley."

"It could be Hardcastle's way of finding out what you know. But then again, Moseley is close to retirement. It's possible he's been bought. Keep it in mind. I sincerely hope he's clean. I've known him for years, but it remains a possibility. If I were your boss, Brian, I'd recommend you continue your investigation on the quiet.

But of course, I'm no longer your boss."
"Don't worry, Don. I'd already decided on that course of action."
"I thought so. Keep me informed."
"Of course."

Brian and his wife left the pub as soon as it felt appropriate to do so without upsetting anyone. He dropped Sarah off at home and continued towards Bradford. He had work to do. He called Teresa.

"Hi Teresa. Any new leads on where we might find Dean Donachie?"
"Not yet, Brian. But we have something else which might be of interest to you?"
"What's that?"
"Lynn, Gary and I have been going through the door-to-door interviews from the addressees close to the mill fire. One of them mentions a young couple. Squatters, it seems. They'd been seen regularly in the area on most nights."
"Did we get a description?"
"Some interesting details. The girl had a plaster cast on her left arm. Her partner, in his thirties, we think, has a fairly recent scar on his cheek. Both were scruffily-dressed, and 'grubby', according to the description."
"Circulate that, Teresa. Let's see if we can find them. They'll need somewhere else to squat now. See if we can get a list of empty properties in the area."
"Will do."

They were lucky. Two officers on night shift were sent to check a report of a break-in at a vacant boarded-up shop in Fagley. They apprehended a young couple and took them in for questioning. The duty sergeant on shift who booked them in immediately left a message for DS Peters. He stated he had two suspects in custody whose appearance matched the details circulated. Brian picked up the information the moment he arrived at work in the morning, and he and Lynn went to pay them a visit in the cells.

Brian realised as soon as he saw the couple that they were going cold turkey. They were anxious and irritable, sweating and complaining of abdominal pain. He felt sure he could do a trade.

"OK, you two. I can get you sorted. I can authorise medication to ease your pain. Just tell me what it is. Heroin? Cocaine?"

"It's H."

"OK. We'll get you medically examined and on to Methadone, for now. We'll also get you checked out for HIV and give you clean needles. If you're lucky, you'll also get something to eat. But first, I want something from you."

"We weren't doing nothing. Just looking for somewhere to shelter."

"I'm not bothered about that. What I want to know is, do you know a guy called Dean Donachie?"

"Deano? Yeah."

"Have you bought drugs from him?"

"No. He used to buy from us."

"Do you know where we can find him?"

"No."

"I'll ask you again. And be very careful how you answer. If you don't answer, or give me the wrong answer, we'll leave you here without treatment for another twenty-four hours."

"You can't do that. We need hospital treatment."

"You get nothing unless you tell me where I can find Dean."

The girl squeezed her boyfriend's hand and nodded to him, giving her silent agreement.

"There's a flat where his girlfriend lives. Bottom of Otley Road. He sometimes stays there."

"The address?"

"19 Brookfield Road. Flat 4."

"We'll go there now. If we find him, we'll get you methadone. If we find you've been telling porkies, you'll sit here and suffer for a few more hours. Just one more thing. Who supplies you?"

"I can't tell you. They'll kill us."

"No methadone, then."

"You can't do that to us."

"So, tell me who supplies you."

"No."

****

Across the city, Terry Stanton had attended yet another interview. He was not optimistic about the outcome but had to attend every interview set up by the Jobcentre simply to continue to collect his Jobseeker's allowance. He walked through the door of the nearest pub, one that he would not normally have given a second glance at. But times had changed. He was a different man. He was no longer choosy about where he drank. Anywhere would do when he was in this mood.

He stood at the bar with his pint, a pint of Smooth which tasted anything but. He was inclined to pour it over the barman's head but resisted the temptation. He'd paid for it and money was tight. He sipped it slowly. He looked around the room. A pensioner sat at one table, cradling a pint, probably the same stuff he was made to endure. At the far end of the room two young men, in their late teens, were playing pool. No mean player himself, Terry wondered whether he ought to ask them for a game, in the hope he could win a couple of quid. He didn't need to think about it; one of the players saw him and called him over.

"You fancy a game, mate?"
"OK. How much you playing for?"
"A quid a game?"
"OK."

Terry beat Daz but was then in turn beaten by Andy. He began to think they were perhaps setting him up and decided to decline another game until Daz put a fiver on the table and challenged him for a re-match.

"If you dare."

Terry's pride forced him to accept and he quickly found himself one shot from winning the game. He lined up his shot on the black and rolled it down the cushion into the corner pocket. He was just about to pick up the fiver when he heard a voice.

"Foul shot."

It was Andy, standing alongside his brother.

"What do you mean, 'foul shot'?"
"You fouled. The white touched Daz's ball before it hit the black."
"It was nowhere near."
"We say it was. And there's two of us."
"I don't care if there's a fuckin' army."

Terry picked up his cue by the shaft with the butt at shoulder height, adjusting his grip so that he could swing it most effectively if the need arose. The two young men didn't move. Each was holding a pool ball, ready to throw it at Terry. Terry's mouth was dry but he wasn't afraid. He spoke slowly and clearly.

"You two are going to take a beating unless you back off. I can't afford to lose a fiver so I'm prepared to fight for it. I'm not frightened of you. I can do a lot of damage with this cue. One end can smash your skull; the other can poke your eye out. I won that game fair and square. I'm taking my winnings and walking out."
"Wait."

Daz had seen enough. He put the pool ball on the table and motioned for his brother to do the same. Reluctantly, he obeyed.

"The money's yours. Put the cue down. Let's talk. I'll buy you a beer."
"Make it a decent one. None of that bitter piss."
"Lager OK?"
"OK."
"Go get three lagers, Andy."

Andy glared at his elder brother but, once again, obeyed and returned shortly with the drinks. They sat at a round table. Daz broke the silence.

"You're probably wondering why the barman kept out of it."
"Probably doesn't get paid enough to mop up the blood."
"Yeah, you're right. He's used to seeing fights in here. He just lets people get on with it."
"Good for him."
"You working?"
"Would I be in here at this time of day if I'd anything better to do?"
"You could be police."
"Not a chance. I wouldn't work for them if it was the only job on offer. Useless buggers!"
"Can you drive?"
"Yep."
"Full, clean licence?"
"Yep."
"You want a job?"
"Depends."
"Mostly evenings into the early hours, including weekends. *Especially weekends*. Occasionally odd hours during the day."

"What's the job?"

"Driver. No. Let's call it 'chauffeur'. Just driving us from place to place while we do business."

"What sort of business?"

"We buy and sell. We need someone to drop us off, drive round the block or park up nearby, then pick us up and take us to the next drop. Easy money."

"What's the pay?"

"We provide the car and fuel, and you get £200 a week."

"Not enough."

"OK. £300."

"Cash."

"Cash."

"I'll take it on a trial basis. See how it goes."

They shook on the deal.

"You're in luck. You can start tonight. We've just had the car repaired after the paintwork got a bit scratched. It's like new. Give me your phone number. I'll call you tonight with instructions."

"OK. See you tonight."

Terry knew full well what he was letting himself in for. Drugs. He told himself he'd earn just enough to pay the bills and keep himself going until he could find a proper job. Then he'd tell them to stick it.

****

Brian decided not to take any backup with him. It was still in the back of his mind that there was someone within CID who could scupper his plans to arrest Donachie. He was taking no risks. He would take only Lynn with him. They were going to a flat. There would be only one exit unless you counted a second-floor window. He was also going without a search warrant, primarily because he didn't want Muesli to know anything at this point. Besides, he wasn't too interested in what was in the flat. He just wanted Dean Donachie.

"Come on, Lynn. Let's see if we can pick him up."

It took less than ten minutes to reach the address but they were too late. A young girl, heavily pregnant, answered the door. Brian showed his ID.

"CID, love. We'd like a word with Dean."

"Bastard's not here."

"Mind if we take a look?"

"Please yerself."

They didn't stay long. The flat was filthy. There were two small dogs and a toddler, maybe a couple of years old, in the one-bedroomed flat. Every available surface was littered with unwashed clothes, dirty crockery and cutlery, and empty takeaway cartons.

"When did you last see him?"

"Couple of nights ago."

"Do you know where he is now?"

"No idea."

"Why did he leave?"

"No idea."

"Did he leave on foot?"

"Someone picked him up."

"Could you give us a description?"

"Didn't see him."

"So it was a male?"

"Don't know. Didn't see."

"Can you describe the car?"

"Four wheels. Don't know much about cars."

"What colour?"

"Dark. Maybe black."

"Hatchback?"

"What's that?"

"Thanks for your time. You've been a great help."

They were thankful to get back out into the fresh air.

"Christ! That place stank! I don't know how anyone could live like that, let alone bring up a family."

"So, what next?"

"We'll call at Dean's mother's flat. The rent's still being paid on it regardless of the fact that she seems to spend all her time in the house in East Morton. I doubt very much if Dean will be there. In fact, I doubt very much anyone will be there, but we need to check."

His instincts were correct. The flat was empty, and a neighbour confirmed she hadn't seen Donna Donachie for several days. Brian made a phone call.

"Teresa, do me a favour, please."
"What do you need?"
"Find out who owns Donna Donachie's flat on Thorpe Edge."
"Will do."

Soon, the result came back. It was what Brian expected. The flat was owned by DPH Holdings.

****

Brian felt he now had one last chance of catching Dean Donachie. He figured the only option left was to go to the house in East Morton. If Dean wasn't there, at least they would be able to question his mother. The problem was, he wanted to search the property, and for that he needed a warrant. And for that, he would have to ask DCI Moseley to authorise it.

"We could go directly to a magistrate."
"Without signed authorisation? It would be refused. And how do you think Muesli would react to that? No. We'll go to the house and ask permission to look around. Odds-on, we'll be refused, but it's worth a shot."

Lynn drove while Brian called Teresa to let her know the state of play so she could cover for their absence if required. The call produced some alarming news.

"Put your foot down, Lynn, and use the siren if necessary. Teresa's just informed me Hardcastle didn't turn up for work this morning."
"Sick again?"
"Don't know. She assumed he was out on a case. But nobody seems to have any idea why he's not in. Either that, or they're not saying."

They were too late. The house was unoccupied. They walked around the property, looking through the windows. Furniture was still in place, though there were dirty plates piled by the sink.

"Let's see if we can get into the garage."

The garage was locked. Peering through the dirty window, Brian could see there wasn't a vehicle inside. He decided to try his luck with a neighbour, ringing the front-door bell until the door opened. He showed his warrant card to the middle-aged man who appeared.

"Excuse me for bothering you, sir. I'm trying to contact my colleague, your neighbour Danny Hardcastle. Have you seen him today?"
"No. Not since yesterday evening."
"Anyone else in the property?"
"No. They all left yesterday."
"Who, exactly?"
"Danny, his partner, and a young man who I think is her son. They all left together."
"Did they leave in a car?"
"Yes. The Mercedes."
"Thank you, sir. You've been very helpful."

Brian made a quick phone call.

"Teresa. We need to trace a two-year-old dark blue Merc. Registered to either Danny Hardcastle or Donna Donachie. Looks like they've done a runner."
"I'll get straight on it. I can get the registration from DVLA or our database. It might take a few minutes."
"Thanks."

He turned to Lynn.

"I know all we've got is suspicion, but I think we'll have to take it to Muesli. First, though, we'd better check Hardcastle's home address."

They drove back to Allerton, during which time Brian took a call from Teresa.

"Brian, I got the registration of the Merc, and I've circulated it to all forces. I can't put an 'arrest' on it, only 'on suspicion'."
"OK, Teresa. Thanks."

Hardcastle's house was unoccupied, but his car was parked on the drive. None of his close neighbours had seen him for the last few days. They were on the point of leaving when an old lady, walking her dog, approached the car and tapped on the window. Brian wound it down.

"Can we help you, madam?"
"Are you looking for that policeman who lives here?"
"Yes."
"Well, I haven't seen him for a few days, but I was walking my dog at about one o'clock this morning – he's quite incontinent, you know – and I saw a young man enter the house."
"He broke in?"
"Oh, no. He went in the front door. He had a key."
"Thank you very much, madam."

He wound the window back up and turned to Lynn.

"Which shift do you want, Lynn?"
"Days, preferably."
"OK. We need another couple of bodies, preferably. So we can do twelve on, twelve off, two to a car."
"Who do you trust?"
"No-one. No, just a minute."

He found the number on his phone and selected 'Call'. The response was swift.

"Hello?"
"Don, it's Brian. How are you?"
"OK. Brian. What can I do for you?"
"Do you know any officers I could borrow for surveillance duty? Trustworthy people, short term. From tonight."
"I can only think of one at such short notice."
"OK. Who's that?"
"Me."
"You sure you're up to it. Don?"
"Absolutely. Is it for the Hardcastle case?"
"Yes."
"Then I'm definitely up for it. Give me a time and the address, and I'll pack a flask and make some sandwiches and be there."
"Thanks, Don. I'll get back to you shortly. 'Bye."

"OK, Lynn. That's one. Leaves me no option now."

He called another number and waited for the response, drumming his fingers on the dashboard.

"Hello?"
"Gary. How are you doing?"
"Oh, hi, Brian. I'm OK. Just shuffling around the office. Nobody seems to be in charge. Hardcastle didn't come in this morning, and we can't get hold of him."
"Can you do a job for me, Gary?"
"Love to. I hate working in this team."
"Can you join me at six tonight for a twelve-hour surveillance?"
"Yeah. If I can get a few hours of sleep while my partner keeps his eyes open."
"I'll be your partner, Gary. We can take turns to grab a few hours' sleep."
"Send me the details and I'll be there at six."
"Will do. Thanks."
"My pleasure."

"That's it, Lynn. You'll be with Don from six am. Gary and I will cover nights. I'd better ring the wife and break the good news."

****

The arrangements Brian had made for round-the-clock cover proved unnecessary. At twelve-thirty, Brian nudged Gary awake and pointed to the slim figure walking up the drive to Hardcastle's door. They were quickly out of the car and sprinting down the road towards the house, but, by the time they reached the bottom of the drive, the front door had closed.

"Go around to the back, Gary."

He gave Gary fifteen seconds before he rang the doorbell. He could hear movement inside the house. He rang again. And knocked hard.

"Open the door, Dean. It's the police."

He heard an anguished scream from the back of the house and ran down the path. Gary was on his knees, pinning a yelling Dean face down on the tarmac.

"Good work, Gary."

"The pleasure's all mine. The little prat threw a punch at me. I'm arresting him for assaulting an officer."

"Let's get him down to a nice, warm cell. The poor mite must be frozen."

"We'll just go through your pockets, Dean. Just to make sure there's nothing in them you could possibly harm yourself with. We wouldn't want you to hurt yourself on this phone."

****

Down at Police HQ, Dean sat alone in Interview room 1. He refused to answer any questions until his lawyer was present. Having dismissed Gary for the night, and informed Don he would not be required for the early morning surveillance, Brian spent his time looking through Dean's phone. Superficially, there was little of interest, apart from messages from and to Hardcastle to confirm the two of them were linked.

Shortly, however, the duty solicitor turned up, not entirely enamoured at having been roused from his sleep to represent a small-time drug-user, and, seemingly keen to return to his bed, advised his client to co-operate fully with the police. Brian was equally keen to trace Hardcastle.

"Right, Dean. There are a couple of issues I want to discuss with you. I want to get to the truth about the circumstances surrounding the death of Amanda Braithwaite in the early hours of January 1st, 2018. But first, I want to know the whereabouts of Danny Hardcastle."

"I don't know where he is. Or mum."

"I don't believe that for a second. You've seen them every day for the past few weeks."

"It's true. I don't know where they are."

"Why would they leave you behind, Dean? Doesn't your mother love you anymore?"

"Danny reckoned the police would be looking for three people travelling together. He told me he'd send me tickets to join them in a couple of days. He told me just to sit tight and the tickets would be sent to his house. That's why I went there every night."

"And you believed him?"

"Yes. Mum said it made sense not to travel together."

"They've set you up, Dean. Left you to take the rap."

"NO! Mum wouldn't do that."

"She'll do exactly what Danny tells her. They just tolerated you. Left you behind. You were no use to them."

Dean started sobbing. Brian continued in a softer voice, a less menacing tone.

"Where are they, Dean?"

"I don't know. Honest."

"You must have overheard their conversations."

"I didn't hear anything."

"OK. When did you last see them?"

"Monday night."

"Tell me what happened."

"We were at the house in East Morton. I was watching TV. They came downstairs with their suitcases packed and told me to get my coat on. We loaded the car and drove towards Bradford. Then they stopped in Allerton and told me I wasn't going with them. They'd only got tickets for two. He bunged me a couple of hundred quid and said I'd be joining them soon. He said they all had to travel separately so we wouldn't be noticed. He said he'd send my tickets. Bastard!"

"So, you've no idea where they've gone?"

"No."

"OK. I'll be back in a few minutes to talk about New Year's Day. I hope you'll have some useful information for me then."

Brian left the interview room and went down to talk to the duty sergeant. He knew him from previous visits."

"Sergeant Barlow. How's the wife?"

"Fine, thanks. How's yours?"

Sarah's fine. Expecting again. Very soon."

"Is that why you're doing overtime?"

"No. Not really. But it all helps. I wonder if you can help me, James. Do you have any cars out anywhere near the airport?"

"Probably."

"Would you mind getting someone to take a quick drive through the car parks? I'm looking for a Merc. Here's the registration number. If they find it, tell them to call it in. Don't touch the car. Just let me know."

"Will do."

"Thanks, James."

Brian went for a quick coffee before returning to the interview room.

"So, Dean. Let's continue. Tell me about your visit to see Amanda Braithwaite."

"Her friend had asked me to bring some stuff to the flat."

"Be a bit more specific, Dean. What stuff?"

"She asked for coke."

"Then what happened?"

"She told me she was going out, but to take it to the flat for Mandy. So, I went around, and she let me in. We talked for a couple of minutes but she wanted to get on with it. So, I cut her a couple of lines and showed her how to snort it."

"Then?"

"She snorted a line and then just sat talking for a bit and then she went all light-headed and giggly."

"Go on."

"She said she was going to do another line. I wasn't sure, but I thought if she got high she might let me poke her. So, I let her do it. But as soon as she'd snorted it, she started wheezing and gasping for breath. Then she fell backwards across the bed and sort of had a spasm. And then she stopped breathing."

"Did you check?"

"Yes. I put my hand close to her mouth, but she wasn't breathing. There was just sick all over her lips. I put my hand on her chest but couldn't feel a heartbeat. She was just still. She was dead. I knew she was dead."

"So, what happened next?"

"I phoned mum. And she put me on to Danny. He told me he was coming over and to wait for him. So, I waited till he turned up. Then he told me to leave, so I did. I was glad to get out, to be honest."

"Did you find out what happened after you left?"

"Yes. He came to the flat."

"The flat in Undercliffe?"

"Yes. He told me he'd cleaned the place up. He took my phone and deleted all the messages, and stuff. Then he told me to keep my mouth shut, or else. He said I owed him."

"Then what?"

"He drove off back to East Morton."

"One more thing. When he arrived at Amanda's did you let him in?"

"No. He had keys."

"Thank you, Dean. You've been most helpful."

"Can I go now?"

"We'll decide in the morning when you've had a nice rest and some breakfast."

Brian was still in the office writing up his report when his mobile indicated an incoming call. His wife, Sarah. He answered immediately, realising it must be something really important for her to call him in the middle of the night.

"What's up, Sarah?"
"Someone's tried to set fire to the house."

She was hysterical. Brian tried to calm her.

"Are you OK, Sarah? Is Daniel OK?"
"Daniel's been crying. But he's sleeping now. But it was horrible. Frightening…."
"Where are you now?"
"Just leaving the hospital. I took Daniel straight there."
"OK. Now listen, Sarah. I want you to drive straight to dad's. I'll call him to let him know you're on your way. He'll put you up for the night. Will you do that for me?"
"Yes."
"I'll get someone round to keep guard on our house, and on dad's. And I'll arrange to get ours fixed. Is there a lot of damage?"
"No. Not really. Just the front door, I think."
"OK. You two go to dad's. I'll sort the house."

He made the necessary phone calls and left the office, driving straight home at speed along the quiet roads and arriving as the fire brigade prepared to leave. He showed his ID to the constable stationed at the bottom of the drive, his gaze fixed on the smoke blackened entrance where there used to be a door with long narrow panes of glass down each side. He stepped gingerly over the threshold avoiding charred lengths of timber which had been pulled from the hall ceiling by the fire fighters.

"What have we got, Allen?"

Allen Greaves was examining the remains of a charred package.

"Ah, Brian. You'll be pleased to know that whoever did this was a complete and utter numpty."
"What do you mean?"

"I mean, whoever was responsible had no idea what he was doing. This was a home-made incendiary device, magnesium-based, with a percussive cap. It was small enough to be pushed through a letter box so that it would ignite on impact inside. Even on a mat. The trouble was, whoever was made responsible for delivering the device had wrapped it in bubble-wrap so that it wouldn't ignite accidentally, and the additional packaging made it too bulky to push through the letter box. I believe the person responsible decided to throw it at the door instead. This theory is borne out by the fact that the device was found burnt out on the path outside the door, although the door and frame had burned through. I believe it struck the door, ignited and rebounded on to the drive where it burned fiercely without causing too much actual damage. Enough incendiary material, however, had already attached itself to the door, causing it to burn through and start a fire in the hall. The noise and the smoke detector woke Sarah and she reacted quickly to get herself and young Daniel out through the back door. A neighbour had already called 999, and the fire appliance arrived in minutes. You couldn't have asked for a better outcome, Brian."

"Any clues to where the bomb originated from?"

"None. There's little of it left. I very much doubt we'll get anything from this, but we'll try."

"Thanks, Allen. It's just as well we're moving house, though I'm not sure the buyers will be too happy."

****

Terry had finished his first shift driving for the brothers. He'd taken the phone call during the evening, told his wife he was going out for a few hours, and drove to the address he'd been given. The black BMW, its front wing having been replaced, was ready for him. His employers sat in the back and gave him directions. During the course of the night, they stopped at a number of pubs and clubs, as well as on street-corners and badly-lit car parks. Terry remained in the car with the engine running, or, if requested, drove around for a few minutes until he received a call to return to pick up his bosses. He knew what they were buying and selling, but that was their business. As long as they paid him, it had nothing to do with him. And at the end of the shift, he took the car back to the lock-up, drove his employers to a point where they indicated he should leave them, and drove home to his wife with a wad of tenners in his pocket. From that point on, he worked every night and saw his pay quickly rise.

****

Dean was no further use to Brian. Either he knew nothing else or wasn't saying. He was eventually charged with possession and supply and released on bail, with strict conditions. Brian's final words to him were,

"Give my regards to Kenny Collins, your probation officer. I'm sure you'll be seeing plenty of him in the future. And plenty of me, too."

Later in the day, a call came through. Hardcastle's Merc had been found in one of the long-stay car parks at Leeds Bradford Airport. He passed the message to Teresa, who arranged for the car to be brought in for forensic examination, then requested that all passenger manifests for flights leaving, or having left, the airport over a four-day period be checked.

It proved to be a laborious process which eventually turned out to be fruitless. Neither Hardcastle nor Donachie appeared on any flight manifest. Brian immediately demanded CCTV footage of the area around the car park where the Merc was found. Again, it took time to produce a result, but it was as Brian had suspected. Images clearly showed Danny Hardcastle and Donna Donachie leaving the car with their luggage and, rather than entering the airport terminal, they'd instead called a taxi to pick them up. Luckily, the taxi was identifiable from the images, but again Brian had to wait until details came back regarding its destination. Three days later, when the news came in, he slammed his fist against his desk in frustration, causing all those in the office to look up from what they were engaged in. Brian was furious. They'd given him the slip.

It took a while longer to piece all the information together. It was the discovery of a body in a Travelodge close to Manchester Airport which finally allowed them to make sense of it all.

Brian read through the report sent by Manchester CID, Lynn looking over his shoulder.

A body had been found in a bedroom of the hotel by a cleaner. A man and a woman had booked in three nights earlier. They had booked for a week, requesting that they should not be disturbed under any circumstances. The cleaner, an East European, had failed to check for special requests and entered the room to clean. The body of a woman, quickly identified as Donna Donachie, was found dead on the bed. Initial forensic examination suggested she had been manually strangled, with the marks on her neck indicating she had probably been strangled by a left-handed person. Examination of CCTV showed a man leaving the hotel late at night. He was identified from photographs circulated by Bradford CID as Danny Hardcastle. Further enquiries showed he had boarded a flight to Schiphol Airport the same night.

"Danny Hardcastle is left-handed, Brian."
"I know. Let's get Dean in again, Lynn. Maybe we'll get something out of him when we tell him Danny has killed his mother."

What bothered Brian most at this point was the fact that, somehow, he was going to have to break the news to Muesli that he needed authorisation to issue a European Arrest Warrant for one of his most experienced detectives, Danny Hardcastle, on suspicion of murder, amongst other offences.

****

By the time Dean was located and brought in, Danny Hardcastle was already in Albania, having taken a train from Amsterdam to Paris, and from there, the TGV to Marseille. There, a small boat, the type which regularly ferried contraband and drugs around the Mediterranean, had a berth reserved for him, along with false passport and papers and would take him to the port of Durres. He would continue to run his drug-smuggling empire safely out of reach of UK jurisdiction. He would worry about Europol in due course, though his contacts assured him they wouldn't bother him as they had 'an arrangement'.

****

Dean was left to sweat in the interview room with his legal representative for a few minutes, until Lynn entered the room, smiling. She apologised for Brian's absence before starting up the recording equipment and introducing herself.

"Dean, love. I'm afraid I have some bad news for you."

"What? You can't find mum and Danny?"

"On the contrary. We found your mother, or, more accurately, a hotel cleaner found her. Lying naked, face down on a bed. Dead."

"No!"

"Afraid, so, love. She'd been strangled by your mate, her lover, Danny Hardcastle. The man you're protecting."

"You're lying."

Lynn pushed a crime scene photograph across the table in front of Dean. His face turned the same colour as the face in the photograph. Deathly white.

"Thought you could trust him, did you, love? Think again."

Dean was silent for a moment, though visibly struggling to keep his composure. Then he cracked, sniffing, and trying desperately to hold back the tears.

"He told me to sit tight, keep my head down and he'd send me flight tickets to join them in a couple of days. He said he didn't want us all to travel together because the police would be looking for us. He promised. He said it was best. We were all going to live in Spain together."

"On a police salary? That wouldn't afford much."

"He was loaded! You don't know anything about him, do you?"

"Why don't you tell me?"

"He's the biggest drug lord in the north of England. He's *the* Mister Big."

"He imports?"

"'Course he does. Didn't you lot know anything about it? You must be right mugs."

"So, tell us."

"Why should I?"

"To get your own back on Danny for what he's done."

Again, she pushed the photograph under his nose, just to reinforce the message.

"He told me all about it one night, after he'd pulled off a big deal. He was drunk. Boasting."

"Go on."

"What's in it for me?"

"Revenge?"

"I don't want to go back inside."

"I think we can work something out about that."

"I want a promise."

"Give me a second."

She announced she was leaving the room, for the benefit of the recording. Brian had been watching proceedings through the glass.

"Good work, Lynn. You handled that well."

"Can we promise him no time inside?"

"Providing he doesn't re-offend, yes. Suspended sentence, probation. We'll work out the details when we get the information."

Lynn re-entered the room and announced her presence.

"OK, Dean. You'll do no time. Provided you keep your nose clean. So, tell me all you know. How did this all start?"

"A few years ago, he arrested me for dealing drugs. He gave me a choice. He'd either seek a prosecution or I could become his informer."

"And?"

"I took his offer."

"You became his informer?"

"Yes. That's basically how he managed to close so many cases. How he got promoted. Then he met my mum, and they hit it off. Then, about three or four years ago, he was on a drugs case. Just by luck, he cracked it. He was just following a low-level dealer one night, when he stumbled upon the man at the top of the chain in a drug bust. Basically, Mr Big bought him off in return for his silence. For a few months, Danny and his team took bribes. Then he decided he wanted more. He set up a meeting with Mr Big, and shot him. He said it was in Manchester. He buried the body somewhere on the moors and took over his business. They import, and supply to big dealers who cut it and sell on to street dealers. He's made millions."

"You mentioned his 'team'. Any names?"

"No. But they were police."

"Would you be able to identify them?"

"I think so."

She turned to the mirror and nodded. Brian understood and soon returned with a large pile of staff photographs. He took them into the room, passed them to Lynn, and left. Lynn spread a random selection in front of Dean and waited for his comments. He picked out three photographs and passed them back to Lynn. She gasped.

"Are you absolutely certain, Dean? Are you prepared to swear to this in court?"

"As long as you can give me protection."

"You think they might come for you?"

"Too right."

"OK. I'll let you talk to your lawyer for a while. When I come back I'll ask you to make a formal written statement. And if it's any consolation to you, I'm sorry about your mother."

"Thanks."

"We'll get you off drugs, Dean. You can see where it can all lead...."

"I've been pushed out of the market anyway. My suppliers got beaten up and run out of town."

"Who by, Dean?"

"I daren't say just now."

"We'll protect you."

"Let me think about it. It's not fair. Thugs pushing people out of making a living. I thought restraint of trade was illegal."

"Go see your union rep."

CHAPTER 18

Brian was glad to get through the next day, to his booked day off, even though it meant an entire day moving house and settling with his family into their new home. He'd been fortunate that the buyers of his Wakefield home had been happy to postpone completion until it was repaired and habitable and had asked for a full redecoration by way of recompense, arguing that there had been some smoke damage to the rest of the house. Brian agreed and by seven in the evening, young Daniel was fast asleep in his new bedroom, Sarah was sipping a glass of white wine and Brian was walking down the hill to get a takeaway meal for the two of them. But first he slipped into the Draper. As he approached the door, he could hear the sound of raucous laughter.

Jamesy's in, he thought.

He was right. Jamesy was engaged with the Foghorn, Mick and Dawn, Rick and a few others in an animated, nonsensical conversation. Every customer in the bar was laughing hysterically and it continued despite his presence.

He was pleasantly surprised to find a rather beautiful young lady behind the bar. On each previous visit he had been served by males, some more hirsute than others, but all unmistakeably male. She gave him a warm smile and introduced herself as Louise. Scouse Billy was quickly at his side.

"Don't tell him anything, Louise, without your solicitor being present."
"What are you on about now, Billy?"
"You do not have to say anything. But it may harm your defence if you do not mention when questioned something which you later rely on in court. Anything you do say may be given in evidence. This fella's Brian, from Bradford CID. Are you all right, la?"
"Fine, Billy. How are you?"
"Mustn't grumble. But I will anyway."
"And you've no room to talk. Your credo is 'Anything you say will be taken down and spread around the village in half an hour'."
"Touché."
"What would you like, Brian?"

He settled for a pint after saying hello to the other customers he recognised.

"So, when do you move in, Brian?"
"We moved today."
"Today? Well, you'll be a regular from now, then. We can look forward to a reduction in local crime."
"And I can look forward to a decent pint."

****

The old whore had grown progressively worse. She'd hardly stirred for a week, spending most of her time sprawled on the settee wrapped in a blanket which stank of stale urine. She ate nothing, drank and smoked copiously and swallowed painkillers in profusion. Still she complained of the pain yet refused to go to the doctor's surgery though it was close by. Andy was more worried than his brother. Apart from the fact that her ill-health curtailed the extent of their night-time activities – and Terry was complaining he was losing money by not working - Daz's concerns centred on the fact that he had to keep turning away the punters. The way he saw it, if his mother had the strength to open her legs, she had the potential to earn money. Some of her Asian customers weren't fussy. All they wanted was an 'empty'. They'd shag a cod on a fishmonger's slab if that was all that was on offer. Reluctantly, he sent them away, though, keen to keep their custom, he insisted she'd be fine in a week or so and would have some 'special offers' for her regular customers. He was optimistic she wouldn't stay on the settee for too long. He was right. Three days later, she evacuated her bowels where she lay, her eyes glazed, her skin ash-grey.

"Get yourself cleaned up. Fuckin' dirty whore!"

Daz was gipping, fighting to keep himself from vomiting at the stench from the thin, almost black liquid running down the settee and forming a stinking dark pool on the carpet.

Andy was more sympathetic and phoned for an ambulance, and as soon as it departed with their mother in the back they called Terry and commenced their evening sales routine.

At the same time as the ambulance arrived, over in Idle, Brian's wife Sarah went into premature labour.

****

An exhausted Brian phoned in a little after nine in the morning. Sarah had a little girl. Seven pounds. Mother and baby doing fine. Then he went home to sleep. His parents had responded immediately by looking after Daniel and they were waiting when he arrived home. The bad guys could wait. He poured himself and his father a large Glenlivet, toasted the new arrival, then collapsed fully-clothed on his bed.

After visiting the hospital the following morning, he returned home where his parents, and young Daniel, assisted him in unpacking boxes and placing their contents in their intended destinations. Brian knew for a fact that, the moment Sarah came home, she would move everything around anyway. But still, the effort made him feel useful. By the end of the afternoon, he couldn't wait to return to work. But that was tomorrow. Right now, he fancied a pint.

****

A group of around a dozen youths had congregated outside the bank. Brian was in no mood to walk around them and simply ploughed through the middle, shouldering a pimply young man, dressed in street uniform of grey hoodie and fake Adidas sweatpants, out of the way.

"Knobhead!"

Brian stopped and turned.

"What did you say?"

None of the group spoke. Brian fixed his gaze on the pimply lad and spoke slowly.

"You lot have got thirty seconds to clear off before I phone for the big van with the big men to arrest the lot of you. Go now or face the consequences. Go on, go home and do some colouring-in, or something."

Grudgingly, they slowly began to disperse.

"Not you, Pimples. You come here. Now empty your pockets."
"What for?"
"Because I'm telling you to. You've heard of 'stop and search', right? Well, then, empty your pockets."
"I've got nothing to hide."
"Well, then. Prove it."

The youth pulled out a tobacco tin and a lighter.

"Open the tin."
"It's only tobacco."

Brian smelt the contents. It was tobacco.

"Now, the other pocket."

Reluctantly, he produced a small pen-knife.

"Why do you carry a knife?"
"Protection."
"From whom?"
"There's a gang from Ravenscliffe. They carry knives."
"And as long as they know you have a knife, you're a target. Do your parents know you carry a knife?"
"No. But they don't care."
"Shall we go and ask them?"
"No."
"OK. I'm taking your knife. You can keep the tobacco, though you're too young to be smoking. How old are you anyway?"
"Fourteen."
"How would you like to earn a little pocket money?"
"No way, you pervert."
"No. I'd like you to be my eyes and ears around here. I'll pay you for information if it leads to an arrest."
"How much?"
"Depends. But it will be money you will have earned from working. From being useful. Doing something positive with your life. Or do you just want to be an arsehole all your life?"
"I want to be a footballer."
"Well, maybe I can help you with that. Maybe I can arrange for you to attend a training camp during the school holidays. How would

that be?"

"That would be good, yeah."

"OK. Keep your nose clean, and your eyes and ears open. What's your name?"

"Adrian Roberts. Adie."

"OK, Adie. Here's my card. Call me anytime you hear or see something that might be of interest to me. OK?"

"OK."

"Away you go. And don't tell your friends. You'll lose your street cred."

Brian walked into the Draper to be greeted by a round of applause. Louise, behind the bar, thanked him.

"We've been trying to get those kids moved on for weeks now. And you disperse them in seconds. What's the secret?"

"No secret. I just get angry whenever someone stands in my way when I need a pint. And it's not all the kids' fault. Half the time, their parents take no interest in them. They've no ambition, no goals, no interests. They're all graduates of the Universities of Google, Facebook and YouTube. That's all they know. Sometimes, all they need is someone to guide them in the right direction. Though sometimes, I have to say, they need a good slap. A pint of Gold, please."

He spent an hour chatting with the regulars, proudly showing the pictures of the new baby on his phone, before taking his leave and walking back up the hill towards his new home. The street corner, by the bank, was deserted.

The following morning, Brian brought mother and baby home from the hospital. He spent an hour with them before returning to work.

****

Having arrived at work after a night of interrupted sleep, his first action was to call Lynn, Gary and Teresa into a meeting room. He locked the door behind them before beginning.

"You three are the only ones I can trust with this, and the information we share here must go no further. Understood?"

They nodded in assent.

"Good. Earlier in the week, Lynn interviewed Dean Donachie. In return for certain 'concessions', he told us that our colleague, or should I say ex-colleague, Danny Hardcastle has been importing Class-A drugs on a massive scale for a few years. It may or may not surprise you to discover that three members of his gang are, in fact, serving officers in this division."

He paused to let the information sink in.

"DS Schofield, DS Ward, and DC Tarkovics were part of the gang. Between them, they supplied a network of dealers in the north of England. We have no information to suggest that anyone else in CID is implicated, but it is possible. My next move is to take this to NCA, and hand it over completely to them. We have enough to do without investigating our own."
"So, what do you want us to do?"
"Business as usual, Gary. Hardcastle has already left the country. Neither Schofield, Ward or Tarkovics are in the office, so we have to assume they've been alerted and are on the run. They're no longer our problem. What I want to do is get the street-dealers, and their suppliers. I want to bring the whole house of cards down."
"Do you want me to bring Amanda Braithwaite's flatmate in?"
"Yes, Lynn. She knows more than she's been telling us. Teresa, I'd like you to set up a teleconference with the officers at NCA, the ones I spoke to."
"OK"
"Gary, you go with Lynn. Get the girl interviewed by the end of the day. No later."
"Right."
"I'm going to break the news to Muesli. I want to see his reaction."

DCI Moseley's face went ashen when he heard the news.

"Are you absolutely 100% certain of this, Brian? This is not a witch-hunt?"
"The son of his live-in partner has given a statement under oath. After we had told him Hardcastle had murdered her in a hotel bedroom and left the 'Do not disturb' sign on the door. Hardcastle was last seen boarding a flight to Amsterdam. Europol has been informed."
"I see. If you've made even the slightest mistake in this, Brian, I'll have you off the force in no time. You'll never even get a job in

supermarket security after this."

"There's no mistake. He's as bent as a Curly Wurly. Now, if you'll excuse me, sir. I have work to do. By the way, do you happen to know where the rest of Hardcastle's team are?"

"I had a phone call. They all have food poisoning. It seems they were all on a stag night together last weekend. They've all gone down with the same thing."

"I hope you're not expecting them back soon."

He didn't wait for Muesli to speak before he turned and left the office. Teresa, looking clearly embarrassed, stopped him on the stairs.

"Brian, I'm so sorry. I've cocked up."

"What's wrong, Teresa?"

"I've just been on the phone to NCA. The two officers you met, the ones I supposedly checked out for you, well, it turns out they've never met you."

"But you checked them out."

"I only checked they worked for NCA. I never actually *saw* them. It was the sergeant on the front desk who told me they were here to speak to you. I just relayed the news to you. I assumed the desk man had cleared them, so I didn't check any further. The people you met were not the real officers, not the real Fox and Sinclair. They were imposters, Brian. I'm so sorry."

"So, someone who knew NCA officers set me up to divulge what I knew about Hardcastle. He knew we were investigating him."

"Or at least, someone else knew we were suspicious."

"What do you mean, Teresa?"

"Muesli could have sent them, and then tipped off Hardcastle. Or Hardcastle might have sent them."

"Well, that would explain things. Call NCA again and give them this information. They'll be able to check Muesli's finances. Let's see if *he* was on Hardcastle's payroll. Oh, and Teresa?"

"Yes, sir?"

"We all make mistakes. My ex-boss used to say that. The important thing is to learn from it and make sure the same mistake isn't repeated. So just forget it."

"Yes, sir. Thank you, sir."

"It's Brian."

"Sorry, Brian."

"OK. Set up a teleconference with NCA, please."

"Will do."

"And circulate descriptions of Hardcastle's team countrywide."

Brian went down to have a word with the desk sergeant.

"A quick word, please, James?"
"OK, Brian. What can I do for you?"
"A couple of weeks ago, you passed a message to Teresa that two officers from the NCA wanted to talk to me. Remember?"
"Let me check the log. It was a while ago, and I see a lot of people in and out every day."
"Sinclair and Fox were the names."
"Yes. Here we are. Two officers, Sinclair and Fox. They went straight back to their car after I'd called Teresa."
"Did you check their IDs?"
"Yes."
"Did you do a photographic check against the database?"
"Well, no. I just checked their IDs on their warrant cards. Why?"
"They weren't genuine."
"Shit! Sorry, Brian. They weren't trying to access the building, though."
"Forget it."

Brian spent the best part of the afternoon in the teleconference. He laid out the full case and ensured that Teresa sent printed copies of all reports and all relevant photographic evidence, including photographs of the implicated CID officers, by fax and e-mail immediately afterwards. He asked if, as a matter of courtesy, NCA would keep him up to date with progress in the investigation. Finally, he phoned Sarah to explain he would unfortunately have to work late that evening. Sarah was not pleased, but then again, neither was Brian. During the course of the afternoon, Gary had once again been re-assigned, to help shore up the manpower due to the surprise vacancies arising from the absences of Hardcastle and other members of his team.

****

Lynn was able to trace Vicky Armstrong, the flatmate of the late Amanda Braithwaite, at her work in a call centre in Leeds. She agreed to come in to HQ on her way home at the end of her shift. This was the reason Brian was working late. He needed names of those further up the chain of supply. He and Lynn were able to grab a sandwich and a drink from the vending machine in the canteen before Vicky Armstrong arrived with her legal representative. Brian put the anxious young lady on the spot immediately.

"Thanks for coming in, Vicky. We appreciate you've had to make time to talk to us."
"OK. But I haven't done anything wrong. Have I?"
"There are certain aspects around Amanda's death that we still need to clear up. We hope you can fill in some of the gaps."
"Is my client being charged?"

Brian looked at the young man who'd just spoken. He looked about eighteen, was smartly-dressed, but wearing a shirt two or three collar-sizes too big. Probably his first assignment, he thought. Everyone has to start somewhere.

"Your client is not being charged at the moment but may well face future charges unless she co-operates fully with our inquiry. She's already withheld information, so I think you should stress to her it would be to her advantage to answer all our questions fully and honestly."
"Answer the officers, Victoria."
"Thank you, sir. Now, Victoria. Or do you prefer Vicky?"
"Vicky is fine."
"OK, Vicky. We've already established that you acted as a go-between, arranging for cocaine to be supplied to your flatmate Amanda Braithwaite. Is that correct?"
"Yes. We were both going to use it on New Year's Eve, but then I got invited out, so he brought some just for Mandy."
"Dean Donachie brought it?"
"Yes."
"He was your supplier?"
"Yes."
"Did you ever buy from anyone else?"
"No. Only Dean."
"How did you meet him?"
"In a club in Bradford. About nine months ago. It was a party. A girl from work's birthday. He just got talking to us and offered us a small dose of ecstasy to sample. Free. It was just a night out and we were having fun. We thought it was harmless. Anyway, one of the girls got his phone number and then he started turning up regularly when we were all out together. It became a regular thing. And eventually some of us tried coke."

"And are you now a regular user?"

"Most weekends, I suppose."

"And had Amanda ever used it before?"

"Not to my knowledge."

"Vicky, have you ever heard the name 'Danny Hardcastle'?"

"No."

"Are you sure."

"I'm certain I've never heard it. Why?"

"No reason. Do you know where Dean got his supplies from?"

"No. He never said."

"You never asked?"

"No. Why should I?"

"Well, every time a product like cocaine passes through a pair of hands, the price goes up. Every dealer takes a cut."

"I never thought about it. I could afford it. I was like a special treat."

"A special treat that could kill you, like it did Amanda. Think about that the next time you fancy a snort."

"I will."

"That's all for now. You can go."

"Thanks. I never meant for any of this to happen. It was just supposed to be a bit of fun."

"That's not how it turned out for Amanda, is it?"

****

The previous night, Daz and Andy had practically exhausted their supplies. They had a little MDMA, a few poppers and some Special K, but they were all but out of heroin and cocaine. However, they were awash with money and had already arranged to buy a large quantity to replenish their stocks.

Terry started work a little earlier than usual, leaving immediately after having his evening meal with Linda. She didn't yet know the nature of his work, only that he was employed as a driver. Terry had been deliberately vague about it, saying only that his employers were well-off people who liked to be chauffeured around to parties. Linda imagined they were footballers or some other kind of minor celebrities and thought no more about it, glad simply that her husband's mood had improved now that he was working and earning a living again. He kissed her on the cheek and left the house. Soon, he was on his way to Manchester with Daz and Andy in the back of the BMW, and a holdall full of banknotes in the boot. Daz and Andy had already worked out what they would buy, and the sellers were delighted that their business had become so successful so soon.

The rendezvous was a closed-down petrol station near Moss Side which they found with the aid of satnav and directions relayed via mobile phone. Within a minute of their arrival, a black Volvo XC90 pulled up about twenty yards in front of them. The driver remained in his seat while the two passengers got out and walked towards the BMW. Daz and Andy got out, after instructing Terry.

"You stay there and say nothing."

He did as he was instructed, watching while the transaction took place, Andy removing the holdall from the BMW's boot, while one of the Volvo's passengers unloaded several boxes from the back of the Volvo. After a quick check of the contents of the respective containers, the deal was sealed with a handshake and the Volvo drove off with the holdall while Daz and Andy loaded the boxes into the boot of the BMW. Throughout the transaction, Terry had remained silently in his seat, as instructed. He was worried though. He'd recognised one of the occupants of the Volvo, the driver. He was still racking his brain trying to place him when his employers jumped into the car and told him to drive back to Bradford. He wondered if the man had recognised him. Hopefully not. He'd been in the car all the time. In the dark.

He was quiet throughout the rest of his 'shift', but fulfilled his role as required, and took his wad of notes in reward at the end of the night. His employers were cock-a-hoop; the money was pouring in. The plight of their mother, in hospital, was forgotten. Forgotten, that is, until Andy received a phone call from the hospital to inform him she had died.

****

Brian and Lynn were still struggling to identify the higher links in the chain of supply. Neither Dean, nor Vicky, were prepared to divulge any information. It was Teresa who unwittingly made the breakthrough.

Knowing that the car thefts case was Muesli's bête noire, whenever she had any spare time, even during her lunch hour, she sought access to various databases, called in favours, and used logical and lateral thinking to seek that one small piece of information which would move that particular inquiry forward. Then, eventually, her persistence paid off. She sent a message to Brian.

"Car thefts. Found a possible link."

Brian put the files he was working through in his desk drawer, locked it and practically ran up the stairs to Teresa's desk.

"What have you got, Teresa?"
"I'll tell you as soon as you get your breath back."
"Now, please."
"OK. I've been cross-checking every piece of information I can find about car crimes for which youths have been questioned, suspected or convicted. And I found a couple of likely suspects. And guess what?"
"Come on."
"These two lads, Darren and Andy Fisher, were at the same school as Dean Donachie. In fact, Darren was in the same class as Donachie before Donachie was expelled."
"That's interesting, Teresa. What else have you got on these two?"
"The older boy, Darren, was arrested several times from the age of thirteen for damaging vehicles. His brother, Andy, who's a year younger has committed similar offences since he was fourteen. Both have been caught driving without a licence and without insurance and taking without consent. Their names didn't come up in earlier searches due to their age."
"How old are they now?"
"Darren's eighteen. Andy's seventeen."
"OK. Any other background stuff."
"Mother's been done for prostitution and petty theft in the past. Father's a career criminal, currently in Hewell Prison in Worcestershire."
"What's he in for?"
"Armed robbery. Ram-raids, mostly. Jewellery shops and the like."
"Thanks, Teresa. Put it all together and send me a copy, please. Oh, and see if you can get me an address, please."

****

Daz and Andy had another busy night. Their customer base had widened considerably through their use of Snapchat to advertise their products to susceptible teenagers and their sales area had expanded to take in Leeds, Halifax and Keighley. At the end of the shift, Andy was already making arrangements to buy another consignment. The money was pouring in and they were working seven nights a week and even considering driving up to Cumbria during the day, once a week. Demand for crack and heroin in Barrow, apparently, was at an all-time high in the area around Egerton Court. Terry didn't mind the extra hours. His finances now were better than they'd been for several months. His wife, Linda, had cut back on the extra work she'd been taking on and was glad that Terry seemed to be handling his job without feeling the stress he'd previously encountered working in the factory. She didn't question his role too deeply. He was a driver. That was it. It wasn't illegal to drive for a living. Nevertheless, she had a feeling it was not all above board. He never received a wage slip, for example, and was always paid in cash.

****

The following morning, Brian took a phone call from DCI Moseley.

"Brian, I'd just like to put your mind at rest concerning DI Hardcastle's team. DS Ward rang me this morning to apologise for his absence and on behalf of DS Schofield and DC Tarkovics. It seems they expect to be discharged from hospital probably tomorrow and will be back at work next Monday. So, you can stop worrying about them."
"Can I ask where their stag night was, sir?"
"Scarborough, Ward said."
"Thank you, sir. That's good news."

As soon as he put the phone down, he looked up the number for Scarborough Health Authority and requested information regarding the three absent officers. The return call fifteen minutes later confirmed his suspicions. No patients with those names had been treated in any of the area's hospitals in recent weeks. They were buying time to make good their escape. He silently congratulated himself for pre-empting their deception by putting out the APW – the All Ports Warning – on them.

By early afternoon, he was on his way to an address in Rawdon. Teresa had passed it to him; the last known address of Darren and Andy Fisher. No-one came to the door in response to his repeated knocking and ringing the doorbell. He went around to the back door, through a low wooden gate falling off its hinges and swinging in the breeze. Looking through the kitchen window, he could see signs of recent habitation, but no signs of life. He was on the point of leaving when a middle-aged woman emerged from the house next door, a basket full of washing under her arm. He called her.

"Excuse me."

"Yes."

"Can you tell me when the occupants will be home? I'd really like to speak to them."

"You won't get anything out of Sheila. She died."

"Oh, I'm sorry to hear that. Sheila Fisher?"

"Yes. She sometimes used that name."

"What about her kids?"

"Those two. Good luck in finding them. There's always people looking for them."

"What sort of people?"

"Kids. Druggies. That sort."

"Are you saying they dealt drugs?"

"Can't prove it, but that would be my guess. They kept some odd hours. Seemed to sleep most of the day and go out at night, till the early hours."

"When did you last see them?"

"Three or four days ago. When their mother went into hospital."

"Any idea where they might have gone?"

"I assumed they'd gone to stay close to the hospital, but Mrs Pickersgill down the road had visited Sheila and it seemed she was the only visitor. It was Mrs Pickersgill who told me Sheila had died."

"Any idea when the funeral is taking place?"

"No, sorry. You could ask Mrs Pickersgill at number 72. She might know, I suppose."

"Thanks very much for your time."

Mrs Pickersgill was unable to help. Brian returned to his car and drove to the hospital to see what information he could get from there. His initial enquiry at Reception resulted in his being sent from pillar to post until he finally arrived at the mortuary where he was told the body of Sheila Fisher would be kept pending efforts to contact a member of her family. So far, their efforts had been without success. No-one knew where her kids were, and their father no longer had any contact with their mother, nor any interest in her. It seemed as if the arrangements, and the expense, of her funeral would be met from public funds. He returned to the office. Another wasted afternoon.

****

Rather than stay in the rented house in Rawdon, Daz and Andy moved in with a customer of theirs on a short-term basis. In lieu of paying rent, they supplied her with the drugs she needed to continue her chaotic life. In return she supplied them with shelter and regular sex.

****

Lynn and Gary continued with their efforts to trace the owner of the car which had caused the death of Mark Bell's fiancée. So far, all their enquiries had proved fruitless. The eye-witnesses were unable to give enough specific detail about the incident, and many of the traffic cameras in the area were annoyingly offline at the time. Every line of enquiry had petered out. Every avenue they explored had come to a dead end.

Mark Bell had become morose, withdrawn. He lost interest in his work to such an extent that his boss felt obliged to issue him with a written warning. He had begun to drink regularly in the local pubs, often on his own. On one such occasion, an acquaintance had offered him something 'to cheer him up'. He went with him to a flat on the Thorpe Edge estate and experienced crack cocaine for the first, but not the last, time.

CHAPTER 19

Brian, as was rapidly becoming his custom, called in at the Draper on his way home. Sam greeted him from behind the bar.

"Evening, Brian. How's your day been?"
"Frustrating, Sam. Like most of them at the moment. A pint of Draper's please."
"Coming up."

At that moment, Kenny walked in, wearing one of his trademark brightly-coloured shirts. Brian was quick to offer.

"And a drink for Kenny, please, Sam."
"Oh, cheers, Brian. How's it going?"
"It's going nowhere, Kenny."
"Shame."
"Actually, maybe you can help me again."
"Yeah. Whatever you need."

Brian fished into his pocket and pulled out the photos Teresa had printed for him. He showed them to Kenny.

"Do you know either of these lads, Kenny?"
"Let's have a look. Yes. I think I know this lad. I've seen his face before. It's a few years ago, though."
"Those are old photos. Taken in his youth-offending days."
"I can't think of the name at the moment."
"Fisher. That's Darren, and his younger brother, Andy."
"Yeah. That's him. I dealt with Darren. Vehicle damage and the like. His brother was never on my case book, though. What have they been up to?"
"Nicking cars, joy-riding, drug-dealing probably. They were at the same school as Dean Donachie. Knew each other. I don't suppose you would have any idea where I can find them?"
"Not really. It's a long time ago. They used to live in Rawdon then. With their mother."
"Their mother died, and they've moved on. I need to find them."
"Sorry, Brian. I can't help you with this. I'll keep my ears open, though."
"Cheers."
"Yeah. No problem. Darren Fisher, yeah. No use to anybody, him.

As much use as a blind one-legged tightrope walker with gout. Anyway, how's the missus and the kids?"

"All fine, Kenny. Young Daniel's starting to feel a bit jealous of all the attention the baby's getting, but he'll be fine. I do my best to spend as much time as I can with him before he goes to bed. Which reminds me, I need to be on my way. See you another time, Kenny. Cheers, Sam."

"See you, Brian."

Brian crossed the road towards the car park. At its entrance, he found pimply Adie waiting for him.

"Now then, Adie. You behaving yourself?"

"Yes, sir. I know something you might be interested in."

"What's that, Adie?"

"Depends how much it's worth."

"I don't know unless you tell me what it is."

"Drugs."

"You'll have to be a bit more specific."

"I've seen someone selling to a local dealer."

"Names?"

"The buyer's called Deano. He's been dealing on the streets around here for a long time."

"I know Deano. What about the sellers?"

"Two young blokes. Not local, but I've seen them around a few times. They turned up in a black Beemer to make the sale."

"You sure? You sure it's a black BMW?"

"Yeah. I know cars."

"Did you get the registration?"

"No. I was too far away for that. And it was dark."

"Well, that's something at least."

"More. There was another man with them. A driver. An older man."

"Is that the best description you can give me?"

"Like I said, it was dark. And he never got out of the car."

"And where exactly did this take place?"

"Just at the end of the road. Just down Howgate, at the back of the Alex."

"When was this, Adie?"

"Last Friday. About ten."

"Is that everything?"

"Yeah."

"OK. You did well, Adie. If ever you see it happen again. Call me immediately. You've got my mobile number."

"OK."

"Here's a fiver. Don't spend it on drugs."

"I won't. I know an off-licence that sells cider to lads my age."

"We'll deal with that another time. I'll see you again some time."

"Yeah. See you."

Brian continued to his car and drove home where he played the role of husband and father until he went to bed. He and Sarah talked for a while before she put out the light and went to sleep. Brian, though, was restless. He waited just long enough to be sure Sarah was asleep, then slipped out of bed, pulled on his dressing gown and crept quietly down the stairs. In the lounge, he switched on a table lamp before moving into the kitchen where he took a tumbler from one cupboard and selected a bottle of malt from another. He poured himself a very generous measure and tasted it before returning to the dimly-lit lounge. He settled in his armchair to ponder the day's events, while also thinking back to the previous October when, he imagined, John Braden would have spent many an hour late at night, in his armchair, sipping malt whisky while trying to make sense of what was happening around him.

He went back to bed around two o'clock, just before Sarah got up to attend to their crying baby.

****

Driving to work in the morning, the question was still on Brian's mind. A black BMW. Could it be the car which forced another car off the road down Pool Bank, causing the death of a young pregnant girl? If it was, that would suggest there may be a link between drug dealers and the joyriders. He wondered if it could be the same people. The only way to find out would be to find that car – and its occupants.

Teresa was already at her desk when Brian approached her. She smiled.

"Good morning, Brian. What can I do for you today?"

"Morning, Teresa. The Fisher case. Can you get on to DVLA, please? I want to know if either of those kids has registered ownership of a black BMW."

"Any more details of the car?"

"No. that's all we've got."

"OK. I'll get on to it."

"And see if you can get any camera footage of a black BMW in the Idle area last Friday. About ten o'clock."

"Will do."

He returned to his desk and briefed Gary and Lynn on his news.

"So, there's not much we can do until Teresa comes back to us."

"No, but if there's any footage, you could be in for a long session of watching hours of it."

"Won't that be fun!"

At least Muesli was just letting them get on with their enquiries without the need for constant updates. It seemed to have sunk in that his absent officers would not be returning to duty, and he spent much of his time on the phone to other areas begging to borrow staff to fill the gaps until he could fill the vacancies on a permanent basis. It was by now common knowledge that Hardcastle and his team had been involved in criminal activities and that, as a consequence, Muesli faced some serious interviews with his superiors. Apart from Brian's team, morale in the department was low. Many of the officers, solid, competent detectives, felt they might be drawn into a shitstorm if, or when, it became public that there were corrupt officers in the Bradford CID. They'd all be tarred with the same brush when the press got hold of it. If any member of Brian's team felt the same, nobody showed it. They all remained focused on what they were paid to do.

Brian picked up the phone on the first ring.

"What have you got, Teresa?"

"Good news. A friend of mine at DVLA has managed to trace the car."

"Fantastic!"

"It took a while, but she found a black BMW registered under the name of Sheila Fisher, the boys' mother. It's insured, but not taxed. Reg is FG07 BFG."

"Well done, Teresa. Circulate the number, please."

"Will do. Bye."

He put the phone down and passed the news to Lynn and Gary.

"Now we've got a chance of catching these sods."

"As long as they're not driving on false plates."

That was a sobering thought.

"Let's hope they haven't thought of that."

****

That evening, Terry drove to the lock-up as usual. Daz and Andy were waiting and unlocked the garage when they saw his car approaching. He parked up and they all climbed into the BMW. Terry put the key into the ignition and turned it. Nothing happened. He switched off and tried again. Nothing. Not even lights on the instrument panel.

"Fuck's up, Terry?"
"Don't know. I'll have a look. See if it's anything obvious."

He opened the bonnet, got out of the car and poked and prodded around the engine compartment, looking for anything obvious like a loose connection. He could see nothing.

"What's wrong, Terry?"
"No idea. Nothing I can see. We need someone who knows about cars. I'm no expert."
"Well, we'll have to get someone to look at it tomorrow. We're going to be late. We'll use your car, Terry."
"It's not insured for business use."
"Who gives a fuck? Come on. Move."

They transferred the goods to the boot of Terry's Astra, got in and drove to their first rendezvous. The deal was quickly concluded and the bundles of twenty-pound notes tossed casually into the holdall in the boot. As usual, the boys were on a high. This game was easy!

They ended the night in Sheffield, in an industrial estate just off the MI. As usual, Terry stayed in the car and let his employers conduct the business. These were new buyers and there was a little tension before a deal was struck and goods and money changed hands. There was a palpable sense of relief as they drove away back towards the motorway.

"Good deal, that. Twenty grand profit for ten minutes' work. They'll want the same again at the weekend. Maybe more."

"Should we put another order in with the Manchester boys?"

"I'll do it in the morning. When we count up how much we've made tonight. Right, Terry, back to Bradford."

****

Aware of the possibility that the BMW might be bearing false plates, officers in the region were alerted to look out for a black BMW, possibly with the registration number FG07 BFG. Though a couple of BMWs were stopped, nothing suspicious was found.

Brian was dismayed at the lack of progress as he read the overnight reports the following morning. He had arrived early at the office hoping to hear good news, and it was fortunate that nobody else was in the office to hear him vent his rage with a string of expletives. He had calmed down by the time other officers reported for duty and was drinking, but not enjoying, a cup of coffee from the vending machine when Teresa rang.

"Morning, Teresa."

"Morning, Brian. You have visitors."

"Who?"

"Sinclair and Fox, from the NSA."

"You're sure they're the real guys this time?"

"Absolutely. They're outside, parked across the road."

"OK. Tell them I'm on my way."

He walked down to the car park, absent-mindedly whistling the Eminem song "The Real Slim Shady". He was singing by the time he reached the car where the two officers were waiting.

"I'm Slim Shady, yes, I'm the real Shady
All you other Slim Shadys are just imitating
So won't the real Slim Shady please stand up
Please stand up, please stand up?"

He grinned.

"Sorry, guys. I'm in a funny mood this morning."

"Well, I can assure you we're the real Sinclair and Fox. We'll stand up, if you like."

"It's fine. What can I do for you?"

"We've got some good news for you. We've, or rather, our continental friends have, traced your old pal Hardcastle."

"Where is the bastard?"

"Last known location was Albania."

"Albania?"

"Albania. The problem is we don't have an agreement with Albania for extradition. They haven't signed up to the European Arrest Warrant agreement. But the good news is, we have people over there keeping an eye on him. If he moves, we'll be ready to nail him."

"And if he doesn't?"

"We're doing our best to freeze all his assets, hoping we can lure him out. We know he's still running his business. We're just trying to make things difficult for him."

"You know about his accomplices in CID?"

"Yes, thanks. Your clerical officer forwarded the details."

"Do you think there's anyone else involved?"

"We've no doubt there are others. We're still gathering evidence."

"Anything I can do?"

"Not really. This is just keeping you in the loop. We appreciate the fact that you're feeding information through to us."

"It's worth it if we get the bastard. I'd love to see his face when he's arrested."

"We'll bear that in mind."

They shook hands and Brian watched as they drove away. He reflected on their words. "We've no doubt there are others." Who was under suspicion? His best guess was DCI Moseley.

****

The following morning, Terry drove Daz and a mechanic friend to the lock-up where he examined the BMW. After fifteen minutes probing, he announced there were some electrical problems which he could only trace with the help of some computer diagnostic equipment which he had at his garage. Terry suspected he was exaggerating the complexity of the problem either because he hadn't much idea what he was looking for, or, more likely, he wanted to grossly inflate the bill. Either way, it wasn't Terry's decision, and he was forced to accept the fact that he would have to use his own car to drive his employers around until the BMW was fixed. So far, his employers hadn't seen the Astra misbehave but he felt that was only a matter of time. They waited until the low-loader arrived to take away the BMW before driving to Manchester in the Astra to replenish their stock in time for the weekend.

As luck would have it, the Astra's engine cut out twice on the way to Manchester and as a result they were twenty minutes late for the rendezvous. On the way home, Andy asked why Terry continued to drive around in 'this old piece of shit'.

"Because I can't afford anything else."
"Well, we've a big weekend coming up. If we sell all this lot, you just might find you can afford to trade it in for something a bit better. We used to nick better cars than this."

It was a flippant comment but Terry bit his tongue and said nothing. But it had him wondering.

****

Lynn and Gary had spent a full day watching camera footage. Occasionally, a black BMW appeared, and on each occasion, they had to check its ownership and ascertain what it was doing in the area at the time. And on each occasion, the cars, their drivers, and the reason for their being in the area all proved legitimate. Their spirits were low until Brian reported the good news that DS Ward had been arrested attempting to board the cross-channel ferry at Dover. One down, three, or more likely four, to go.

CHAPTER 20

On Saturday evening, Brian finished the washing-up, helped put Daniel to bed and asked his wife's permission to go out for a couple of pints. He'd always sought permission; she'd always given it. It was a charade they'd gone through all their married life. She understood the stress his job brought and, besides, she felt more comfortable at home, being a housewife and a mother. They were both comfortable with the arrangement.

Coat collar up against the cold wind, he walked down the hill towards the centre of the village, noting the group of youths assembled near the entrance to the car park. Seeing him, they split up and walked away. He knew they'd be back together in five minutes or so. The power of mobile phones.

The Draper was heaving. Standing room only, but as usual the customers were courteous enough to make room for anybody who needed to get to the bar to be served. If only all pubs were like that. He could name a few where you had to fight your way to the bar. Where regulars would deliberately block access to anyone whose face they didn't recognise. Thank God the Draper was more civilised than that. He nodded a greeting to all those he recognised and thanked those who made way for him to get his pint. For a change he chose one of the guest ales and squeezed himself away from the bar and against the wall from where he could keep an eye on the behaviour of a small group at the table by the door. He caught Nick's eye and called him over.

"Hello, Brian. Nice to see you again."
"Hi, Nick. Do you know those four lads by the door?"
"No. Never seen them before. Why?"
"I've just seen one of them passing what I think may be drugs under the table."
"I'll throw them out now. We don't want that sort of stuff in here."
"Let me deal with it, please."
"OK. I'll be right behind you if you need any help."

Brian put his glass on the bar and approached the table. The young man facing him dropped a small white packet under the table. Brian had seen it.

"You've dropped something, lad."
"I don't think so."
"Well, I do."
"It's none of your business, anyway."

Brian took out his warrant card.

"You're wrong, lad. It's very much my business. Pick it up and give it to me."

Nervously, he looked at his mates, hoping they would help him out in some way. He was wrong. Brian made the consequences quite clear.

"If any of you lads want to make any sort of objection, think again. You're all implicated here. Any objection from any of you and I'll make sure you'll be under observation for the rest of your lives. Is that clear?"

They all nodded.

"OK, you lot, stay where you are. You, lad. Outside."

Brian hoisted him out of his seat by his collar and accompanied him outside and into the alley at the side of the pub. In the dimly-lit passage, Brian pushed him up against a wall and snarled.

"Empty your pockets. Put the contents on the ground."

The lad complied, placing a wallet, some small change, a mobile phone and a bank card on the ground.

"And the rest."
"There's nothing else. Honest."
"Empty your pockets. Or else I'll tear them open and look myself."

He extracted three small clear plastic packages, each containing a small quantity of white powder, and placed them on the ground.

"What are these?"
"I don't know. Someone just gave me them on the street."
"Try again. What are these?"
"I don't know."

"I'll tell you what they are. They're illegal class A drugs. Cocaine, I would guess. Do you know what the penalty is for being in possession of a class A drug?"

"No. Like I said, someone just gave them to me."

"You could go to prison. Maximum sentence, seven years. I don't think you would like that, a pretty boy like you."

"Look, I've never been in any trouble before. I promise it won't happen again."

"I'll tell you what we'll do, then. This time, I'll take your word for it. If I ever catch you with drugs again, I'll arrest you and seek the highest possible penalty. So, I want you to tell me you're sorry and it won't ever happen again."

"I'm sorry. It won't happen again."

"Just one more thing. Don't ever go in the Draper again. I don't ever want to see either you or your mates in there in future. Clear?"

"Yes."

"The staff have clocked you. I'll tell them to make sure if any of you walk through that door again, they ring the police. I can be here in five minutes. And I'll give you all a really hard time. Understood."

"Yes."

"So, who did you buy the stuff from?"

"A couple of guys were dealing just up the road."

"Know their names?"

"One was called Andy. I don't know the other one. Or the driver."

"What sort of car?"

"Astra, I think."

"Colour?"

"Don't know. Dark."

"Can you describe Andy?"

"Young. Seventeen, eighteen, maybe. Slim, average height. Short fair hair."

"Is that all you can give me?"

"Yes, sorry."

"OK. Pick up your possessions. Apart from the drugs. Get on your way. Your mates will be joining you in ten seconds."

Brian bent down and picked up the plastic packages, opened each one, and let the wind disperse the contents. He turned and walked back through the pub door. Seconds later, the three other young men left, looking sheepish.

"Thanks, Brian. I'm glad you sorted it out without making a fuss."

"No problem. They won't be back. But if they do ever wander in, just give me a call and I'll be straight down. I don't want drug users in my local."

Brian went back to his pint and engaged in conversations with other customers. At the back of his mind was the thought that the lad had mentioned someone called Andy as the dealer. And an Astra. If this was Andy Fisher and his brother, with their driver, then they were now using an Astra, rather than the BMW his team had been looking for. Once again, they were keeping one step ahead of the police.

****

On Monday morning, as soon as he walked into the office, he was met with the news that two more ram-raids had taken place over the weekend. An off-licence in Wilsden had been the target on Saturday night and a Minimarket in Shipley on Sunday night. In both cases, an ATM had been wrenched from its stand. Gary and Lynn had already been despatched to investigate, leaving Brian to continue alone with his case load.

****

Daz and Andy slept in. They'd had a long night to cap off a busy and successful weekend. They'd taken more money than ever before and now had a team of street dealers beneath them. This arrangement meant they no longer had to drive to every pub and club to sell their merchandise. Now they just sold to dealers, making fewer drops than before, and were thus able to expand their operation to cover a wider geographical area. They'd come up against occasional resistance from other sellers when they'd encroached on someone else's patch but had quickly overcome any objection as a result of an extra purchase made during their previous collection of goods from Manchester. It was at Andy's side as he slept. A Russian military pistol, plus ammunition, a bargain at £150, according to the seller. Nobody would argue with them now. The fact that Andy, at the moment, was terrified of the thought of actually *using* it was immaterial. In fact, he'd bought it on trust. He didn't even know for sure if it worked. But, nevertheless, it would give them instant respect on the street.

When he woke, he found two new messages on his phone. Both

were from street dealers requesting more stock. He would answer them once he'd consulted his brother.

****

The first thing Terry did when he woke up was make himself a mug of coffee. Linda had already gone out to work so now was the best time to check his finances. He emptied out his pockets. Over £400 in notes. He walked across to the chest of drawers in the bedroom, removed the bottom drawer, and pulled out a locked metal cash box from underneath at the back. He unlocked it and took out the contents, counting out the notes. £1960. It had quickly mounted up. He smiled, imagining the look on his wife's face when he eventually showed her the stash. Then, on reflection, he put the lot back in the box and locked it away. He'd tell Linda some other time. Maybe when the amount had reached £3000. Another couple of good weekends should do the trick.

He checked his phone. A message from Andy.

"Pick us up at nine tonight."

He replied 'OK' and went for a shower.

****

Brian spent the morning looking at traffic camera footage taken over the weekend in the local area. He could find no trace of a dark Astra. He was puzzled. Had they changed the car again? It was possible. Another possibility was that they had moved their sales operation to a different city. A third was that they had stopped selling. At that point, he didn't even consider the fourth option – that they'd moved up the chain and were now supplying the street dealers.

There was little he could do at the moment. He just had to wait for a break. He put the file aside and instead looked at all the intelligence they'd gathered so far concerning the car thefts. Since Muesli had been screaming at him to make some progress, he thought he'd better make the effort. He was still poring over the notes when Lynn and Gary returned.

"Hi, you two. I hope you've had a better morning than I've had."

"I'm not sure about that, Brian. But at least we've got some CCTV to look at, from both incidents. Do you mind if we show you? See if you confirm what we're thinking?"
"Go ahead."

Gary inserted the disc into the monitor.

"This one's from the Wilsden store on Saturday night. Watch. See the Range Rover driving past? Here it is again. Reversing at high speed. There. Straight into the shop entrance. Now the three men, masked and hooded attacking the ATM with sledgehammers. Loading money into a holdall. And out. Back in the Range Rover and away they go. Look at the clock. Less than a minute."

Lynn continued the narrative as Gary ejected the disc and prepared the second disc to play.

"The Range Rover was found abandoned in Harden. An eye-witness thinks he saw three men leaving the vehicle and get into a dark-coloured VW, possibly a Golf, which drove off at speed in the direction of Cullingworth. SOCO have been examining the Range Rover but have found no prints nor any useable evidence as yet. The vehicle, by the way, was stolen a short while earlier in Bingley."

Gary continued, as the second disc played.

"The second incident on Sunday night is slightly different. Here it's an Isuzu D-Max pickup reversing outside the minimarket. Three men again. Smash the glass door and in. Heavy duty chain looped over the ATM. Then dragged through the door. The whole ATM loaded into the back and they're away. Again, less than a minute. I think it's the same crew."
"Me too", continued Lynn. "Again, SOCO got nothing from the vehicle, which, again, had been stolen earlier and abandoned on the moor at Baildon. This time nobody witnessed the transfer to a second vehicle. These guys are good."
"OK. I presume you've asked Traffic for footage of the areas where the robberies took place?"
"Still waiting for news from them."
"Can we link these to any of the earlier ram-raids?"
"Only in the respect that it's possible the earlier raids were part of their learning curve until they were ready to move up to this sort of

stuff."

"I don't think we've seen the last of these guys."

"At least, the more we see of them, the more likely we are to catch them. Let's hope they make a mistake next time. But apart from that, let's hope that Traffic come up with something."

****

Linda and Terry had finished their evening meal together, washed up and were watching TV. They were still a couple, but some of the warmth of their relationship had recently evaporated. Terry knew that his wife suspected his job wasn't entirely legal and was worried about the consequences should he get caught. Terry, too, knew that it was just a matter of time. He just needed a few more weeks. Then he would quit and walk away. What worried him most, though, was whether the brothers would allow him to walk away bearing in mind what he knew about their criminal activities. He would have to choose his moment carefully.

He didn't yet know Andy had a gun.

At eight-thirty, he kissed Linda and got his coat.

"Don't wait up, love. It'll be late when I get back."

"OK. See you in the morning."

He met the brothers at the lock-up where they were waiting with the holdall full of cash. Together they set off towards Manchester. Andy was on a high. He'd recently taken to sampling some of the merchandise to his brother's dismay and disapproval. Andy shrugged it off. The way he saw it, he was simply quality-checking the product they bought. It needed to be done. They paid for it. They needed to ensure the quality was consistently high.

****

The meeting went without a hitch. Andy selected a kilo pack at random, opened it and took a small sample which he snorted and pronounced acceptable. Minutes later, they were driving towards Sheffield to a small unit on an industrial estate near Rotherham. Here, they handed over the packs of cocaine in exchange for wads of twenty-pound notes. They drove off to take the M1 north, fully aware that their cocaine would once again be cut before resale, doubling its value, but unconcerned. They'd made a massive profit without having to take the risks of being arrested for selling in bars and clubs and on the streets.

Andy was still on a high.

"Let's have some fun. Daz. Let's take a car."
"OK."

The brothers felt the need to celebrate, instructing Terry to drive around the outskirts of Leeds and taking a route through Headingley and on to Horsforth. Unable to find a suitable vehicle, they continued on to Yeadon, where Daz spotted an old Audi 100. They circled the area and approached from a different direction. The Audi was parked on a quiet street, under a street light which was not illuminated. They had enough cover. They could take it easily without detection. Again, they circled the area to find somewhere to leave the Astra, somewhere safe, somewhere it wouldn't attract undue attention. Daz was uneasy about leaving it with all the money in the boot and aired his concerns.

"What if someone nicks it?"
"Let's take the money with us."
"Yeah, but when we trash the car, we'll have to carry the bag all the way back to the Astra."

Terry suggested the compromise.

"Why don't I follow you in the Astra and leave it near where you're planning to do your joyriding?"
"No chance. I'm not leaving you with all that money. What if you do a runner?"
"I'm not that stupid."

The brothers discussed it in whispers while Terry drove around the area. Finally, the agreed their plan.

"Here's what we do, Terry. We stop the car at the end of the street. Andy stays in the car with you while I nick the Audi. Then you follow me. When we get near the race track, I'll pull over and you can leave the Astra in a layby. We'll all go together to the race track. Afterwards, we walk back to the Astra and you drive us home. How does that sound?"

"We leave the money in the Astra?"

"Yeah. It'll be safer than in the Audi. It might end up damaged so badly that we can't get the boot open."

Andy laughed, high-pitched, hysterically until they parked the Astra at the end of the street, some fifty yards from the Audi. While Daz walked over to the Audi, Andy snorted another line of coke. He felt invincible.

In less than a minute, Daz had the steering lock off and the Audi's engine started and was racing away with the Astra in his wake. The two cars were heading towards Oakland. Soon, Daz indicated as they approached a layby. Both cars pulled in. Terry locked the Astra and he and Andy got in the Audi, Terry sitting alone in the back, as Daz and Andy swapped seats in the front. Tonight, it was Andy's turn. He wanted to show off his driving skills to the man they employed as their driver. He engaged first gear, released the handbrake and hit the accelerator. The Audi, despite its age, responded immediately and raced towards Oakland.

CHAPTER 21

Bill picked his way through the trees in the dark. In his left hand he carried his torch, flicking it on at intervals to check his path. He knew his way well enough without it, knew where the obstacles were. But you could never tell at this time of year. Branches often snapped and littered the path, and if he tripped and fell, if he broke his ankle or something, he could lie there all night. And if they eventually found him, still alive that is, he'd have some explaining to do. His right hand patted his coat where the two dead pheasants were stuffed into the deep inside pockets. "Perk of the job", he murmured to himself. "Two good cock birds. Heavy buggers." He'd need another whisky when he got back to the cottage, though as he stumbled along, his unsteady gait gave away the fact that he'd already consumed plenty. Breathing heavily, and coughing, he didn't hear the car.

He emerged from the woods and stepped on to the concrete track, pausing to stamp his boots to shake off some of the cloying mud which added so much extra weight to the heavy footwear. He stood for a second or two, breathing laboriously. He could hear it now. Was it a car? Where was it? It was getting louder.

Andy whipped the car round the bend at breakneck speed. Even without the headlights he knew the lie of the track. The last thing he expected was an obstacle in his way. He saw it at the last second. A dark shape in the middle of the track. Too late. Bill's leg snapped as the car hit him. His face smacked into the windscreen, splattering it with blood. His body jerked upwards, somersaulting over the roof, and hit the cold hard concrete, where it lay, lifeless. Andy brought the car to a slewing halt about thirty yards away. Daz jumped out and ran back down the track, slowing as he approached the body lying face down. A dark pool of blood spread slowly outwards from the smashed head. The old man's shattered right leg was splayed at an impossible angle to the rest of his body. Gingerly, he put his foot under the man's side and tried to turn him over but couldn't move the dead weight. He noticed the trickle of urine as it soaked through the old man's trousers and smelt the stench of the involuntary bowel movement. A black sickly smell. He vomited at the side of the road, and ran, stumbling, back to the car.

"Is he...Is he badly?"

Andy spoke slowly but with a nervous edge to his voice. He already knew the answer to the question.

"Badly? You've fuckin' killed him! He's fuckin' dead!"
"Sure?"
"'Course I'm fuckin' sure. His brains are all over the fuckin' place. I'm telling you, he's fuckin' dead. Jesus!"
"Well, he shouldn't have fuckin' been there. He shouldn't have been there! What the fuck was he doing there?"
"He works here. He worked here. He was the gamekeeper."

They both turned to face Terry in the back seat. For just a few seconds, in their panic, they'd forgotten about him. But now they turned their attention to him and eyed him suspiciously. He was a witness! They were brothers. They would stick together. And their mates would alibi them, for a few quid. But the man in the back seat was a different proposition. They realised it almost at the same time. They didn't really know him. Or anything about him, apart from what he'd told them.

Terry could see it in their eyes. They were weighing him up, trying to decide what to do about him. He knew whatever decision they came to, he couldn't be a part of. It had gone too far now. He'd come tonight with the intention of finding out if they were the ones who'd taken his car. And if they were, he meant to beat the shit out of them. But it was past that stage now. He had to think. Fast!

"Move it, Andy! Drive up to near the main road. We'll ditch the car, and leg it."
"What about him?"
"I'm thinking."

Andy shoved the car into first and turned back up the slight incline. He drove into the field to avoid running over the corpse on the track. The tyres took a good grip on the firm ground and he increased his speed. Terry didn't notice as Andy's right hand reached inside his jacket for the gun. Daz broke the silence.

"So how do you know the old guy, then, Terry?"
"He's the one who informs the police when he finds wrecked cars on the estate. Cars that have been stolen by twats like you for a bit

of fun. He told the police when he found mine. A Focus. Nice car. Best one I ever had. Never let me down. I needed it to get to work. And when I lost it, I lost my job. Just because someone took it. For a bit of fun. And drove it round these fields. And left it pancaked in the ditch. And you know what they did then? They pissed in it. They fuckin' pissed in it!"

Terry was becoming angry. He clenched his fists as he spoke, hissing the words through his teeth. He was seething. His heart pounded, and the veins stood out from his temples. He was sure they were the ones. He was certain. And then he knew. Any doubt, even the slightest possibility he might have been wrong, dissipated in an instant as he watched as Daz turned to face forward. He could hear him clear his throat, and he knew what was coming next. He'd imagined it so many times. Woken in the middle of the night thinking about it. And his anger welled up as he watched the ball of phlegm issue from Daz's mouth and land square on the rear-view mirror, before slowly dribbling down.

"You bastard!"

He threw a punch which caught Daz on the side of the face. Only a glancing blow, but it was all he could manage as the car bumped its way over the rough ground. He threw another which Daz deflected with his arm. Rising from his seat, he pushed his left arm between the side of the car and the head rest, and locked it under Daz's chin, pulling him back against the seat in an attempt to choke him. Daz's hands came up to try to prise the arm from his throat. He gasped to his brother.

"Do him, Andy. Do him. Now!"

Terry saw the dull steel as Andy's right arm came up between the seats. He was steering left-handed, half watching where he was heading, half watching behind, as he tried to aim the barrel at Terry's face. The car lurched to the left as the front wheel hit a rock, drawing Andy's attention to the front for a split second. It was enough. With his right hand, Terry picked up the discarded Krooklok on the back seat beside him, and as Andy re-sighted the gun, brought it down hard just above his wrist. The explosion was deafening in the confines of the car. Blood spurted on the windscreen, as Daz started to convulse and scream. His hands were no longer trying to prise Terry's arm from his throat. They were holding his groin. Trying desperately to staunch the flow of blood which pulsed and arced between his fingers. The bullet had severed his femoral artery. He was bleeding to death. And he knew it. And was powerless to stop it. He looked pleadingly at his brother, who still held the gun in his limp hand. But Andy couldn't raise the pistol. He couldn't grip it. He had no grip. His fingers tingled, and his forearm throbbed with the agony from his broken radius and ulna. He tried to shut out the pain. To ignore the cries of his dying brother. Daz's eyes focused on his brother for a fleeting second. They blazed defiantly. In little more than a whisper he gave Andy his final instructions.

"Kill the bastard!"

His eyes closed. He leaned back in his seat, still holding his groin. The blood was still pulsing out, though not so forcefully now. His cries were little more than a whimper, like a wounded animal.

Andy put his foot down, turning the wheel from side to side with his good left hand. Trying to keep Terry off balance in the back as he raced towards the oak tree. Terry shifted across into the seat behind the driver, his left hand frantically scrambling among the broken diamonds of glass strewn on the seat until he located the seat belt mounting. He pulled the clasp from its reel with his right hand. Too quickly. The inertia reel locked. He kept calm and tried again. This time it came free and he pulled it across his body and locked it in position. He felt the sudden change of direction, the rear wheels locking and skewing abruptly to the right as Andy wrenched hard on the handbrake. The impact was violent and immediate and jerked Terry against the door as it caught the tree a glancing blow. His head struck the door frame, dislodging another shower of glass fragments. He could smell the bark. He was so close he could actually smell it.

Andy turned for another circuit. Another rapid charge at the tree. Foot hard down on the gas. Daz lolled in the passenger seat, unrestrained, leaning against his brother, unconcerned at the bouncing and battering motion of the car. He was beyond it now. Andy pushed him roughly away, wincing at the pain pulsating in his forearm. He dropped the gun in his lap and locked his broken right arm through the spokes of the steering wheel. He moved his left arm from the wheel and felt for the weapon.

Terry was alert to the danger. He picked up the Krooklok at his side and opened it out. He moved forward quickly before Andy could get a grip on the gun. Andy's eyes widened in alarm as he felt the cold metal against his throat. He began to gag as Terry pulled backwards with both hands, increasing the pressure, choking him. Fighting for breath, he instinctively dropped the gun and brought his hand up to his throat to prise away the Krooklok. The type he could remove in seconds from the gear stick and handbrake. The type he would always toss casually into the back seat or out of the window in triumph and disdain. The type which was now crushing his Adam's apple and throttling him.

"Game's over, Andy. Know what I mean?"

Andy knew he hadn't the strength to free himself. With one good hand, he just couldn't break the stranglehold. And with his throat being compressed tight against the head rest there was no room to manoeuvre. He had one last chance. Side-swipe the car against the tree. He could do it. It would work. He'd practiced dozens of times, in all kinds of cars. It was all a matter of concentration. And timing. If he could just ignore the pain. Keep his head clear. Just for a few more seconds. That would be enough. It would shake the bastard off. Then he'd grab the gun and finish him. And then the game would be over. He knew Daz was gone. But he still had a chance. He'd finish it. Here. Now. Once and for all. This is it. This is for real.

The oak tree loomed out of the darkness. Directly ahead. Terry held his nerve. And kept the steady pressure on Andy's windpipe. Counting down as the distance to the solid oak rapidly decreased. And its trunk seemed to broaden until it filled the whole windscreen, blotting out what faint light there was in the sky.

"Now!", Andy thought to himself. "Now. Do it now! Spin the wheel, full lock!"

But the wheel refused to turn. His broken forearm prevented the signals from his brain reaching his hand. His muscles took over, urging his wrist to turn. To grip. Sending frantic, painful messages back to his brain. Inducing nausea. Shutting down the nerves in his arm, in his hand, to prevent further damage.

At the last instant, Terry released his grip on the Krooklok. He put his head down between his crooked arms, elbows locked. And his knees against the back of the driver's seat. And braced himself for the inevitable impact.

The car struck the trunk of the oak tree full-on. For a second, the rear lifted off the ground, and then settled again with a thud, the boot lid springing open. The impact forced Daz's lifeless body forward as the airbag inflated and immediately exploded. His head struck what remained of the windscreen, shattering it into tiny squares, and his body followed through the gaping hole, settling on the crumpled bonnet, as his trainers caught on the dashboard, tearing his ankle ligaments but stopping him from being launched further. His lifeless body was already spread-eagled on the bonnet as his brother, restrained by his seat belt, felt the full force of the impact. The engine was forced from its snapped mountings and tore through the bulkhead. Andy screamed as metal ripped into his flesh. The clutch pedal snapped off his left ankle. The steering wheel lashed into his diaphragm as he crumpled round it. Shards of glass tore at his face as he bucked forward, and then was thrown back hard against his seat. But he was alive! In agony, but alive. The fact that his airbag had failed to deploy never occurred to him.

Terry groaned in the back. His whole body ached. Despite his evasive action, his neck had whiplashed. He couldn't move his head. He daren't move his head. His left kneecap had dislocated. He knew it. It had happened once before when he was at school. He'd gone in for a tackle, playing football. And felt the immediate pain. And looked down at his leg, and noticed the egg above his knee, and the void below, where his kneecap should have been. He tried to relax for a second, to take in the extent of his injuries. And he just wanted to sleep. To get away from this nightmare. Forget it all. Wake up in the morning, and none of it had really happened. He closed his eyes to shut out the horror. But it wouldn't go away. The dark blood arcing from Daz's groin. The gamekeeper's shattered body on the track. But now it was over. The game was over. And he'd survived.

And then he could smell that familiar smell. The one he'd grown accustomed to every couple of weeks for the past god-knows-how-many years. When he'd pulled into the local service station to fill the tank. Petrol! He could smell its sweet, sickly scent. He fumbled with the seat belt release. Panicking. He had to get out. Quick. He released the catch and pulled on the door handle. It moved but the door remained tightly shut, its frame buckled by the impact. He leaned back, lying almost flat on the back seat, and kicked hard, but to no avail. The smell seemed stronger, more pervasive. He tried the other door. Yes! It opened immediately. He scrambled out, falling to the ground as his knee gave way. He dragged himself to his feet, and stumbled away, looking back at the tiny momentary flashes, like fireflies in the night, emanating from the torn electrical system of the wrecked, smouldering vehicle. And he could see slow, laboured movement from inside. Andy. He was still alive!

Terry stood transfixed in the dark as the bloody mask turned slowly towards him. He could see the pain etched deep into the eyes staring, unfaltering, straight at him. The bloody mouth uttered something, but Terry couldn't hear it.

"It's not over yet, bastard."

Andy hissed through broken teeth. His instinct to survive was still strong. And his instinct to avenge the death of his brother was stronger. He reached for the gun, marvelling at its power, its weight, and levelled it at Terry's face. He struggled to keep it steady. Keep his eyes focused. Ignore the pain. The game may be in its final stage, but he would have the last play. It was his choice. Who lived. Who died. And his mind was made up. This bastard in his wavering sights had set them up. He was responsible for Daz's death. And even if he didn't make it himself, he had to kill this bastard. For his brother's sake. For his sake. For his mother's sake. And for his dad. Wherever he might be.

"Say your prayers, Terry."

The words came out as a hoarse whisper from his crushed throat. He took careful aim, using the window frame to take the weight from his broken arm. Sighting through one eye, he beaded his target. He squeezed carefully on the trigger, with a slow but steady pressure, ignoring the fumes filling the car. He paused to wipe away the blood and the sweat trickling into his eyes. And once again he held his breath and took careful aim at the hunched figure in his sights.

The spark was brief, but enough to ignite the vapour from the broken fuel line. Hungry flames sought oxygen and licked round the bonnet. Daz's hair frizzed and burned, and his clothing ignited spontaneously as the heat increased. And in an instant came the deafening explosion, lighting up the night. The force blew Terry off his unsteady feet. He turned to face the car which was already burning fiercely. Flames erupted beneath the bonnet and engulfed the corpse barbecuing on it. Inside, he could see Andy enveloped in fire, staring at him, pleading.

Terry rose again to his feet, struggling to retain his balance as he watched the flames devouring the vehicle. Thick black smoke rose straight into the calm night air. He could feel the intense heat, smell the burning flesh. He walked unsteadily towards the car. He could see the flicker of hope in Andy's eyes as he approached. But Terry had no intention of helping him. He wanted Andy to see him smiling, and had not the heat been so intense, he would happily have pissed on him. Instead, satisfied that he'd got his revenge, he stumbled away from the inferno to seek the safety of the bushes.

****

The police helicopter had completed its patrol down the A1 and was returning to base when the pilot noticed the sudden flash of bright light in the darkness below him and some miles off his starboard side. He radioed base and banked to investigate.

Terry heard the whirring sound, faint at first, but becoming louder. He strained to recognise it but his senses were confused as they struggled to take in the enormity of what had occurred. Three lives lost. Almost four. But now he had to get away. He headed, limping, towards the ditch, hoping to follow its course to the comparative safety of the woods. Each step sent bolts of pain up his leg. But he had to keep moving. Had to get away from the scene. His neck ached as he turned his head slightly to look back at the very instant when a beam of strong light illuminated the inferno from above. He scrambled across the ditch and threw himself into the hedgerow whose thorny branches tore at his hands and face. He managed to crawl through a small gap and lay hardly daring to breathe in the darkness. The searchlight beam swept the area, but he was safe in the shadow of the hedgerow. But for how long? He knew the helicopter would report the incident, and the police would be quickly on the scene. Keeping close to the bushes, he lurched towards the woods.

It took him a good fifteen minutes to cover the quarter mile or so to the relative safety of the thick copse. He leaned back against a tree to regain his breath. Fully aware of his pain, he chose to ignore it. If he succumbed, if he lay down here and sought the relief of sleep, they may find him. Or worse still, they may not find him. He could die of exposure. Keep moving! He could hear the distant whirr of the helicopter and see its searchlight beam. But it seemed to be moving away, criss-crossing the top fields. He emerged from the woods and picked his way towards the main road, keeping close to the hedgerow.

The police BMW raced down the dual carriageway, sirens blaring, and took the slip road at speed. The driver braked hard at the roundabout to allow the fire engine, coming from the opposite direction, to take precedence. The BMW followed it down the dirt track and into the fields, then pulled out and overtook, bouncing its way across the dark hard earth towards the still burning vehicle. In the distance, the wail of sirens on the speeding paramedic ambulance grew more audible. As it reached the slip road off the dual carriageway the driver received the crackling message over his radio. His services would not be required at this incident. He switched off the siren, turned around and returned to base.

The police had found the body of the gamekeeper splayed on the concrete track, illuminated starkly by the searchlight of the hovering helicopter. HQ was informed and a mobile incident room requested at the site. The helicopter was despatched to sweep the area in ever wider circles. The officer in temporary charge at the scene had a faint, nagging suspicion that someone may have escaped the carnage. The rear nearside door was wide open, and while the explosion or the impact with the tree might conceivably have caused it, at the moment he concentrated his efforts on locating a possible third occupant of the vehicle.

Terry lost count of the number of times he tripped and stumbled as he skirted the perimeter of the estate. He was exhausted and thought of holing up for a while in one of the copses. He decided to keep moving. To put as much distance as possible between himself and the scene of total horror he was fleeing. He had no idea whether the police were hard on his trail, whether they had dogs, whether the helicopter would return. He had no idea that, instead of concentrating all their efforts on finding him, the police were in fact scaling down the search; two bodies had been found shot dead some ten miles away and a murder investigation was underway.

Eventually, exhausted, Terry reached the lay-by. He remained on the other side of the hedgerow for a couple of minutes. Watching, listening. Once he reckoned it was safe to continue, he found a gap in the hedgerow, squeezed through, and sought the comparative safety of the Astra. He prayed it would get him home without problems and, to his immense relief, it did. The last thing he wanted was to draw attention to himself. He drove carefully, trying hard to ignore the excruciating jolt of pain in his knee every time he changed gear and was relieved to reach the car park near home. He had no fears about leaving the car. If someone stole it, so what? But he had a feeling it would be safe with Daz and Andy out of the picture. First, he made sure he took the holdall from the boot. There was no point in tempting fate.

Limping heavily, and in excruciating pain, he managed to open the back door of the building, drag himself along the corridor and up the stairs to his flat. Relieved, he dumped the holdall in the kitchen, took a bottle of whisky and a glass from the cupboard, sat at the kitchen table and poured a large measure. The nightmare was over. He took a large mouthful of whisky, held it in his mouth for a few seconds and then swallowed, feeling the welcome heat in his throat. Finally, he dragged himself into the bathroom, stripped off and washed himself as well as he could. He inspected his knee, knowing he would have to go to the hospital sooner rather than later. He would worry about that in the morning. Right now, he needed to sleep.

****

Brian's phone woke him. He checked the time. Five-forty-five. He slid out of bed and took the phone downstairs to take the call.

"Sorry to disturb you at this time of the morning, sir. It's PC Hartley from Harrogate. I've been told you are the one to contact concerning wrecked cars on an estate north of Bradford. Oakland, they call it."

Brian's ears pricked up and he was suddenly wide awake.

"What have you got?"

"Well, sir. We had a helicopter out last night over the A1. He noticed a fire off in the distance and went over to investigate. He reported it and a call was sent out. They found a burnt-out Audi, sir, with two bodies inside."

"Thanks. I'm on my way."

"There's more, sir."

"Go on."

"There is also the body of a man thought to be the gamekeeper on the estate. Looks like he was run over. And the SOCO team we sent believe there may have been a third occupant of the car, who may have escaped alive. They're searching the area now, sir."

"Thank you, PC Hartley. I'll be there as soon as I can."

As Brian showered, he considered the situation. Three occupants in a car. On Oakland. Joyriders, probably. But there was a separate scenario. Three men in a car. They could possibly be the drug dealers Adie had described. He was out of the house and driving north as quickly as he could.

****

When Linda awoke and saw the state of her husband groaning in pain, she dressed quickly, helped him get dressed, and helped him down the stairs. She leaned him against the doorway while she ran to the car, reversing it as close to him as she could. She got out and laid him across the back seat before driving at speed across town to the BRI Accident and Emergency department.

She was lucky. At that time in the morning, traffic was light and A & E relatively empty. Terry received prompt attention from the duty doctor who was able to ease the patella back into position once the painkillers had taken effect. After an hour, Terry was wheeled to the physiotherapy department where a knee brace was fitted and a program of recovery was explained to him. He was discharged with a prescription for painkillers and an appointment for further out-patient treatment. At no time during his examination did he mention the other cuts and bruises he had sustained. They would heal in their own time without treatment. Linda drove him home to rest.

****

Brian had arrived at Oakland and left his car at the roadside, outside the gates. He made his way on foot towards the vehicles he could see close to the single large oak tree in the middle of the field. Drawing closer, he could clearly see the burnt-out vehicle at the base of the tree. He saw a face he recognised and called to him.

"Allen!"
"Ah, good morning, Brian."

Allen Greaves approached him, arm outstretched.

"What have we got, Allen?"
"In all, three bodies. One, further down the track, was obviously hit by a vehicle. The injuries suffered are consistent with his being struck head-on by this vehicle, or at the very least a vehicle of this make and model. His right leg was broken. The point of impact matches the height of the front bumper of the Audi. His face had evidently hit the windscreen, broke it, and his body went over the vehicle and landed face down on the track behind it. I would imagine he died more or less instantly. We'll match the blood on the car bonnet and windscreen to the body down the track, I'm sure."
"What about the other bodies?"
"The passenger died from a gunshot wound to the groin. My initial thought is that he was shot by the driver."
"Interesting. How about the driver?"
"Severe injuries caused by impact with the tree. These were probably enough to cause his death within a few minutes. But he actually burnt to death, I believe. Once we get them back to the mortuary, we'll have a more complete picture."
"The PC who called me this morning seemed to think there may have been a third passenger in the car."
"It's a distinct possibility. A rear door was wide open, and I don't believe it flew open during the collision with the tree or in the resultant explosion. We'll be towing the vehicle back to the lab to see what else we can add."
"Any identification of the victims?"
"The old man, we think, was the gamekeeper. We're awaiting conclusive identification, when the estate owner arrives. The two men in the car? I don't think we'll ever be able to identify them conclusively unless we're lucky enough to have their DNA in the database."
"OK, Allen. Give me a call the minute you get any more news."

"I will."

Brian returned to his car. He was about to call Teresa to let her know he was on his way when his phone rang.

"DS Peters."
"It's PC Hartley from Harrogate again, sir. Sorry to bother you but I thought you needed to know that the helicopter pilot has just filed his shift report. He says he thinks he saw movement in the hedgerows when he flew over the crime scene. He's not certain whether it was human, or some sort of animal, but he said whatever it was, was limping. Could be the third passenger, sir."
"Thanks, PC Hartley. That's useful news. Thank your pilot for me."
"Yes, sir. Thank you, sir."

He called Teresa.

"Teresa, we've just had a report of a car crash at Oaklands…"
"It's just come through to us, Brian. I'm reading it now."
"This may be the break we need. I'll be in later. I just want to make a house call first."

He parked up in the large car park and walked around to the front of the block. At the entrance he pressed the bell for number 44. He waited a minute and pressed it again. No response. He'd have to call again in the evening.

Walking back to the car, he had a sudden thought. He made the call.

"Martin Black."
"Martin, it's Brian Peters."
"Hello, Brian."
"Martin, have you got the bodies from the car fire yet?"
"Just come in. I was just about to start on them."
"Well, from what I've heard, identification may be difficult, but I was wondering, do you still have the body of Sheila Fisher?"
"Yes, Brian. Still awaiting funeral arrangements. Still trying to get her next of kin to pay."
"I wouldn't bother. I've a feeling two of her kids are on your slab now."
"Ah."
"So, would you do me a favour and take a DNA sample from

Sheila Fisher? I've a feeling we'll identify the bodies that way."

"OK, Brian. I'll let you know as soon as I have something."

"Thanks."

****

From his kitchen window at number 44, Terry watched Brian drive away. The sound of the doorbell had woken him, but it took him so long to get out of bed that the caller had given up and left before he got to the door. Seeing Brian, he was glad he'd missed him. He'd need to speak to his wife first to concoct a feasible alibi for the previous night and explain his injuries.

CHAPTER 22

When Linda arrived home from work, she wasn't in the best of moods. Her supervisor had 'one of her days' and took it out on Linda. Linda was used to it. It was even plotted on her calendar. She knew when to expect it and was prepared. So, she was pleased to see her husband up and limping around, with a mug of tea ready for her.

"How was your day, Linda?"
"Just as expected. What about yours?"
"Fine. I had a visitor, but he'd gone by the time I got to the door."
"Oh. Do you know who it was?"
"Yes. And I know why he was here. Are you prepared for the whole story?"
"I think I deserve to hear it, don't you?"
"Yes. I do. OK, here goes. The caller today was a policeman. Peters, I think his name was."
"Yes. I remember his name. You spoke to him when the car was stolen."
"That's right. Well, after I lost that lousy job at the factory I was really down. Dad had died. The car had been wrecked. The replacement kept breaking down. I couldn't find work anywhere and I was seriously depressed. Well, one lunchtime, after visiting the Jobcentre yet again, I went into a pub and got talking to two young guys. They offered me a job, driving. I was a bit suspicious. It sounded a bit dodgy, but I accepted. It paid well. Cash in hand. I think I knew what they were up to right from the start, but I went along with it. I was just the driver. I didn't handle the drugs."
"Drugs? Oh, my God, Terry. What were you thinking of?"
"Earning money. To pay the bills. That's all it was about. Anyway, business took off and from just selling on the street and in the pubs and clubs when I started, soon they were buying direct from the importers and selling to a group of lower-level dealers. They were making a lot of money, Linda. Several thousand pounds a week. And all I was doing really was driving them from place to place."

He paused as Linda took his hand. She squeezed it gently, supportively.

"Then, last night, they'd concluded a big deal and wanted to celebrate. So, they stole a car and drove it to Oakland. You know, where our car was found. That's when all the pieces of the jigsaw started to fit into place. These were the two lads who stole our car. I was sat in the back, listening to them boasting as they threw the car around the estate. They knocked over an old man. I'm sure they killed him, but they just carried on. The driver had been using cocaine and was as high as a kite, and I just lost it. I got my arm round the passenger's throat. The driver pulled a gun – I didn't know he had it – but I hit him with the Krooklok and broke his arm as he fired. The bullet hit his brother. I hooked the Krooklok around the driver's throat and tried to strangle him. He threw the car around to try to dislodge me and ran it into a tree. The passenger went right through the windscreen. The driver was seriously injured. I managed to scramble out before the car exploded in flames. I survived. They both died."

"Oh, God, Terry!"

"I didn't kill anyone, Linda. The crash killed them. And you know what? I'm glad. It's over. It's finally over."

"So, that's why the policeman was here?"

"I guess so. I'm not sure I'm a suspect. He may just want to let me know they've got the guys who were stealing cars. But, the thing is, he'll be back, so, we need to agree on an alibi and explain the injuries."

"I'll say you were here all evening. We had a few drinks and went to bed...."

".... Then, during the night, I got up to check the car. I thought I heard the alarm, so I got up and went downstairs. I tripped and fell down the stairs...."

".... And then, when I realised you'd been gone for more than half an hour, I went looking for you. I found you on the stairs and drove you to A & E. They treated you and you've been here since. How does that sound?"

"It will have to do. It's not totally convincing. But it will be hard to disprove. Thanks, Linda."

"Don't worry, love. We'll get through this. But promise me you'll never do anything like this again."

"I promise."

****

The following morning, Brian got the call he had been waiting for.

"Brian. Good morning, it's Martin Black."

"Morning, Martin. I take it you've got some news?"

"I have, Brian. You were right. The DNA samples we took from the two teenagers are a close match to the sample we got from Mrs Fisher. There's little doubt she was their mother, Brian. Well done."

"Thanks, Martin. Things are becoming much clearer, now."

"There's more, Brian. The front seat passenger had been shot in the femoral artery. That would have been enough to kill him unless he'd received immediate medical attention. As it was, he would probably have survived long enough for the fire to have killed him. The driver, though, is a more interesting puzzle."

"How so?"

"Well, for a start, his right arm suffered a compound fracture to both radius and ulna. This I believe was caused by a direct blow from a heavy object. I think the car security lock that was found on the floor of the car was the implement used to cause the injury to the forearm. Here's what I believe happened. Are you ready for this?"

"Fire away, Martin."

"OK. The rear seat passenger gets his left arm around the front seat passenger's neck, pulling him backwards in a stranglehold. The driver pulls out a gun. As he moves to point it at the rear passenger, that passenger, while still maintaining the headlock, grabs the Krooklok in his right hand, and brings it sharply down on the driver's right arm, breaking it and in doing so, deflecting his aim as he fired, so that the gun was pointed at the front seat passenger and the driver, in fact, shot his brother in the groin by accident. The rear seat passenger then got the Krooklok around the driver's throat and tried to strangle him. The driver lost control of the car and it hit the tree. Again, the evidence backs up this theory, as despite the body being so badly burned, it is clear he had suffered throat injuries consistent with a solid object being held tightly across his trachea. One other thing, though."

"Go on."

"The position of the driver's body was puzzling. He was splayed across the passenger seat. His arms were extended through the open window, with the gun still in his grasp. My only explanation for this, is that he was trying to shoot someone outside the car."

"In other words, the third man?"

"Yes. I believe so."

"Thanks, Martin."

He ended the call and went out to his car. Ten minutes later, he'd parked up next to Terry's Astra and had pressed the doorbell of number 44. This time, he got a response. Terry opened the door and ushered him in.

"Good morning, Mr Stanton. I have some good news for you."
"What's that?"
"The thieves who stole and destroyed your car will not be doing it
again. We found their bodies out at Oakland the night before last."

Terry did his best to feign surprise.

"Their bodies? They're dead?"
"Yes, sir. It seems they stole another car and took it to their usual
race track. Seems they lost control and it hit the tree."
"Oh."
"You sound surprised, Mr Stanton."
"Yes. Yes, I am."
"Well, I find that a bit strange. Since you were there at the time."
"No. I wasn't. I spent all that night at home with my wife."
"Which night was that, Mr Stanton?"
"The night they died."
"Which was when, exactly?"
"The night before last. You just said."
"I said we *found their bodies* the night before last."
"Oh. I just assumed."
"Well, let's say you're right. By the way, that seems to be a nasty
injury to your leg. How did that happen?"
"I fell down the stairs."
"When was that?"
"The night before last. The wife took me to A & E."
"While you were there, you should have asked them to treat those
little cuts to your face. Don't tell me you cut yourself shaving. How
did you get those?"
"Must have been when I fell."
"I'll tell you what they look like to me. They're the type of wounds
consistent with those sustained by a passenger in a car crash. You
know, when the windscreen shatters when something heavy, like a
body, for instance, hits it at high speed and those tiny squares of
glass fly everywhere."

Terry was silent, not knowing what to say. Brian pressed his point
home.

"We know you were in the car, Mr Stanton. Forensics are
completing their examination at the moment and they will be able

to prove you were there. They will find fingerprints. Fire doesn't destroy everything, you know. Do you have anything to say now?"
"No."
"In that case, I'd like you to come down to HQ with me and you'll be questioned under oath. So, if you would like to leave a message for your wife, or call your solicitor?"

Terry exploded.

"Who's the criminal here? I've lost everything. They've made all this money from crime. They tried to kill me. I'm the victim, not them. They're scum."
"Let the court decide. Vigilante justice is not the answer, but, for what it's worth, I'm on your side."

They drove in silence. Terry knew he faced charges, but what type he was unsure. Probably aiding and abetting at the very least. He decided to say nothing unless a solicitor advised him otherwise.

They were walking through the reception area when Terry recognised the face behind the reception desk. It wasn't immediately clear to him where he'd seen the man before, but he had definitely seen him. It was still playing on his mind when he entered the interview room and sat next to his solicitor as Brian went through the formalities and started asking the questions.

"Mr Stanton. We know you were in the car. Why?"
"Has it occurred to you that they might have kidnapped me at gunpoint? Took me out there to kill me? Just a random event."
"Well, that would certainly be a random event. I'll tell you what I think happened, shall I?"
"Be my guest."
"The driver of the car and the front seat passenger were brothers. Darren and Andrew Fisher. They were drug dealers. You were their driver. We have a witness who has seen you in a car with your employers while they were out on the street selling drugs. On Howgate, in Idle. I have that information in a sworn statement. So, unless you co-operate fully, I'll charge you with aiding and abetting for a start. Understand?"
"Yes."
"You see, I'm not overly concerned with the shit at the bottom of the pile. It's just necessary to trample through that to get to the shit at the top. Those are the people I really want. So, what can you tell

me?"

Then it came to Terry. The face he'd recognised in Reception. He'd seen him at one of the deals. He was sure. Yes. He was driving the sellers' car. He knew he'd seen him before. The day when he'd first come down to HQ to see if there was any progress in finding the car thieves, he was behind the reception desk. Then when he'd driven to Manchester for a bulk purchase, that same man was behind the wheel of the sellers' car. He was absolutely certain. And just today, when he'd walked into the building with DS Peters, he'd seen the same face again. This was it. His 'Get out of Jail free' card. He spoke slowly.

"I may be able to help you get to the shit at the top of the pile."
"Please, go ahead."
"Only if you'll go easy on me."

Brian considered his options, then responded.

"If you're totally honest with us, and what you tell us is useful in our inquiries, I'll do everything I can to ensure your co-operation is fully recognised."

Terry recognised he had little option.

"You need to talk to the desk sergeant. He drives for some people higher up the supply chain than Darren and Andy."

Brian's eyes widened and his pulse increased. He would have reached for a cigarette had he not stopped a long time ago. This was one of those moments when he needed to remain totally calm and dispassionate.

"How do you know this?"
"I recognised him as soon as we came in. I've seen him previously in the supplier's car."
"OK. I'm just going to leave the room and I'll be straight back to show you some photographs. Won't be long."

He stopped the recording and left, his heart racing. He took the stairs two at a time and raced to Teresa's desk.

"Urgent job, Teresa."

"What is it, Brian?"
"Get me a photograph of every officer who works in this building. Get them from the personnel files if you have to. You'll get them right back. I just want to show them to a witness. This is desperate, Teresa."
"Give me five minutes."

Brian went over to the vending machine and selected a coffee which he sipped until Teresa returned with an envelope full of photographs.

"I presume you want to preserve their anonymity. Their names and ranks are printed on the back, Brian. Just so we can file them properly afterwards."
"Thanks. This shouldn't take long."

Back in the interview room, with the recorder on, he showed the photos one at a time, until Terry stopped him.

"This one. That's the guy."
"You're absolutely sure?"
"Absolutely."
"This is the man you've seen in the driver's seat of a car used by drug suppliers, while a transaction was taking place?"
"Yes."
"For the benefit of the recording, Mr Stanton has just identified a serving officer in the Bradford area's police force. Sergeant Barlow. Sergeant James Barlow."

The interview concluded and Terry was allowed to go home, aware that the police would be speaking to him again, and that there was no point in running away from it. Being honest about his involvement was now his only option.

When Linda arrived home from work and he told her of the day's events, her relief was evident. She held him, told him she was proud of him. And that she would stand by him as long as he told the whole truth.

"Have you looked in the holdall?"
"No. Should I?"
"If you want me to be honest about everything. Put it on the table and open it. It's heavy."

Driving home, Brian was elated. He'd contacted Sinclair at the NCA and he'd agreed to drive up to arrest Sergeant Barlow the next day. He wondered how Muesli would react to that. Probably give him a bollocking for not informing him first.

Brian got a bollocking as soon as he walked through his front door.

"You've forgotten, haven't you?"
"Forgotten what?"
"Never mind."

He found it hard to get much conversation with his wife as they sat at the table. Finally fed up of the silence, he asked outright.

"Have I done something to upset you?"
"It's not important."
"It obviously is. So, what is it?"
"You don't remember what today is? What we were doing eight years ago today?"
"Oh, Christ! I'm so sorry. How can I make it up to you?"
"It doesn't matter."
"We'll go out for a meal at the weekend. I'll get mum and dad over to look after the kids."
"OK. That'll be nice."
"I'm so sorry, love. I've been really busy at work."
"I know. It's not a problem. Don't let it happen next year."
"I won't. I daren't."

They both laughed. Brian knew the crisis was over. He vowed it would be that last time he forgot their wedding anniversary.

****

The following afternoon, DI Sinclair and DS Fox arrived, showed their ID to Sergeant Barlow and went straight to Muesli's office.

"This is just a courtesy call, sir. We just thought you should be aware that we're here to arrest a member of your staff."
"And who might that be?"
"Your man on reception at the moment. Sergeant Barlow."
"Sergeant Barlow? On what grounds?"

"He's involved in the sale and supply of Class A drugs, sir."

"And what proof do you have?"

"He's been identified by a member of the public, sir. We just want to interview him."

"Who else is aware of this?"

"I'm not at liberty to disclose that at the moment, sir."

"Well, if this is an act of malice, or some spurious accusation, I will be speaking to your commanding officer."

"Like I said, sir. We're just informing you out of courtesy. We'll let you know the outcome."

"See that you do."

"Since Sergeant Barlow will be unable to complete his shift, I'm sure you will be able to provide cover in Reception."

"It's all very inconvenient."

"Look at it this way, sir. If there weren't any criminals, we'd all be out of a job."

They were discreet and Barlow went with them without a fuss. Fox called Brian from the car to thank him and asked him to keep it quiet for now. He agreed but knew that rumours would soon spread. Still, so far it had been a good week, apart from the forgotten wedding anniversary. They'd cleared up the vehicle thefts and made inroads into the drugs supply chain, with another corrupt officer arrested. Now, he hoped, his team could put all their efforts into catching the ram-raiders. At least his team had not been given the task of investigating the recent double shooting.

Driving home, Brian reflected on the events of the day, and smiled. He didn't know Sergeant Barlow too well but hoped that he would come clean about his extracurricular activities and name others involved, in return for a more lenient sentence. The house of cards would collapse. Now he understood why his arrival in CID was met with so much suspicion; he and Lynn were a perceived threat to the established order of things. Even Muesli had been obstructive. Brian wondered about the extent of his involvement.

On the way home, he made a couple of stops to buy peace offerings for Sarah – a bottle of wine and a bouquet of roses. That should do it. That, and the fact that Teresa had added all his significant dates into her Outlook calendar, should ensure there would be no repetition.

****

Terry and Linda were seated at the kitchen table, the holdall on the floor and its contents piled neatly on the table between them. They had counted it again today, twice, in fact. There were twenty-four thousand, eight hundred and eighty-five pounds in total, in different denominations of grubby banknotes.

"And there's another £1960 in a tin in the bedroom. Wages."
"What are we going to do, Terry?"
"As far as I'm concerned, we should keep it. All of it. Call it wages. I've earned this."
"I'm not sure, Terry. What if someone comes looking for you?"
"Who? Why? This money is the legitimate payment for goods provided. I don't owe anybody anything. The *real* owners are both dead. They left it for me, for safe keeping, in *my* car. They entrusted it to me. We're keeping it. And you know what I want to spend it on?"
"What?"
"A new car. To replace the one that they stole and wrecked. I want to get rid of that piece of shit out there in the car park and buy a good car. Maybe not new, but one from a reputable dealer, with a warranty. This is their compensation to me for wrecking our car. We deserve this. They started it."
"OK. Let's wait until the dust has settled. Then we'll go looking for one together."
"Deal."
"Let's drink to it. It's over."
"Let's hope the police think the same."

CHAPTER 23

It was business as usual in the CID office, though Brian could sense the general mood was much lighter. The other officers who had previously cold-shouldered Brian and his team were now much friendlier. They all sat together at a long table in the canteen. They shared jokes, discussed each other's cases and were much more open to input. For the first time since Brian arrived, the department felt like one big team. He was beginning to like it there. Homophobic remarks previously aimed at Gary and Teresa had stopped. The only comments now heard were light-hearted piss-taking, such as those aimed at the sole Manchester United supporter in the office.

The different teams continued to work hard, and morale was high, due to the increased rate of criminal convictions and fewer incidents of antisocial behaviour on the streets.

As the newspapers got hold of the stories of police corruption and the arrests made, it seemed that public confidence in the remaining officers had risen to the extent that more minor crimes were reported, and the public became more likely to pass on information regarding suspected criminal behaviour. But there was still more to come.

Brian got the tip-off via his mobile.

"Brian, it's Sinclair from the NCA."
"Hello, Alex. What can I do for you?"
"Could you please make sure you're in the office at ten o'clock tomorrow morning?"
"Why?"
"Can't tell you. But you wouldn't want to miss it."
"OK. I'll be here."
"Thanks. I think you'll enjoy it. 'Bye."

"That was a bit cryptic", he thought, but he still made a note to be there, then pushed the thought aside and returned to reading the reports which had come through that morning. Another ram-raid. Lynn, Gary, and another recent recruit, DC Forrest, had already set off to visit the scene.

His mobile rang again.

"DS Peters."
"It's Adie, sir."
"Hello, Adie. What's up, son?"
"I've just heard about the robbery, last night. The cash machine off Bolton Road."
"Yes. I'm just reading the report now. What do you know about it?"
"Well, I was up there at teatime last night with a couple of mates. We were just messing about on our bikes in the car park. Well, I noticed a car come in and park up. They were there about half an hour. One of them got out and went into the shop, then came back out and they sat a bit longer. Then, the other man got out and went into the shop, came out, and then they drove off. I just thought it was really a bit suspicious. It was like they were sizing it up. Then, when I heard about the raid, I sort of thought, it might have been them, like. What do you think?"
"It's worth following up, Adie. Can you give me any further information? Details? Descriptions, that sort of thing?"
"Better than that. I got the car registration. You ready? ST17 YXU. It's a red Mondeo. Two white men. Both mid-thirties, I guess. One bald and tall, the other dark hair, short beard, medium height, I suppose. Both slim. Is that any good to you?"
"Brilliant, Adie. Thanks, son. If this leads anywhere, we'll get you to that football training camp this summer."
"Awesome!"

He asked Teresa to check the DVLA database for details of the car's owner and went for lunch in the canteen, sitting at the same table with some of his colleagues, his new friends. He was not surprised to learn that many of them secretly despised Hardcastle and his team but were afraid to raise any of their concerns about his 'methods' for fear of reprisal.

He checked his phone. A message from Lynn.

"Where are you, Brian?"

He replied, "Canteen."

"May be good news for you when you get back to office."
"On my way."

Lynn was sat in front of a monitor when he arrived. She had a big grin on her face.

"What have you got, Lynn?"
"Video footage from last night's raid. Watch this. You won't believe it."

She played the video from a point a few seconds before the pickup came into view and smashed through the glass doors. They watched as a hooded figure got out of the passenger door, ran into the store, and hooked a heavy chain around the cash machine. He stood aside and signalled the driver to move. The vehicle was powerful enough to tear the cash machine from its mountings and drag it towards the door. The pickup reversed, a second man got out, and the two men manhandled the machine on to the back of the vehicle.

"Now watch this."

The first man went back into the store and grabbed a chocolate snack. Wearing gloves, he was unable to get the wrapper off, so he took off a glove, unwrapped the snack, took a bite and threw the discarded wrapper to the ground beside the pickup. He got into the pickup which drove off at speed. Lynn reversed the DVD to the point where the suspect unwrapped the snack and stopped it.

"I couldn't believe it the first time, so I watched it again. How can anyone be so stupid?"
"You'd be surprised."
"Gary's gone back to retrieve the wrapper. He's taking it straight to Forensic."
"Well, let's hope they can lift prints. And let's hope they're in the IDENT1 database. Can you enhance the image? Zoom in on his hand?"
"OK."
"There! Look. On the back of his hand. The tattoo."
"Let me zoom in a bit more. Yes. It looks like a skull."
"See if you can get anything from HOLMES 2."
"OK."
"We've got another potential lead, by the way."
"What's that?"
"A member of the public informed me he'd seen two men acting suspiciously at the scene yesterday. He gave me descriptions, but,

better still, he got the registration number of the car they were in. Teresa's tracing it at the moment."

"This is turning into a good week for us."

"Keep it to yourself, but it could get even better tomorrow."

"Why?"

"Wait and see."

It wasn't long before Teresa provided the name and address of the car owner, Kevin Dwyer, who had been released from prison six months earlier after a long spell inside for armed robbery. The HOLMES 2 database identified the possible owner of the tattoo as Colin Allsopp, another ex-convict, who had served his time in the same prison, at the same time, as Dwyer. They decided to wait for the result from Forensic before paying the two of them a visit. Once they'd nailed those two down, they fully expected they'd give up the name of the third person involved.

****

Sarah noticed the change in her husband's mood the moment he walked into the house. The big grin on his face gave it away.

"It looks like you've had a good day."

"I have. And I've a feeling that tomorrow will be even better."

"I'm glad to hear it. I haven't seen you smiling much recently."

"You will. I promise."

"Good. Daniel's been asking me where his happy daddy's gone."

"Well, I'd better go and make it up to him, then."

"Go on, then, while I make tea."

As Brian entertained his son, there was only one other thing on his mind, one target that had so far eluded him. He vowed he'd never give up the hunt until that man was behind bars. That man was Danny Hardcastle.

****

The following day was a fine Spring day, set clear and sunny, with a light breeze. For the first time this year, Brian drove to work with the window half down. He was looking forward to his day at work and contemplating the surprise event the NCA had in store for them.

It was evident that only his team were aware that something was to happen but Brian was the only person who had any inkling what it might be. He kept glancing at the office clock ticking its slow way to ten o'clock. Bang on time, Teresa called his desk phone.

"Brian, I think you should come upstairs immediately. Sinclair and Fox are here. Your presence is required."
"On my way."

He took the stairs two at a time and walked quickly down the room towards Teresa's office where the officers were waiting.

"Morning, Brian. Thanks for coming. We'll get on with it."

Fox knocked on Muesli's door and waited for permission to enter. Both NCA officers entered but left the door open so Brian and Teresa could clearly see and hear what was happening. Brian's face broke into a wide grin as he heard Sinclair ask Muesli to come with him to NCA HQ for questioning concerning allegations that he took 'hush money' from officers under his command in return for his silence regarding their criminal activities.

Muesli's face was ashen. He stood up meekly and walked silently out of the office between Sinclair and Fox, who both winked at Brian and Teresa. Sinclair told Brian,

"I think you should brief the staff downstairs. They need to know what's happening before the papers get wind of it, I suppose. As a result of the information you previously passed to us, we executed search warrants on all the properties we identified as being owned by Hardcastle's company. We found a great deal of drugs, cash, and incriminating evidence on a desktop computer at his East Morton address. It had been wiped hastily but the data was easily recovered and, as a result, a number of people have been taken into custody following dawn raids this morning. We have also been able to freeze many of his bank accounts. Oh, and another thing. Your new Chief Inspector is waiting in the car park. You should formally introduce him to the staff. I think you might have met him before."

Brian followed them down the stairs and into the car park. Waiting outside was the last person he was expecting to see.

"Don!"

"Morning, Brian. You seem surprised to see me."

"I suppose I should have been expecting it. But I thought you'd retired."

"I had, but I need something to occupy my time now I no longer have Janet for company. Don't worry, Brian. It's only temporary. Until they find the right man to run the unit on a permanent basis. I'm just a stop-gap."

"Well, I'm very glad to see you. Come in. I'll introduce you. Then I'll brief you on our on-going cases."

"Lead the way."

Don McArthur followed Brian into the open-plan CID office where staff had congregated to discuss the momentous event of the morning, news of which had just reached them. Brain called for silence.

"Can I have your attention, please, folks? Just quieten down for a minute. I have an announcement. I'd like to inform you that DCI Moseley has been put on 'gardening leave', pending investigation into his performance as a DCI of this unit."

"You mean he's bent?"

Brian had anticipated the possibility that the rumour mill had been operating.

"At the moment, it appears that he may have abused his position. I must stress that no charges have yet been brought, so we should not pass judgment at this time. I'm sure, when the time is right, and all the facts have been uncovered, the truth will come out. In the meantime, we don't plan on having a collection for him."

He paused until the laughter subsided.

"So that we're not left rudderless, we have a new boss on board, on a temporary basis. He's a man I know well and for whom I have the highest regard. I'd like to introduce to you my former boss as head of the North East CTU, Detective Inspector Don McArthur."

When the applause and whistles had died down, Don addressed the gathering.

"I'm here to steady the ship. I won't be making any sweeping changes. All I ask from you as serving officers and support staff is that you do your job to the best of your ability and to the standards the public expect. Some of you I have never met before, but I will be taking the opportunity to talk to each of you individually so that you are in no doubt what I expect of you while I'm in charge. I don't care whether or not you like me as long as you do your job. Any questions?"

"It's customary to meet for a drink after work to welcome a new member to the team, sir. Will you be joining us?"

"Yes, but only if you'll let me pick the venue."

****

A short while after the gathering dispersed back to their individual groups, Gary took a call from Forensics. It was only brief but he couldn't wait to let his boss and Lynn know.

"Forensics have identified the prints, boss."

"Anyone we know?"

"Colin Allsopp."

"So that's print and tattoo identification. Good work. Why don't the two of you bring him in, and then go and pick up Dwyer."

Brian called Teresa and asked her to get copies of photographs of the two men. He sent a message to Adie's phone asking to meet him in Idle after work. At that meeting, Adie confirmed the photographs were of the two men he'd seen at the scene of the ram-raid the afternoon before it occurred.

The following morning, Allsopp and Dwyer were both charged and remanded in custody. They grassed on the third member of the gang. He was arrested at his home later that day.

****

As the officers were interviewed individually by Don over the next couple of days, each one was surprised by how much he knew about their background, their strengths and weaknesses and the cases they were currently investigating. Don's appointment had not been a spur-of-the-moment decision, and he had clearly done his homework. Within two days he'd earned their respect, and on the Friday evening, after work, a fleet of cars and taxis headed out of town towards Idle, to the Draper.

As they all filed in through the front door, heads turned, and The Foghorn shouted,

"It's a raid. Hide the counterfeit crisps! Honest, officers, they fell off the back of a lorry."
"Behave yourself, lad, or I'll arrest you for being in possession of an offensive haircut. How are you?"
"Fine, Mr McArthur. Yourself?"
"Fine. We're not here on business, except the business of having a couple of drinks, so if you'll kindly let us get to the bar...."
"Sorry. Make some room for the Serious Alcohol Squad, lads."

There being more than a dozen of them, the officers were shown round the back where the recently-opened Brewery Yard was available. The weather was pleasant, and Jim was happy to show them all around his pride and joy – the newly-completed Bone Idle Brewery and Event space – with his customary enthusiasm. Later, Jim took Brian aside.

"I don't know what you've been up to, Brian, but we don't get any more undesirables in here, and the kids on the street are less disruptive just now. I hope it's not just a short-term thing."
"It will always be a problem, Jim. I think we're managing it at the moment."
"Well, it's good to see you more often these days. We might even name a brew after you."
"CID Cider?"
"Sorry, we don't do our own cider. Yet."

The officers dispersed over the course of the next two hours, leaving only Brian and Don, before they both eventually admitted defeat, shook hands and made their way home. It had been a good week for both of them.

****

The following Monday, having discussed the matter first with McArthur, Brian had a short meeting with a representative from the Crown Prosecution Service. As a result, it was decided that the case against Terry Stanton would not be presented to court. On hearing this, Brian breathed a sigh of relief. He had argued that the evidence they had was inconclusive, and that a trial would not be in the public interest, also pointing out that Stanton had played a major role in exposing a serving police officer's drug-related activities and helped smash an organised crime ring.

At the end of his shift, Brian drove to visit Terry Stanton at home. Pulling into the car park, he could see Terry polishing a pale blue Ford Focus. He pulled up alongside.

"Nice car, Terry. Yours?"
"Just picked it up this morning. What do you think?"
"Looks in good nick. Paid cash, did you?"
"Got a loan."
"Aye, from the Bank of Darren and Andy Fisher, I bet."

Terry grinned, embarrassed.

"So, to what do I owe the pleasure?"
"I just popped over to give you some good news, Terry. They're dropping all charges against you."
"Really? That *is* good news."
"That doesn't mean the evidence is destroyed, Terry. Just that we won't be acting on it at this time. So, keep your nose clean in future."
"I will. I certainly will."
"Unless we ask you otherwise."
"What do you mean?"
"Well, Terry, I know it's been difficult for you to find a decent job, so I was just wondering...."
"Wondering what?"
"If you'd consider doing a bit of undercover work for us, maybe, in the future, should the need arise."
"Let me think about it. On second thoughts, forget it. My wife would go mental. Count me out."
"OK, Terry. It was just a thought."
"No hard feelings?"
"None."

Terry took Brian's outstretched hand and shook it firmly.

"Thanks, Brian. Linda and I will never forget this. I know our luck is going to change for the better. I just know it."
"I hope you're right, Terry. Goodbye and good luck."

CHAPTER 24

On Tuesday morning, Brian had been called to McArthur's office. It was a short but fruitful meeting, during which Don informed Brian that he was being promoted to the rank of Detective Inspector with immediate effect for a probationary period, for his tenacious work and team-leading skills in solving a number of serious crimes during his short time in CID.

"I didn't expect this, boss."
"Well, there's a vacancy and you've earned it."
"My team did a lot of the work."
"But you lead them. And don't worry. Their roles will be recognised, Especially Teresa's. Keep it to yourself, Brian, but I've got a more important job in line for her. Just subject to approval from higher up."
"Good. She deserves it."
"And there's something else for you."

He rummaged through his drawer before handing an envelope to Brian.

"Here you are."
"What is it?"
"Your flight tickets."
"Going on holiday, am I?"
"A working holiday, courtesy of our friends at NCA. Open it."

Brian tore open the envelope to find a one-way ticket to Malta, flying at 09.05 on Friday morning, along with five hundred Euros.

"One way. Does that mean you're not expecting me back?"
"We don't know exactly how long it will take. You can book your return when the job's done."
"And the job is what?"
"That will be explained to you when you get there. There will be someone to meet you when you get off the plane. Good luck."
"Thanks, boss."

He went back to the office and briefed his team, asking only that they react quickly and effectively if any new cases came in, and to contact McArthur if they needed guidance.

"How long are you going to be away, Brian?"

"Not exactly sure. I'm hoping it's only going to be a few days. We'll see."

"Enjoy the sunshine, then."

"I will."

At the end of the working day, he went home to Sarah and the kids, and broke the news of his trip abroad after they'd put Daniel to bed.

"It'll only be a few days, Sarah. I'll get mum and dad to pop over to help with the kids."

"We'll be fine, Brian. It's your job. Bring us all something nice back."

"I will."

The more he thought about the trip, the more he hoped he had guessed its purpose correctly. Unknown to Sarah, he couldn't wait for Friday to come around. He sat up that night after she'd gone to bed, cradling a glass of malt and wondering how the trip would pan out.

****

He was up early on Friday morning and took a taxi to the airport. He had an immense dislike of airports. Cavernous places, where every walkway, every corridor, seemed to be designed to take you past shops selling over-priced designer goods. He was glad to get through the boarding gate and onto the plane, but was becoming impatient, cursing when take-off was delayed, even though it was only for fifteen minutes. At least it gave him time to reflect on the one puzzling point which had started the chain of events leading to this confrontation. Why did Muesli initially ask him to take a second look at the file on Amanda Braithwaite's death? Did he think that, just because it had already been dealt with by a more senior officer, he'd just sign it off? Brian shook his head. He doubted he'd ever get the answer.

Once in the air, he relaxed a little, allowing himself a small whisky and a snack to pass the time, trying his best to keep his temper in check every time the passenger in the adjacent seat decided she needed to go to the toilet.

"How much piss can one person generate? Even one as gross as her? I wish they hadn't booked me on a budget flight."

However, after a three-and-a-half-hour flight they touched down at Malta International Airport. The temperature was 24C and hit the passengers as they disembarked. After clearing customs, Brian approached the exit, scanning the waiting crowd, looking for a face he recognised. Finally, he saw a board held out in front of him; the name Brian Peters was written on it in large black letters. He approached the man holding the board.

"I'm Brian Peters."
"Ah, DS Peters, or should I say, DI Peters. Congratulations on your promotion, sir. I am Police Constable David Muscat. Please, come with me. A car is waiting."
"Thank you. Lead the way."

A white police Mercedes was waiting in the short-term car park. PC Muscat loaded Brian's small suitcase and flight bag into the boot and motioned Brian to take the passenger seat. He drove quickly, with much swearing and muttering, to the Police HQ in Floriana. Brian noted the imposing stone building, but soon discovered it was in need of a little updating, with noisy air-conditioning. Nevertheless, it was fit for purpose, and charming in its own way, unlike many of the soulless buildings he'd been in back home. He was ushered down a corridor and into a small office where some familiar faces were waiting.

"Hello, Brian. Good flight?"
"Tolerable. Good to see you again, Alex. You too, Chris. So now you're going to tell me why you've brought me all this way?"
"I thought you would have guessed by now."
"I was hoping you were going to say you had Hardcastle in custody."
"Close, but not quite. Let me fill you in. Thanks to the help we got from your team in Bradford, we were able to more or less close down Hardcastle's operation in the UK. We were also able to freeze most of his bank accounts and seize his assets. We knew he was hiding out in Tirana, Albania..."
"I know where Tirana is."
"Sorry, Brian. Just be patient while I finish the story."
"Go on."
"Thank you. So, we knew he had escaped to Albania - one of his

team we arrested confirmed that. And we also discovered that he was in the process of having a villa built in Malta, and, crucially, that he had a bank account here. We've left that account open and accessible, and with the help of his builder and the authorities, have concocted a situation where he needs to present himself in person at the bank in order to release funds to complete the housebuilding and pay outstanding taxes. We expect he will do that, so that he can at the same time arrange for the balance of his account to be transferred somewhere we can't touch it. The meeting is scheduled to take place tomorrow morning. We will be ready to meet him whether he comes by air or sea."

"Can you really monitor all the places he can land here?"

"Yes. The Maltese police have made all their resources available for this operation. And we have contacts in Albania who are monitoring all passengers leaving the country. Even if he is using a false passport, facial recognition software will be able to identify him. We are ready for this and we are confident."

"So, what do we do in the meantime?"

"We take you to your hotel, then we go for lunch."

"Sounds like a good plan to me."

They drove him to the 4-star Victoria Hotel in the centre of Sliema, waited long enough for him to sign in and drop his bags in his room and took him to a nearby restaurant where they enjoyed a leisurely lunch while chatting about the case.

"The European Arrest Warrant has already been issued by the International Criminality Unit at the Home Office, and extradition papers have also been forwarded. As soon as he sets foot on Maltese soil, the local police will arrest him. Once the paperwork is completed, they will then hand the bugger over to us to take home. So, basically, we're just waiting for the local force to inform us when he's in their custody. They'll inform us as soon as they have him."

"How long does it take?"

"Maybe twenty-four hours, if we're lucky."

"And in the meantime?"

"We wait."

****

After lunch, Brian asked for some time alone during the afternoon so that he could buy some souvenirs to take home for his wife and kids. They were happy to let him, provided he took his phone with him. And so, he found himself wandering around Sliema and taking the ferry across to Valletta, taking in the sights. He was captivated enough to make the decision to come back some time for a holiday with his family. It was so far removed from life back in Bradford. A different world, a different age.

They met up again in Sliema for an evening meal, rounded off with a few drinks. The three of them got on well, and swapped stories of some of the memorable moments in their careers. They were about to turn in when the call came through Alex Sinclair's phone.

"He boarded a plane and flew out of Tirana at 9pm. After a stop and a switch to another airline, he's due to land at 9.50 in the morning. Get some sleep. We'll pick you up at 9am. We'll go to the airport and watch the fun when the local police arrest him, then we'll follow them back to police HQ. As soon as we are sure there'll be no problems with the extradition, we'll book the flight home."

****

Shortly after his plane had landed and its passengers had disembarked, Hardcastle was detained at immigration and handed over to the waiting Maltese police. He was taken out through a private exit to a waiting police van, alongside which stood the British officers. As a gesture of goodwill, the Maltese police allowed Chris Fox to take a photograph, using Brian's phone, of Brian handcuffing a miserable-looking Hardcastle.

"There's a souvenir for your scrapbook. It'll look good on your CV as well."
"Thanks. I'll treasure that."

They followed the police van back to HQ and waited until the formalities were completed. PC Muscat broke the news to them.

"You can take him home as soon as you are ready. Everything is cleared."

Chris Fox was able to book seats for three to Manchester the following morning. Brian's flight to Leeds was scheduled for the afternoon. He immediately rang Don with the good news. They were then left with little option as to how they would spend the rest of their time on the island. They went for a drink. And then another drink.

****

Thanks to the alarm call he'd booked, Brian was down for breakfast in good time. He booked out of his hotel and took a taxi to police HQ in time to see Sinclair and Fox take custody of a miserable, and angry-looking Hardcastle. He followed them in a police car to the airport and refused to let Hardcastle out of his sight until he'd seen him go through the boarding gate in handcuffs, with the two officers. Only then would he allow himself to relax. Again, he called Don.

"He's on the plane, boss. We've got him."
"Good work, Brian. While you've some time to kill, get me a nice bottle of malt from Duty Free. We'll celebrate with it in the office when you get back."
"Will do, boss. Pass the good news to my team, will you?"
"Of course, I will. They've all worked hard on this."
"I'm sending you a photo of the arrest from my phone. Show it to the team for me, please. They'll love it."
"I'll put it up in the 'Hall of Fame' I'm starting in the office. From now on, all photos of significant successes will go on it."
"You need to take the job permanently, boss. You've only been in the job a few days and you've already netted an international criminal."
"We'll see. We'll talk about it over a drink when you get back. Safe journey. See you in the morning. By the way, Brian: the firebomb at your house was a random event. Two schoolkids."

He had some lunch in the airport and loaded up on gifts and whisky in the duty-free shops before sending one final text.

"On my way home. Landing around 7. Be home by 8. Kiss the kids for me. See you soon. B. xxx"

He boarded the plane for the flight home. He couldn't wait.

THE END

Printed in Poland
by Amazon Fulfillment
Poland Sp. z o.o., Wrocław